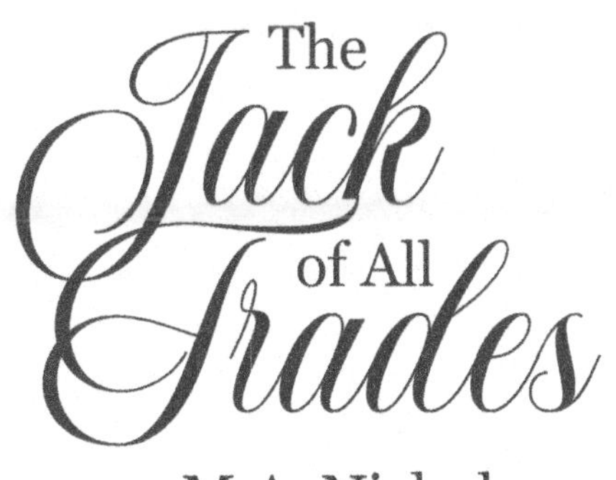

M.A. Nichols

www.ma-nichols.com

Books by M.A. Nichols

Regency Love Series

Flame and Ember

A True Gentleman

The Shameless Flirt

Honor and Redemption

The Jack of All Trades

A Tender Soul

Victorian Love Series

A Stolen Kiss

The Honorable Choice

Hearts Entwined

A Passing Fancy

Tempest and Sunshine

The Villainy Consultant Series

Geoffrey P. Ward's Guide to Villainy

Geoffrey P. Ward's Guide to Questing

Magic Slippers: A Novella

The Shadow Army Trilogy

Smoke and Shadow

Blood Magic

A Dark Destiny

Table of Contents

Prologue

Sussex
Spring 1805

The study did not boast a grand view of the grounds around Dewbourne, but trees and grass were a vast improvement to barracks and the press of the city. Not that Deal was bustling compared with London, Liverpool, or Manchester, but it was busier than this quiet corner of Sussex. That town was little more than a cesspool populated by soldiers and sailors who gave no attention to anything other than public houses, gambling, and all the other places bored men used to fill their time.

Lewis Finch took a deep breath, savoring the scent of the outdoors wafting through the open window; he could not pinpoint the exact odor, but it was a distinctive mixture of local flora and fauna that smelled like home. And infinitely preferable to the stench of stables and soldiers.

Finch shook himself free of that thought, shoving aside memories best left undisturbed, and focused on the greenery before him. There was no need to wallow in thoughts of Deal or the future that place provided when faced with such beauty.

Tugging at the bottom of his jacket, Finch adjusted his uniform. How were the light dragoons supposed to fight when restrained by this wretched thing? Fashion dictated a snug fit, but it did no good on the battlefield. Enemy soldiers wouldn't surrender due to their awe over the fine cut of his jacket or the vast amount of silver braiding decorating it. And though ladies noted how brilliantly the rich blue and scarlet facing complemented his fair hair, the French had never expressed any appreciation.

Puffing out his cheeks, he turned away from the window. It wasn't providing much solace at any rate, so Finch resigned himself to pacing. The heels of his polished boots alternately clicked and thudded as he passed from the hardwood floor onto the rug and back, his feet tracing a haphazard path around the study.

He needed to focus. If he was to explain himself properly, he needed his wits about him. Not that it would do much good, for his wits failed him in such moments. But Finch rehearsed the forthcoming discussion, lining out every argument succinctly.

Surely Father would see reason—

"It is good to see you, my boy," said the gentleman in question as he strode in through the study door, shutting it behind him. With a bright smile, Father gave Finch a hearty handshake. "We hadn't expected you to visit. You should've sent word."

"It was rather unexpected, but this conversation could not be postponed any longer," said Finch as his father motioned for him to take a seat.

"Your visit is rather precipitous, son, for I have wanted to speak with you about your future," said Father, taking his own seat behind the behemoth expanse of polished wood that served as his desk. "It sounds as though the French are causing quite a stir on the Continent, and I would like to get everything settled before your regiment is sent abroad."

Finch straightened as the pressure in his chest eased. His smile grew as he nodded. "That is the precise reason I wished to speak with you. I fear the army does not suit me."

Giving a nod, Father leaned back into his armchair with a shake of his head. "I blame myself for your current predicament. I should've known you would not fare well as a soldier after your abysmal time at the Royal Naval Academy, but I had hoped the army would suit you better. After all, purchasing a commission in such a prestigious regiment could make up for any of your..." Father waved a hand, pausing before he settled on the proper word. "...deficiencies."

Finch's heart shriveled, though his passive expression remained fixed in place.

"You've caused me quite a bit of worry and frustration, my boy. All I have ever wanted is for you to establish yourself in a worthy career and achieve the level of prestige due a Finch, but all my effort have been for naught, as you do not excel in any area."

Heat ran up Finch's neck and along his face, and he gave a faint nod, hoping it might be enough to keep his father from treading down this familiar path.

"I do not understand why you struggle so. You are competent enough in various fields but cannot seem to master a single one in any meaningful manner," mumbled Father, turning his gaze away from his son to stare sightlessly at the wall. Then with a chuckle, he added, "The Finch family's jack of all trades."

Finch's words fled him, and he stared at Father while the silence stretched into an eternity. Had the clocks stopped ticking? It felt as though the world were turning in a vat of molasses. His ribs constricted, and his hand itched to rub at his chest and ease the pain, but Finch refused to move, not allowing his shoulders to drop even a fraction as he watched his father.

But that was when his faculties finally snapped back into place, and Finch recalled precisely what he had intended to say before the conversation had turned down this path.

Finch cleared his throat. "You have done much for me, Father, but I believe I've discovered the proper path for me."

Father turned his gaze to his son, brows raised. "Have you?"

"Though I am not suited for soldiering, I have done well as the aid to our regimental agent. He has decided to sell out—"

Father's brows rose again, and he leaned forward. "And you are poised to take his place?"

The words stuck in Finch's throat as his fingers tapped a staccato beat on his knee, and he searched for a truthful response that wouldn't disappoint his father.

"Son?" Father watched him with raised brows, and Finch let out a breath, his gaze dropping to the rug.

"I will not be given his position."

Finch still could not believe they'd chosen Lieutenant Thomas, but that thought was followed by an intense desire to roll his eyes at that blatant self-deception: Finch may have hoped for a different outcome, but in truth, no one was surprised at Thomas's appointment. The fellow was ingratiating and a skilled negotiator—both of which were necessary for a regimental agent. And the 15th Light Dragoons was too popular a regiment to allow any but the best to handle the intricacies of selling its commissions and its many financial affairs.

With a huff, Father leaned back in his armchair. "Then you are stagnating in your current role and have little hope of advancing."

Finch unclenched his teeth, the muscles in his jaw throbbing. "And I have no desire to return to the battlefield—"

"Nor are you likely to distinguish yourself there," replied Father with another vague wave of his hand.

Steeling his nerves, Finch ignored that and focused on the task at hand. "As I was saying, Lieutenant Bentley has done well as regimental agent and is leaving to start a bank. He wants me to serve as his partner—"

"At a bank? Ridiculous."

"It is a good profession, Father."

"For the son of a vicar or physician, perhaps, but it is hardly fit for a Finch. You hail from a long line of proper gentlemen, and I would not have you stoop to being a money lender."

Finch's brows furrowed. "My responsibilities would be nearly identical to that of a regimental agent, yet you have no qualms about me pursuing that option."

Father leveled an incredulous look at his son. "Don't be ridiculous. Bankers are hardly better than tradesmen, and I cannot countenance you joining their ranks. Your brothers and I would not be able to admit the relation, and we'd be forced to sever all ties with you. But an officer in a prestigious regiment like yours is a gentleman through and through. An honorable addition to any family."

"I am not being ridiculous. The skills I've honed while assisting Lieutenant Bentley are the precise reason why he is interested in partnering with me even though I can offer little in the way of capital," said Finch. "Though I do not have his way with people, I have a talent for numbers that would be valuable to his venture."

Father's expression shifted to that of paternal exasperation as though Finch were an errant child and not a man of seven and twenty. "My dear boy, keeping good ledgers is hardly noteworthy or every steward in the country would be hailed a genius. It is only basic arithmetic."

Finch opened his mouth, but Father spoke over him. "I am proud to see you've developed that skill, for I would hate to think my son a dunce, but it is hardly worth pursuing. You are also skilled at the pianoforte, yet you would never pursue music in a professional capacity."

Father watched him with an open expression of concern, his greying brows resting high on his forehead, waiting for Finch to agree with that undeniable fact. A rebellious part of his heart wanted to argue, but Finch knew all too well how that would end: there was no battling Father. Though only his last few years were spent in the army, Finch had been a lifelong soldier, standing at attention, awaiting his commander's orders—

even if Father gave them with a paternal air. As there was no point in disagreeing, Finch nodded; he had no more sway over his father than an ensign had over a general.

With a wry smile, Father shook his head. "The Finch family jack of all trades, indeed. Skilled at many things yet master of none."

"Perhaps I could attend university? It is a little late for me to pursue the church, but I would welcome that possibility," mumbled Finch. Anything would be better than the army, and Father could not argue against the gentlemanly nature of that profession.

Resting his hands on his desk, Father gave his son a warm smile. "This is precisely what I wished to speak to you about, for I have spent much time thinking through the options and have landed on a perfect solution."

Father's fingers drummed against the wood as he continued, "I have already invested far too much capital in bolstering your career. Your brothers and I have done all we can to provide you with connections and opportunities to distinguish yourself, and yet you've floundered. In the six years since you joined the army, you've yet to advance up the ranks or distinguish yourself in any capacity despite the family expending vast funds to purchase you such a coveted commission."

His hands stilled while Finch kept his eyes riveted to the polished desktop. He wished there was some excuse or explanation he could give, but there was no denying the fact that he had failed. Again.

"My grandsons will soon begin their professions and shall need the family's assistance, while the time is long past for you to be independent of our purse strings." Letting out a soft sigh, Father shook his head. "And though we have funds enough to continue aiding you, we've exhausted all our connections. Even if you displayed an aptitude for the church, you have little chance to gain a prosperous living without some familial tie to that profession. We would waste more funds educating you only to find you languishing for years awaiting an appointment to a parish. Assuming you could secure one."

He leaned forward, drawing Finch's gaze, and there was a worried furrow to his father's brow. "That is not the life I want for you. Endless waiting for something better to appear and forever disappointed."

And then a spark returned to his father's eyes, drawing with it a smile. "Which is why I have decided on the proper course of action for you, my boy. With battles looming, there is high demand for your commission. That, along with the sale of your horse, saddle, and all the rest—"

"Ares?" Finch winced at his father's implication and the beast's silly name, which was far too on the nose for his liking. Though Finch supposed if any horse deserved to bear the name of that god of old, it would be that fine creature.

"You will have no need for a horse, and he will fetch a pretty penny," said Father with another airy wave. "A gentleman about Town can forgo such a luxury without it being remarked upon."

Finch blinked at his father, though the gentleman hardly noticed.

"If you sell all and invest the funds, you will have enough capital to earn a modest interest," said Father, as though that explained all.

When Finch did not reply, Father gave another sigh and shake of his head.

"It will allow you to be a gentleman of leisure," said Father, as though that were the finest prospect a fellow could aspire to. "The family will secure you lodgings befitting a Finch and your interest will cover the rest of your expenses. You would have to economize, but a bachelor does not entertain and London does not require a carriage or horses. You have no need for a large house or anything more than a valet, and when you take that all into account, there is no reason you cannot thrive. It is the only proper option for you."

There was some merit to the scheme. Leisure's siren call provided him with images of what that life would mean. The gentry's eldest sons haunted London with little thought beyond their own pleasures, indulging in frivolity and all the entertainments the city had to offer. Finch had hardly visited Town more than a time or two and had little knowledge of it other than the fanciful tales he'd heard his peers exchange of ballrooms and clubs, merriment and excitement.

Yet there was an aspect of his future that Father had not addressed.

"And marriage?" asked Finch.

Father's brows rose. "You've never shown an inclination towards matrimony."

"I've been occupied with establishing myself in a profession," said Finch, not bothering to add that his father had seen little of him since he'd left home at twelve, so the gentleman hardly knew a thing about his son's inclinations. "This course of action would leave me without sufficient funds to marry and no means of securing a greater income."

Father waved that concern away. "Your brother Julian has done well for himself in the navy, yet he cannot afford to marry. Your present course in the army is no more likely to provide that opportunity."

"And that is why I wish to pursue this business venture with Bentley—"

"This is not a negotiation, son." Though neither unfriendly nor biting, Father's tone was hard, his expression unyielding as he held Finch's gaze. "A father's duty is to guide his son, and a son's duty is to abide by his father's decision. You are long past the age where you ought to be independent of the family finances, yet still, you require assistance. I have been patient, my boy, but I cannot allow this to go on any longer."

With a sad shake of his head, Father's gaze drifted away once more while he considered things. When he met Finch's eyes again, his smile warmed. "This new course of action will be mutually beneficial to us both. You would gain a modest lifestyle in London society, and the family would no longer have such a drain on our resources. Your time in the light dragoons has been expensive—"

"I try to economize."

But Father held up a hand to forestall any further excuses. "I understand, my boy. Your regiment has certain standards of living, which you've had to follow, and I do not begrudge you a single penny of it. But the fact is that one year's worth of expenses in the army could pay the rent for your London rooms ten times over. As you are unlikely to rise any higher than your present position, it makes better financial sense for us to pay your rent in perpetuity than continue on as we have."

Finch opened his mouth to reply, but Father spoke over him.

"And being a gentleman of leisure is admirable. It would bring far more prestige to the family than your current course of action or any of your unsavory propositions."

Mouth agape, Finch sorted through his thoughts and arguments, hoping to land on something that might convince his father otherwise, but there was little point. Finch had proven himself useless in all the other professions his father had proposed, and if he viewed Finch's proposals as "unsavory," then there was little hope of changing his mind.

"And if I refuse?" Finch didn't know why he bothered asking that question, for he knew full well the answer would not swing in his favor. But asking such ridiculous questions was one of the many reasons why he had failed at the law as well as the navy and army.

Father's fingers drummed against the desk, the sound harder and more unyielding than the gaze he leveled on his son. And when he launched into a lecture about family honor and a son's duty, Finch merely nodded at various intervals, knowing there was no point in going to battle.

For better or worse, Father had chosen Finch's life path, and there was no deviating now.

Chapter 1

Devon
Winter 1812

Propped up on her elbow, Felicity leaned across her desk, her eyes tracing the lacy patterns of frost across her study window. The clouds had cleared enough to allow slivers of sunlight through, which caught the crystals clinging to the masonry. The city sparkled, begging her to abandon her work and explore the world outside.

Felicity longed for proper trees. In this portion of Plymouth, there were few to be found among the buildings, and one of the most beautiful sights was a copse coated in a thick layer of ice crystals, twinkling in the sunlight. She yearned to bundle herself in her cloak and gloves, explore the frigid out of doors until her fingers and toes were numb, and return to a crackling fire and drinking chocolate.

Sighing, she turned away from the window's enticements and stared at the ledgers on the desk. Her free hand fiddled with her quill, ignoring the mess the remnant droplets of ink made on the wood. Felicity stared at the numbers until her eyes blurred, and she leaned back, rubbing her temples as though that might ease the mounting pain.

Felicity wriggled her shoulders, massaging the knots that had formed as she hunched over her work, and leaned back to survey that which was yet to be completed. The stacks of letters were organized according to their urgency, but the truth was that few would be answered to either her or the sender's satisfaction.

Invitations for balls, parties, and entertainments she had not time to consider. Missives from friends remained unanswered. Petitions begging her to join various societies and charitable functions would only receive funds in her stead; it eased her conscience minutely but did not salve the longing she felt to participate in more meaningful matters.

No, questions from solicitors, clerks, and Uncle's business partners took precedence. Endless queries about investments and expenses appeared in those piles like the hydra of old; for every answer she gave, three more questions arose.

Again and again, Felicity wondered if Uncle George had known how much of a mess she'd make of his business. Or how great a cost it would exact from her. Of course, Uncle had intended her to have assistance as he'd had.

Felicity stared at the work to be done and pleaded with herself to continue picking away at it. But heaven help her, it was all so inordinately boring. She was no stranger to completing distasteful tasks, but as far as she could see, there was nothing to love about investments and commodities.

The study door opened, and a footman strode in with a salver on hand. He offered it to his mistress, and she retrieved the calling card and sighed, her shoulders slumping.

"Show him in, Thomas," she said, replacing the card.

Standing, Felicity straightened her skirts and patted her hair, which by some miracle remained perfectly coiffed, though many hours had passed since the pins had been placed in her unruly mass of red curls.

"Miss Barrows," said Mr. Johnson, striding in and giving her a quick bow.

Felicity curtsied and snatched a handkerchief from the desk to wipe at her ink-stained hands. "Good afternoon, Mr. Johnson."

"My, that looks frightful," he said, gesturing towards the letters and ledgers. Mr. Johnson picked up an envelope from a pile and glanced at it with raised brows. He tossed it back with a casual flick of his hand. "Have you been at this tedious work all day?"

Felicity put the discarded letter back in the appropriate stack. "All week, more like, and I am at my limit with no end in sight."

"You poor thing," he said, ushering her to the pair of armchairs positioned by the fire and calling for a maid to bring some refreshment.

"I do not need tea and cakes," she said.

But Mr. Johnson waved that away. "Nonsense. You take too much upon yourself, and you need a respite. You are quite pale, you know. It would be a shame to spoil your complexion."

Felicity nearly laughed at that, for the fellow had managed to say that flimflam with a straight face, as though her complexion was foremost of concern. And as though it hadn't been spoiled long ago.

"Your concern does you credit, sir," she said, barely containing a laugh. "I assure you that tea and cakes are by no means a remedy for my ills."

"It is no wonder that your mind is so burdened when faced with such strenuous work."

"I would hardly say ledgers and correspondence are strenuous. Tedious, yes. But by no means strenuous." As she spoke, Felicity eyed the gentleman, wondering if he would seize this opportunity to say that which he'd hinted at for the past few weeks.

Perhaps she ought to be more charitable and feel a modicum of shame for finding humor in the situation, but she hadn't encouraged his advances nor were his motives by any definition pure. Perhaps if she were in better spirits she might allow this farce to continue, but Mr. Johnson was pulling her away from more important things.

"Ah, me," she said with a dramatic sigh. The whole thing was ridiculous, yet there was pleasure to be found in it. Affecting her most contrite expression, Felicity prodded the fellow by adding, "There is so very much to do."

Mr. Johnson shifted in his seat, drawing closer to hers. "I fear it weighs heavily on you, Miss Barrows, but perhaps the solution is right in front of you."

Covering a chuckle with a cough, she turned a sweet smile in his direction. "And what solution might that be?"

"You need a husband to assist you."

"That is precisely what my last man of business believed." And he'd thought himself suited for that role as well, but Felicity was not going to admit that aloud. "However, an employee is far easier to replace than a husband."

"But you've yet to find a man of business who suits your needs."

Felicity leaned back. "What do you know of that?"

Mr. Johnson leaned forward, taking her hand in his as Felicity's lids lowered. "Hush now, that is of no importance. I have come today to speak with you concerning a personal matter."

"My finances?" she asked, unable to resist twitting him.

Patting her hand, he shook his head. "Surely you've noticed my marked attentions the past month, and I do feel as though I have reason to hope that your feelings have grown as mine have."

"Oh, so you do wish to speak of my finances."

Brows pulled together, Mr. Johnson stared at her. "I wish to ask you for your hand in marriage."

Which were one and the same, but Felicity did not bother pointing that out. "Whyever would you want my hand? Marriage requires more than a single appendage."

Mr. Johnson's eyes narrowed. "You are being obtuse on purpose."

Felicity gave him an apologetic smile. "I am teasing you, Mr. Johnson. The only way to find joy in life is to laugh at our own expense."

"I am speaking of love and matrimony. I hardly think now is the time for jests."

"And I think there is none better." Especially when faced with such a proposal, but Felicity held back the eye roll lurking beneath the surface and patted his hand in return. "I apologize if I offended you, Mr. Johnson. You were saying?"

The fellow stared at her with a scrunched expression. "That I adore you and wish to spend the rest of my days by your side."

"You hadn't actually said either of those things."

"I am saying them now."

Felicity clasped her hands in her lap and turned an assessing glance in his direction. "And why do you adore me?"

Mr. Johnson's brows rose. "Pardon?"

"You say you adore me, but I wish to know precisely why you long to spend the rest of your days by my side." She punctuated that with a challenging raise of her brows.

Sliding to his knees, Mr. Johnson drew closer, and Felicity fought back a groan. It was so much easier when the gentlemen held onto their dignity and refrained from such ridiculous overtures.

"You are a goddess among men, and you question why I love you?" he asked.

"I am asking for specifics. What is it about me that you love?"

Mr. Johnson inched closer, taking Felicity's hand in his and pressing a kiss to her knuckles. While his attention was occupied, she raised her eyes to the heavens, begging for patience, and dropped them once again when he turned his gaze to meet hers.

"I have never seen a lovelier creature than you, Miss Barrows. You are beauty personified," he murmured. "With titian tresses that glow in the sunlight and the fairest eyes in all creation."

Felicity covered a laugh with a cough. For all that gentlemen claimed honor was paramount, the fellow had just spouted several blatant falsehoods all in a row. Her hair could not be called titian any more than a mule could be called a horse. Though it did glow in the sunlight, it was less a burnished copper and more a blaring orange with disobedient curls that her lady's maid cursed daily. And Felicity had no delusions concerning her eyes; though a decent shade of brown, there was nothing remarkable or particularly fine about them.

Unconsciously, she brushed a touch across the rough bumps that followed the edge of her jaw. She was long past the age of fretting over her complexion, but neither was she one of those ladies who wrapped themselves in the false confidence that claimed such imperfections were lovely. The scars and bumps marring her skin were simply a part of who she was, and Felicity was secure enough to know that whether considered ugly or beautiful, her appearance was of no importance. Even if so many others believed otherwise.

Mr. Johnson rambled on about her various features and their relative loveliness, embellishing them to the point of absurdity, and though there was still humor to be found in his attempts at romance, Felicity's heart gave a sad little shudder. Did every gentleman think her so vain and silly that she would believe such obvious lies? That she would fall into his arms because he cobbled together false compliments about her face and figure?

Perhaps another spinster might cling to the fantasy they presented; Felicity did not miss the fact that the compliments all mirrored each other, blending into a generic mass.

"Mr. Johnson," she said, but before she could interject further, he launched into a bout of poetry.

"'Shall I compare thee to a summer's day?'"

"I would rather you not."

"'Thou art more lovely and more temperate.'"

"Mr. Johnson, please desist," she said, but the fellow continued, giving line after line of the sonnet with growing affectedness, his gaze holding hers in a manner that had her inching backward, though the back of the chair kept her from traveling too far. When she gave another protest, he halted mid-line and watched her with a furrowed brow.

But before she could say another word, he launched into another. "'Love is not love which alters in its alteration finds...'"

"Enough, Mr. Johnson," said Felicity, nudging him aside so she could get to her feet and move to the desk. "I thank you for your kind words, but I fear I must decline your offer."

"Decline?" Mr. Johnson blinked at her, and she held her breath. How the next few moments would unfold varied greatly from gentleman to gentleman, and she hoped Mr. Johnson had enough sense to behave with dignity.

"But, Miss Barrows, I am offering to marry you."

"I am fully aware of what you are offering, Mr. Johnson, but I have no desire to marry for the sake of marrying. I do hope you are not too disappointed," she said, adding a few more trite words of consolation as she rose to her feet.

Mr. Johnson did the same, though his gaze remained unfocused, his brows pulled together in such a tight bunch that Felicity didn't know whether to be offended or amused by his utter confusion. She chose the latter.

With a nudge here and there, she had him out the study door and shut it firmly behind him. Giving a heavy sigh, she leaned against the door and stared upwards as though patience might pour down from the heavens.

Chapter 2

Why did so many proposals include soppy verses? True, love was not love if it altered with the slightest whim, and every young lady hoped for a beau who believed her more lovely and temperate than a summer's day, but such poetry bespoke a romance that was more fantasy than reality.

Of Shakespeare's sonnets, there was none to compare with One Hundred and Thirty, which spoke of true love that was not falsely compared to objects of inordinate beauty; it was written by a lover who recognized his lady's flaws and adored her all the same. Surely that was far more endearing and heartfelt than blind adoration that sees perfection where there is none.

Pushing off the door, Felicity abandoned such thoughts and turned her attention back to her wretched work. She collapsed onto the armchair, staring at the physical evidence of all she needed to do, and felt her stomach sink. Would it ever end? Or was her life to be a constant stream of uninteresting tasks?

"Oh, Uncle," she murmured, not for the first time. Likely the fellow had more pressing matters to attend to during his eternal rest than to watch his niece flounder, but Felicity wished he were seated beside her.

Another knock sounded at the door, and Felicity bade the visitor enter, grateful for yet another distraction from her business. Before she could right herself, Bethany Beaumont swept into the study.

"Tell me you are not spending yet another afternoon cooped up in this dreary place," she said, reaching for Felicity's hand and tugging her to her feet.

"There is work to be done," said Felicity, but Bethany would hear no other protests as she led her friend from the study and into the sitting room where the maids were readying tea and cakes. Though she still did not require any refreshment, a bit of conversation was welcome, so she settled herself onto the sofa as Bethany did the same.

"Was that Mr. Johnson leaving just now? He looked terribly distraught," said Bethany.

"No doubt he expected a different outcome to his declaration," said Felicity as her friend reached for the teapot and began preparing their cups. "I ought to do that, Bethany—"

"Hush, Felicity. If you take no umbrage with my stepping over the bounds of propriety, then I am glad to do it. You have enough weighing on your mind without having to wait on me."

Watching Bethany's efficient movements, Felicity felt the tiniest bit of strain ease from her heart, though that allowed a trickle of disappointment to take its place. Her mind was too clogged and her thoughts too sluggish for even such a simple task, and Felicity wasn't sure if she should weep in gratitude that someone was aiding her or growl in frustration that such ministrations were necessary.

"My thanks, Bethany," said Felicity, taking the proffered cup and plate before her friend prepared her own.

"Someone needs to make certain you are taking care of yourself," said Bethany, moving with such ease that she hardly glanced at the tea and dishes.

"I do not know how Uncle managed it all. I've been without a man of business for little more than a fortnight, yet I am overwhelmed with all that needs doing."

"You are dealing with his work and your own," replied Bethany. "Your uncle had you to manage the household and all that comes with it, and he had assistance in dealing with the minutiae of his business. Was it really necessary for you to sack Mr. Kerr?"

Felicity's brows rose as she took a sip of her tea. "He had designs that included far more than managing my business affairs, and though he was a fine man of business, I had no interest in allowing him a more permanent position in my life. After all, a husband cannot be sacked if he proves unworthy."

Bethany chuckled. "And was Mr. Johnson here to make his application?"

Abandoning her teacup to the side table, Felicity shook her head with a laugh. "He was so ridiculous, Bethany. He spouted the most absurd poetry and called me a goddess, as though I would fall into his arms weeping at his benevolence."

Bethany's gaze softened, her lips twisting into a half-smile. "And what if he was in earnest?"

"You've witnessed my entire frustrating mess of suitors, and you would ask that? Truly?"

"I simply hoped that perhaps..." Bethany shook her head, setting aside her teacup.

Giving a single shrug of her shoulder, Felicity gave her friend a wry smile. "As did I. But these gentlemen paid me no mind when they believed me to be in possession of a minor inheritance. Now that Uncle is gone and the opposite has proven true, they flock to me in droves. One need only look to the shallowness of their declarations to know their hearts are not truly engaged."

Felicity let out a puff of air and shook her head. "No doubt Mr. Johnson will arrive again tomorrow with a posy in hand to show me how much he truly adores me, though his words make it clear how little he knows me."

"You think so?" asked Bethany.

With a grin, Felicity replied, "It is what the last three have done, and I doubt Mr. Johnson is imaginative enough to do more than the standard overtures. Though it seems to me that a 'goddess' deserves a fair bit more than over-recited poetry and a handful of generic blossoms. The florist must have a 'Miss Barrows' bouquet, for it is near identical every time."

The pair laughed as Felicity recalled the various steps the false beaus had taken to secure her heart, and though she varied little from the truth, Felicity did add a few minor—yet deserving—embellishments. Perhaps Mr. Gardiner's breath was not as strong as cooked onions mixed with rotten beef, but it was close enough. Could he not have eaten something less pungent before baring his "soul" to her?

When the mirth died down, Felicity stared at her nearly empty teacup, her smile turning into a hint of a frown. "I do not fear being a spinster. Marriage to the right man sounds blissful, and I would welcome such a happy turn of events, but my current life is too blessed to surrender it for anything less. However, being bombarded by gentlemen who believe their lukewarm offers are heaven-sent is disheartening. And so very overwhelming, Bethany. I cannot get a moment's peace."

Pressing a finger to her temple, Felicity massaged the ache. "And it is all heaped on the business I have to attend to."

"Have you not found a man of business to assist you?"

Felicity leveled an exasperated look at her friend. "Not one who suits my needs."

Bethany nibbled on her lip, her brows twisting together. "And I fear I am no more useful in such matters than a sparrow, for I haven't the slightest idea of how to handle any of it."

Giving her friend a narrowed look, Felicity replied, "You are plenty useful, Bethany. Who else will listen to me complain at length about the blessings of inheriting a fortune?"

"And you do love to complain," replied Bethany with a nod and a wry smile.

Felicity sent her friend a mock scowl, which earned her another grin in return. When it was clear that Bethany felt not the slightest bit of remorse, Felicity sighed. "I am just so excessively fatigued—body, mind, and soul."

Bethany's expression softened, her eyes filling with concern. "Perhaps you ought to consider retiring to Farleigh Manor for a few weeks. A bit of time in the country would do wonders for you. Since much of your business revolves around ledgers and correspondence, there is no reason you cannot maintain most of it while you are away."

Felicity began shaking her head before Bethany finished her sentence. Uncle's estate—or rather, her estate—would not bring any comfort. The house was too large and empty. Felicity bit on the inside of her cheek, her gaze falling to the rug. In truth, it wasn't so much empty as it was filled with memories. Though it had been nearly twenty years since Father and William went to their eternal rest, the only memories she had of that place were tied to them. If she wished to raise her spirits, it would not do to visit a place so haunted by theirs.

"Perhaps not, but I did receive an invitation from Great-Aunt Imogene to visit her in Bristow whenever I wish." While Buxby Hall held some reminders of that which she'd lost, they were fainter and easily dealt with.

"That could be just the thing, Felicity," said Bethany, sitting up straighter. "Some time away from your worries and duties."

"A place where few know me and even fewer would make demands of me," added Felicity with a decisive nod. Bristow was precisely where she ought to go.

Chapter 3

Sussex
A Sennight Later

One could be forgiven for thinking that no time had passed for Lewis Finch. The world had continued to spin about its axis, but little had altered in the past seven years, and never was that more evident than when he stood at his father's study window. Finch's uniform had been cast aside, but still, he awaited his general's orders as he looked out at a view that had remained unchanged in that time.

Turning to face his father, Finch took the seat before the massive desk and waited for him to finish his usual lecture about family honor and obligation. As much as the rest of his world remained constant, he was surprised to see how much the Finch family patriarch had altered of late. Father rarely visited London anymore, and Finch's visits home were often curtailed by the cost of travel, so it was rare for him to see Darius Finch above once a year, and Finch had arrived at Dewbourne to find his father had aged greatly.

The gentleman's light coloring no longer hid the swaths of grey, and new lines cragged his face. But more than that, his posture was stooped and his voice a wispy echo of what it had once been. His sister-in-law had not mentioned this fragility in any of her letters, nor had she or his brother given any hint of the situation when they last visited London. Finch supposed they had not noticed the change that had crept up incrementally over the past year.

"Are you listening, Jack?"

Years of hearing that appellation and Finch still flinched at it.

"You were explaining the current affairs of my nephews," said Finch, rattling off a few vague details he'd grasped during Father's rambling exposition. Finch wished to prompt his father to simply say that which needed saying, but it would do no good to do so. Just as it did no good to fight what was to come.

"It is time to reevaluate your situation. The family will no longer carry the financial burden of your rooms in London. The time is long past for you to be independent and for the family to funnel those funds into better investments. I have so many grandsons, all of whom need as much assistance as we can give them..."

And so, Father droned on while Finch thought through all the rebuttals. His rent was the compensation for sacrificing his freedom and future for the sake of the Finch family honor, after all. But Finch supposed the occasional bank note his brothers or father tossed him was enough to salve their consciences.

Father had once said that the money saved from one year of Finch's army expenses could pay his rent for over a decade, but in the end, it had only been seven years. Or at least that was all they were willing to expend any longer.

Rifling through his mental ledgers, Finch thought through his options. He always managed to live well within his limited income, but was it enough to pay for his London rooms? There was little point in doing the arithmetic once more, for Finch knew it was only possible if he could retrench to cheaper lodgings, but the family could not countenance a son of theirs living anywhere less exalted. No matter that he could not afford it.

Likely, they preferred him to live off credit; collecting crushing amounts of debts was entirely acceptable as long as society did not discover it. Snatching a purse from a fellow on the street was deemed theft, but refusing to pay your grocer or tailor bills was gentlemanly.

"...Surely, you understand that we must do what is best for the family, Jack."

There was only one response in such a moment, for the youngest son had no right to give any other. And so, Finch parroted the words he'd spoken so many times, "Anything for the family."

"Good lad," replied Father with a faint smile, his lips trembling as though that movement required some effort. "I understand you are traveling to Essex this afternoon."

"My coach leaves within the hour. I always spend a few weeks at Simon Kingsley's estate before the Season begins."

And that was another issue all its own. Not a quarter of an hour ago Finch's most pressing concern had been his impending visit to Avebury Park. However, thoughts of Simon's ill-advised rush into a marriage of convenience and the mess Finch would likely find in the Kingsley estate had been unseated by Father's newest edict.

"Are you taking the public coach to Brighton?"

Finch nodded. "And then on to London and Essex."

"The coaches between here and Brighton are shoddy and uncomfortable. I cannot spare the family carriage for the entire journey, but if you speak to Rodgers, you can use it for that first leg," said Father with a smile as though his proffered crumb was a bounteous feast.

"My thanks, Father." Finch rose to his feet and bowed, leaving the study before the fellow had time to bask in his beneficence.

"Good travels, my dear Jack," he called, making Finch's cravat tighten about his neck.

Striding through the empty halls, Finch forced thoughts of his father from his mind and focused on the far more pressing matter. With more economies, he might afford the steep rent, though Finch despised the thought of expending such funds on extravagant rooms that only served as a symbol of his family's status.

Yes, Lewis Finch was a pauper compared to most of society, but he was a gentleman of leisure with the proper address befitting his illustrious family. Regardless of the fact that they held few connections of note and their wealth was not enough to grasp society's attention. Upper crust they may be, but not enough for those lofty standards.

A pain made itself known behind Finch's left eye, and he took in a breath. He would survive. He would. Economy and prudence were old friends of his, and he had ample savings to keep his situation from veering into dire straits in the interim. Yet he doubted he could continue balancing his family's demands and his pocketbook's. How much longer until his father required something that landed him in debtor's prison? Would his family claim their connection then?

Not a sound announced his assailants before they launched themselves at Finch, coming at him with a coordinated attack that did credit to the finest soldiers he'd known. One latched onto his leg, bringing Finch to a halt, and when he bent over to look at the mass of golden curls, the other used an obliging ledge to leap upon his back, her arms wrapped around his neck.

"Uncle Lewis!" Though he could not see which of his rascally nieces clung to his back, that distinct cadence belonged solely to the youngest of his brother's daughters.

"Are you causing mischief, Ginny?" asked Finch, shifting the child's hold so she did not strangle him.

"Don't be silly," she laughed, parroting a phrase that was so often applied to her.

Leaning forward, Finch looked at the leech wrapped around his shin. Barbara looked up at him with the angelic features she shared with her twin, though there was far more truth to the sweetness and innocence in Barbara's case than Ginny's.

"Mama said you were leaving today," said Barbara, loosening her grip enough to meet her uncle's smile.

Finch lifted his foot, giving its passenger a great swing forward. Barbara squealed and tightened her hold once more, while her sister nudged Finch's side with her heels, spurring him to move faster. With a shuffling step, he galloped down the hall as the sounds of squealing laughs echoed behind them. The pair were growing at a rapid clip, and Finch struggled to move their combined weight. A tinge of sorrow colored the joyful moment as he realized the dear girls were rapidly leaving childhood.

And sadly enough, they were some of the only family left who referred to him by his given name. Even the other children called him Uncle Jack, but this sweet pair had yet to adopt that moniker.

Those thoughts (and Ginny's incessant nudges) made him move faster, allowing him to push aside fatigue to steal a few more minutes as their horse.

"Girls!"

That one word, spoken with all the frustration a mother can muster, had Finch halting in his tracks while Ginny ducked behind his back and Barbara hid her face in his shin. Annette marched down the hallway with scorching steps that left the rugs beneath her feet smoldering. Her gaze did not waver from her children, though they refused to meet it.

"Miss Tuck has worked herself into a dither while searching the grounds for you," she said, coming to stand before them with her hands on her hips as though to punctuate an already clear point. "Girls, look at me."

With slow movements, the pair met their mother's eyes. Ginny released her hold on Finch, dropping to the floor before he had a chance to soften her fall. Coming around as Barbara rose to her feet, Ginny took her sister's hand and the two stood before their mother with heads hung low.

"It is unkind of you to treat her so," said Annette. "Miss Tuck is here to help you become the young ladies I know you can be, but you spend more time wriggling out of your lessons than learning. You know you are not allowed in the garden until after luncheon, and yet you blatantly ignore that rule. That is wicked of you."

Ginny's gaze darted upwards. "We didn't go into the garden."

Barbara nodded, her head bobbing up and down in quick movements. "We only left the door to the garden open. That is all."

Annette's brows drew together as she studied the children while a chuckle tickled Finch's chest, threatening to burst out as the implications quickly made themselves known. As understanding grew, Annette's eyes closed, her hand reaching up to massage her temple.

"Did you not think that Miss Tuck might be worried when she saw the door open but did not find you outside?" asked Annette.

Barbara glanced at her sister, and Ginny shrugged. "But we did not put one toe out of doors, Mama."

"How else were we to say goodbye to Uncle Lewis?" added Barbara. "He is leaving today and Miss Tuck would not allow us to see him off. We only wanted a few moments."

Ginny nodded. "She gave us no choice."

Though there was a hint of humor sparking in Annette's gaze, she gave her child a stern shake of the head at that pronouncement. "Do not shift your naughtiness onto someone else's shoulders. You still had a choice."

Ginny and Barbara moved in unison, stepping to Finch and cuddling close, their eyes gazing up at their mother with a sadness and pleading that would melt the devil's heart.

Annette sighed, her shoulders dropping. "Now that you have disrupted your lessons, you might as well give him a proper farewell."

Spinning, they latched onto him, and Finch crouched down. Their arms shifted to wrap around his neck, and the girls strangled him amongst pleas for him to return quickly. Their eyes glistened, and Finch tried to assuage their sadness, but their sentiments echoed his. Though anxious to see Simon and be free of Dewbourne, he would miss these dear girls as he always did.

With a clap, Annette drew their attention, hurrying the girls back to their lesson, adding, "Do not stray one step from your course, girls, or there shall be consequences."

Standing side by side, Annette and Finch watched as the pair walked hand-in-hand towards the nursery.

"I am not equipped to handle children who have the cunning and strategy of Admiral Nelson. What is a mother to do with such daughters?" asked Annette.

"Hope they do not defect to the French."

Annette gave him a gimlet eye, though softened with a smile. "Are you leaving soon, Jack?"

"Almost immediately. Father gave me the use of the family coach to get to Brighton, and I was just going to send word to have it readied."

"I am certain Phineas would wish to see you off, but he is dealing with some issue at present—"

"The drainage project?" asked Finch. "Or is it the investment he's looking at making with Barlow and Styles? He and Father have been debating the merits of different commodities, and I fear they may invest too much in one venture, leaving the family's finances dependent on a single investment."

Annette wrinkled her nose. "Whyever would I know that? Phineas has been taking on more responsibility for the estate of late, and I cannot keep up with all that nonsense. But Jack, can you not wait until luncheon to leave? Then we can have a meal together and see you off properly. I am certain he would like to bid you farewell."

Finch smiled at his sister-in-law and muted the disbelief that threatened to show in his gaze, for his eldest brother never bothered to see him off, and Finch doubted that tradition had altered today.

"I appreciate the sentiment, Annette, but I cannot miss the coach at Brighton."

With a furrowed brow she blinked at him. "Surely they can wait an hour. It would not be such a terrible inconvenience."

Finch coughed to cover a snort and cleared his throat. "Public coaches have a schedule and cannot deviate from it."

Annette's brow pinched all the more as she tried to comprehend, but as the lady had never used public transport, the concept was as foreign as if he'd spoken in German. Finch wondered what she would say if she knew he was not even granted a seat inside the coach but forced to take a seat up top. A shiver ran down his spine at the thought of the frigid cold that awaited him—even with the extra woolen layers he had packed in his valise.

"Then I suppose there is nothing more than to wish you Godspeed, dear brother-in-law," said Annette, giving him a kiss on the cheek and a smile before striding off towards her sitting room.

"Until my next visit," he mumbled, casting one last look around the halls he'd explored in his childhood. At times, it was difficult to believe that over two decades had passed since he'd called this building home. At others, the memories felt as though they belonged to some other Lewis Finch who'd lived eons ago. What would the Finch of the past say if he could see himself now?

Shaking aside such melancholy thoughts, Finch went in search of Rodgers. The sooner the butler called for the horses to be readied, the sooner Finch would be on his way to Essex.

Chapter 4

Essex
Two Days Later

There was nothing lovelier on a winter's day than a thick layer of fresh snow; seeing those plump flakes flittering down from the thick clouds, coating everything in their pristine white, was divine. But this year, Mina Kingsley far preferred barren ground. Though the world was awash in those dread muddy browns and greys, it meant the roads were clear and she could enjoy an outing with her dear Simon.

Winter had curtailed many of their morning rides, and Mina missed those stolen moments when the pair of them had galloped across the fields atop their mounts, the wind rushing by. But the roads had cleared enough to take their curricle out, which was nearly as wonderful as riding.

Simon sat beside her, his hands grasping the reins as he guided the horses along the country roads. While her husband's attention was on driving, Mina examined his profile. The unnatural bend to his nose was more pronounced at this angle, and she felt a strong desire to kiss it. Whoever thought a straight nose handsome was a fool.

"You are staring at me, woman," he said with a mock growl, his dark gaze slanting towards her.

"I am appreciating the view," she replied with a grin, though Mina had no idea what possessed her to say such silly things to him.

"Unfortunately, I have to keep my attention on the road, or I would do the same." The corners of Simon's lips curled upwards. "I've missed our rides together."

"I have as well," said Mina as a wicked thought entered her mind. Without bothering to question it, she followed the prompting and slid closer to him on the seat. "But there are some benefits to this arrangement that we cannot achieve while in the saddle."

Leaning into him, Mina shifted the blankets around them and feathered a kiss on his jaw, just above the edge of his scarf.

"You are hindering my ability to drive." His voice was low with a hint of a laugh laced through it.

"Am I?" Mina snuggled closer, nudging his arm up and around her.

Though simple, this moment was everything. Peace. Contentment. Love. Joy. She'd never thought to feel so much, and these sentiments settled into her soul, whispering to her that life was perfect and always would be.

No man deserved such happiness. Simon certainly did not, but neither was he going to turn aside the blessing that had landed in his lap despite his bungling. His earlier statement had been true; it was more difficult to drive with Mina cuddled into his side, but there was no other soul on the road, and Simon wasn't about to ask his dear wife to give him space.

One of the horses snorted, sending out a great puff of vapor, and the bite in the air had Simon freeing one hand to tuck the lap blanket more firmly around Mina. She smiled in return and rested her hand on his knee, and as much as he enjoyed this trip out, Simon longed to be free of the carriage and turn his entire attention to his wife.

Three months of bliss was not enough. Luckily, they had their entire lives, but Simon doubted decades with Mina would satisfy this longing. At times, the strength of it stunned him. He'd gone from being his own man to being a servant to this need. The change had come without warning, and Simon felt like falling on his knees and praising the Almighty that it had.

Simon loved his wife. His Mina.

The marriage of convenience that had proved most inconvenient at times had grown into something far stronger and deeper than "love." Those four little letters could not contain the emotions thrumming in Simon's heart.

"What is that smile for?" asked Mina.

Turning his eyes from the horses for the barest of moments, Simon met her gaze and said, "I am so very happy, my love."

Her hand rose to his face, and the soft leather of her glove brushed his skin. She gave him no words in response, but the warmth in her gaze filled him until he no longer felt the crisp winter air nipping at his cheeks. But one of the horses nickered, and Simon turned his attention back to the task at hand. All the love in the world would do no good if he overturned their carriage.

"You are shivering," he said, glancing in her direction.

But Mina merely smiled. "I could never be chilly when so close to you."

Simon grinned in response but turned the pair home. As much as he wished to spend the entirety of their day out in this felicity, he wasn't about to let her catch cold. Even with the warm bricks and blankets he'd procured for the drive, their journey could not last indefinitely.

Avebury Park appeared far sooner than Simon would've liked, but he supposed it was no great loss, either. Though there were duties aplenty to commandeer their attention, perhaps he could convince Mina to throw it all over and enjoy an indoor picnic with him. Lazing about as they ate Mrs. White's delectable treats and enjoyed each other's company was about as perfect an afternoon as Simon could wish for. Mina could paint as he read.

Directing the horses towards the stable, Simon tossed the reins to one of the grooms as a pair came forward to take charge of the carriage. He alighted and turned to give Mina a hand down; there was such a light in her eyes as she watched him, as though she held some secret mirth, and Simon marveled that this lovely creature was his wife.

Before releasing her hand, he turned it over and placed a kiss on her palm. Mina's cheeks were already bright as cherries from the cold wind, but she ducked her head in the manner she always did when blushing. Nudging up her chin to meet his gaze, Simon felt the world fade into darkness around them, but before he could make a move, it was Mina who closed the distance and pressed her lips to his.

Simon's arms came around her, and Mina held him with equal fervor. He had enough rational thought left to keep the kiss from becoming far more heated than was seemly, even if the servants were trying to remain invisible. Though poets had expounded at length about the power of a lady's touch, they hadn't captured the unutterable joy that accompanied Mina's touch.

Breaking free, Simon remained close to her, his feet and legs tangled among her skirts. Holding her gaze, he found an equal measure of passion burning there as well. Simon tucked her arm in his and led her to the house, sucking in a deep breath and allowing the chill air to calm the blaze in his chest.

Forcing herself to keep a moderate pace, Mina refused to run back to the house. Simon watched her, and giddiness surged through her. Would she ever tire of seeing him gaze upon her with such longing? Whatever fantasies she'd constructed in her younger years, Mina had never been able to truly imagine what it felt like to have such intensity focused on her.

With his free hand, Simon opened the front door, and all thoughts of her husband evaporated at the sight of the servants scrambling about. At the foot of the stairs sat several trunks, and a touch of the winter's chill settled into her heart.

They had visitors?

Simon helped her with her cloak and bonnet, and Mina called out to their housekeeper as she hurried past the entryway.

"Thank goodness you've returned, madam," said Mrs. Witmore, coming to Mina's side and directing a passing footman to take their master and mistress's things. "A gentleman, claiming to be a friend of Mr. Kingsley, arrived not a quarter of an hour ago. Mr. Lewis Finch. Jennings admitted him, and we are readying the Garden Room for him while he freshens up in the Yellow Room."

There was an unspoken question in the housekeeper's gaze, asking whether or not she'd done the correct thing, and Mina gave her a nod. "Thank you, Mrs. Witmore. I do apologize for the upset this has caused, but I have no doubt you will have everything in order shortly."

With as much decorum as could be allotted for such activity, Mrs. Witmore hurried off to direct the maids in their work.

Mina turned to her husband. "Mr. Finch is staying with us?"

Simon gave a pained smile. "He always visits for a couple of months in the winter. I had meant to tell you, but it slipped my mind."

Months. Not a mere fortnight or two, but months. Though Mina could not claim to have ever spoken to Mr. Finch directly, his words remained fixed in her memory. Mousy and unattractive. The perfect workhorse for Simon's intended marriage of convenience, too on-the-shelf and desperate to think of rejecting such a cold and calculating arrangement.

"What is the matter, Mina? I apologize for not speaking to you about it sooner, but I truly forgot he was coming," said Simon, his brows pulled tight together.

Mina's shoulders began moving in a dismissive shrug, but she held it back, fighting against old habits that demanded she ignore the churning in her stomach. No, this was Simon, and she would not lie to him.

"I do wish I'd had some warning, but I understand it wasn't intentional," said Mina. Simon kept a firm grip on her hand, and she twisted her other in her skirts. "I will admit I am not overjoyed at having another of your guests descend on Avebury Park. The last time did not fare well for us."

Simon already had the pale complexion of one born and raised in Britain, but he grew ashen, his dark eyes widening as he stared at her.

"I hadn't thought," he murmured, his eyes darting around the entryway. Then Simon drew close, his gaze fixing on hers. "You have nothing to fear, Mina. I promise I will never allow you to suffer such treatment ever again. Should you wish for me to toss Finch out, I will do so. Without hesitation."

With each word, Simon's tone tensed, his words coming faster. His grip on her hand tightened, his eyes pleading with her to trust him. There was such an edge of fear to his expression and tone that Mina wished her words recalled. Yes, the present situation brought with it unpleasant memories, but Simon had spent the last three months atoning for those sins, and Mina had no desire to flog him any further.

"Of course not, Simon," said Mina, mustering a smile for him.

Never had Simon paid such strict heed to details. His gaze scoured Mina's expression and posture, looking for all the little signs of her heart. Her shoulders tensed as she spoke. Though her free hand was no longer clenched in her skirts, it had left many wrinkles behind. There was a tightness around her eyes and a twist to the corner of her lips.

Was she speaking the absolute truth? Not that Mina was a liar, but he knew how often she shunted aside her feelings for the benefit of others. Was she doing so again?

After the beauty of their morning drive, this moment felt all the more painful. For that alone, Simon was ready to toss Finch out into the snow.

"Are you certain?" he asked, his eyes scouring for all those little hints of her feelings. Mina usually had such an open expression, but in such moments, Simon wasn't sure he trusted himself to understand his wife. His inability to read her moods had nearly cost him his marriage three months ago.

Mina wrapped her arms around him, holding him close. "Do not fret, my love."

Simon buried his face into her neck, breathing in her scent that held a hint of the lilies she adored so much.

"Finch is a fine fellow, truly," he murmured. "He does not always think before he speaks—"

"I am well aware of that." A hint of a smile colored her tone.

"But he has a good heart, Mina. I do think you'll like him when you come to know him better." Leaning back to meet her gaze, Simon pressed a kiss to her nose. "And should you wish to at any time, simply tell me, and I will heave him out the nearest window."

Mina laughed, a smile lighting her eyes, but Simon did not join in. Giving her a squeeze, he watched her with all the determination of his heart.

"I am in earnest, my love," he said. "You are my heart and soul, and I will not allow you to be mistreated again. If you are in any way unhappy, you need only mention it, and I will do what I can to fix it."

"You sound like a knight of old swearing his fealty to his lady love," she said with a hint of mirth.

Simon squeezed her. "I am. And I swear it. You are everything to me."

Mina's eyes brightened, her hand coming up to brush her favorite spot on his cheek as she always did when particularly moved, and then she closed the distance once more, and all thoughts of Finch and past heartaches faded into nothing.

Chapter 5

Considering his family's pretensions, Finch wondered if his father would suffer apoplexy at the sight of his youngest son tying his own cravat. His fingers moved with the speed and dexterity of one well used to performing such a task, and they flew through the motions with little prompting from their master. No doubt, the Kingsleys' staff thought him odd for refusing the ministrations of their footman, but having forgone a valet long ago, he saw no need to use one at Avebury Park.

Finch examined himself in the mirror, turning this way and that. A stray thread hung from the seam on his sleeve, so he retrieved his sewing scissors and snipped the dreadful thing off, making doubly certain that no imperfection was to be seen.

Striding from his bedchamber, he wished he could banish thoughts of his father's edicts as easily as that. Money was a useful thing, but when one had little, it became an all-consuming presence in one's life. Like a squalling babe, it demanded constant attention but without the promise that such tantrums would fade with time. If anything, the foul thing became more incessant as the years sped by.

Finch paused in the hallway. Was he going to allow this to ruin his holiday? Visiting Simon was his favorite time of year, and yet his mind was determined to spend the entirety of it fretting about that which he could not change.

Shaking aside those worries, Finch focused on his friend. Surely Simon had finished the task that had occupied the majority of his morning, and they could pass the rest of it in their usual pursuits—like a proper ride. His brothers' stables lacked any remarkable mounts, but Simon had quite the collection. Sheba was a pretty filly always game for daring antics across the Essex countryside. The nip in the air was worth braving if he could spend a few moments astride that superb beast.

Lost in his thoughts, Finch did not notice the dining room's sole occupant until he was standing beside her. Halting in his tracks, he stared at the lady, and she stared right back with a piece of dry toast lifted to her lips.

"Mr. Finch," she said in greeting, dropping her gaze away from him. Her muscles tensed, her cheeks pinking ever-so-slightly.

"Mrs. Kingsley," he replied with a nod, thanking his luck that he did not trip over her name. It seemed odd to refer to Simon's wife in such a manner. Of course, it seemed odd that Simon had a wife at all, but to stand on ceremony in a home more beloved than his own was ludicrous. Yet with every look and tone, Mrs. Kingsley made it clear she did not welcome familiarity with Finch.

Sweeping his gaze over the lady, Finch gave her a winning smile. "That is a fetching gown, Mrs. Kingsley."

The lady stiffened at the compliment, yet somehow also shrank before his gaze. For the life of him, Finch did not know why she found him so offensive, yet over the course of the last day, every time he so much as looked in her direction, Mina Kingsley blushed, stammered, and generally seemed ill at ease in his presence.

Serving himself a plate from the sideboard, Finch took the seat opposite Mrs. Kingsley. He'd hidden in his bedchamber to avoid such interludes, and now they were forced together. The silverware clinked against the china, serving as the only sound in the room.

"Lovely weather we're having," said Finch.

Mrs. Kingsley looked up from her plate, her eyes connecting with his for a moment before they moved to the window that looked out on the overcast and gloomy day. She gave no reply and returned to her breakfast, staring at it with grim determination.

"Good morning, darling," said Simon, breaking through the tense air of the dining room as he strode through the doorway and came to his wife's side.

Mrs. Kingsley's face lit with a smile. "Mrs. White has made your favorite."

Simon took her hand and placed a kiss on it. The pair said not another word, their gazes locked in some silent communication that felt far more intimate than a proper embrace. Mrs. Kingsley's cheeks blossomed red, though her lips remained fixed in a glowing grin. Clearing his throat, Finch drew Simon's gaze, and Mrs. Kingsley's blush deepened while Simon gave a chagrined smile.

"I did not see you there, Finch," he said, giving his friend a nod before going to fetch himself some breakfast.

"I was well aware of that," replied Finch, spearing a bit of kipper on his fork. "You two have been married nearly a year. I would think any infatuation would've faded by now."

Simon cast his friend a self-satisfied grin over his shoulder before returning from the sideboard to take his seat beside his wife, who was blushing all the more. As Simon tucked into his breakfast, Finch was forced to acknowledge that sometime between their marriage and the present, Simon had fallen in love with the lady. In truth, Finch was glad to see it. What he'd thought would be a loveless marriage had blossomed into something beautiful, and it did him good to know his friend was so very contented.

And yet each whispered conversation and tender touch opened a gulf between Finch and Simon. Before, Finch's visits had provided a welcome distraction from Simon's never-ending work on Avebury Park. Now, Mrs. Kingsley gave him the daily support and friendship Simon needed. Unfortunately, Finch needed the distraction as much as Simon had, and there was no one left to fill that role.

Getting to his feet, Finch gave his farewells to the pair (one of whom seemed relieved while the other looked only mildly disappointed) and strode from the dining room in search of a new distraction.

...

Fairly pressing her nose against the coach window, Felicity watched the trees pass as she searched ahead for Buxby Hall. So little of the grounds had changed over the years, and it did her good to see it had remained so constant. It was not the proper time of year for berry picking or luxurious picnics among fields of wildflowers, but Felicity was desperate to grasp the peace she found when visiting dear Great-Aunt Imogene.

"Bristow is a little slice of heaven," Uncle George had always said, and they were words that held an echo of her father's voice, though Felicity could not recall him saying such.

The house crawled towards them, a great grey edifice sitting amidst a swath of white. The carriage passed the pond, now frozen over and ringed with trees coated in ice crystals. Felicity had the door open before the footman reached it, and she hurried up the stairs and through the front door to find Great-Aunt Imogene coming down the staircase to greet her.

"My dear, thank heavens you've arrived," said the lady. "I feared something terrible must have happened, for I expected you ages ago."

Felicity widened her eyes and grimaced. "It was not the worst journey I've ever taken, but it was quite possibly the second worst. There were lame horses, broken wheels, and impassable roads between here and Plymouth. It is a miracle I arrived at all."

"My dear, you look pale," said Aunt Imogene, examining her niece with a gimlet eye. "You haven't been taking care of yourself."

"It is the strain of travel, but all will be well now that I am here."

"Come, the servants are preparing a repast for you," said Aunt Imogene, motioning for her to follow down the hall. As much as a warm meal sounded delightful, Felicity's heart sank at the thought of remaining indoors.

"Would you think me terribly ungrateful if I begged off at present? I know I only just arrived, but I have been cooped up for almost a sennight, and I am desperate for a stroll. Might I spend a quarter of an hour visiting your grounds before we eat?"

"Of course," said Aunt Imogene, patting Felicity's cheek with a wrinkled hand as though her great-niece was little more than a fretful schoolchild. "I am the same. I cannot bear to remain caged for too long. I would join you, but I fear I am not as steady on my feet, and this winter is far too frigid and icy for my good."

"Unsteady?" asked Felicity, standing back to examine the elderly lady.

"Not to worry, my dear. It is merely age demanding I pay it more heed," she said with a smile.

Felicity's brows furrowed, but Aunt Imogene waved away any concern, bundling the younger lady out the front door with a promise that she would return before her fingers and toes froze through.

Opening her lungs, Felicity took in a deep breath, filling them to capacity. The air was biting but so very bracing that she took several more before making her way around Buxby Hall. Even in the midst of winter, the gardens were lovely. Or perhaps because of it. Though the blossoms were long dormant, the woody plants boasted a fine smattering of ice that sparkled even though clouds filled the sky.

With a tug of the ribbons, Felicity pulled off her bonnet. It was too cold to do so for long, but she reveled in the breezes tugging at her curls. Her hair must look a fright, but such mundane worries faded to the background as she plopped her bonnet back on, allowing the ribbons to hang free. Each step from the house took her further from the weight of her cares and worries, as though the very land she stood upon held some magical properties to erase heartache and troubles.

Yes, this was precisely where she ought to be. Away from the constant demands of business and false suitors. Free of the unending troubles and strife. Unshackled by the expectations of an heiress. Here, she was simply Felicity Barrows.

Though her promise to Aunt Imogene had her thinking she ought to return to the house, Felicity could not keep herself from wandering towards a particularly lovely copse of trees, their dark trunks contrasting against the winter's white. Just one quick look—

Felicity's left foot shot forward, her right keeping her tethered to firm ground but without the ability to steady her. She had no time to react to the sudden disruption of her balance, and gravity pulled her down. If pressed, she would have no thought as to what it was she slipped on—the ground looked as sturdy as any patch—but such details did not matter, for they did not alter her present course.

The whole of her weight slammed onto the frozen ground, her right foot wrenching as the force of her fall twisted her. Every joint screamed at once, the impact radiating through her. Her bonnet went flying, her cloak and skirt tangling around her as she landed with a thud.

Staring up at the cloudy sky, Felicity lay there, her body throbbing in time with her heartbeat. Like a howling winter wind, she moaned, the noise pulled from deep within. It was a horrid sound, but her rattled bones demanded it, and another built inside her, growing in volume.

Felicity dared not to twitch. She simply lay there amidst the snow and ice and hoped nothing was broken. She needed only a moment—or an hour—and then she could attempt to regain her feet. No doubt, that would be a painful undertaking.

And then Fate played another cruel trick on Felicity, for a voice called out to her, followed by the sound of hurried hooves. Her body was already bruised; did her ego need pummeling as well? A face appeared above her, and Felicity felt like groaning anew.

Chapter 6

"That was quite the fall." The gentleman crouched down beside her and placed a hand on her arm as though to help her upright. But Felicity only wished to lie there. Perhaps forever.

"Allow me to help you," he said.

"There is no need."

"I doubt it. That was a spectacular tumble."

Felicity sighed. "If you are going to do something, do it spectacularly."

The edges of his lips quirked into a smile. "Then you succeeded admirably. Now, sit up."

But Felicity did not move. Her body twinged with every breath, so she knew standing would be an unpleasant experience, and doing so in front of an audience would make it all the worse.

"I thank you for your concern, but I can manage. Please be on your way. I will be right in a moment."

His light brows rose. "You think I could leave without assuring myself you are well?"

The gentleman reached for her foot, and Felicity jerked it away, a surge of pain accompanying the movement.

"What do you think you are doing?" she demanded.

"Checking for breaks. I wouldn't be surprised if you did yourself serious damage."

"I assure you I am whole." Despite wishing for more time, Felicity forced herself upright. Her muscles and joints protested, and her head spun, but the world righted itself in quick succession.

"And how would you know?"

Felicity frowned. "As they are my bones, I would know if they were out of sorts."

Straightening, the fellow looked at her with a matching scowl. "Are you always so obstinate? I am merely offering my assistance."

Cursing her wretched tongue, Felicity sighed. "I am not obstinate. I am merely embarrassed beyond words that anyone witnessed my 'spectacular tumble' and wish to be left in peace while I lick my proverbial wounds."

"They may be more than proverbial, but we cannot know for certain unless you allow me to check you," he muttered.

Felicity's shoulders dropped. "I apologize. I appreciate your assistance."

Finch eyed the young lady, wondering if he was bound to feel the bite of her tongue once more, but the previous show of temper faded, leaving her looking quite contrite. Untangling her skirts from around her feet, Finch removed the slipper and felt her ankle. The chill already had the young lady's cheeks a bright red, but there was a quality to it that made him wonder if she were blushing.

"Are you a physician?" she asked.

"No," he replied, and her foot stiffened, so he added, "While in the army, I had thought to pursue medicine and studied with a surgeon. Though my education is limited, I have enough experience to tell if a bone is broken or whole."

With a few prods, Finch replaced the slipper and moved to

her other foot. "They appear to be perfect."

The lady gave another sigh. "That is a compliment I haven't heard before. If you begin to wax poetic about my lovely appendages, I may have to brain you."

Leaning back, Finch stared at her before letting out a wholly sincere scoff. The lady wasn't an antidote and wholly unpleasant to gaze upon, but neither was she some Aphrodite who ought to be concerned about swains tossing themselves at her feet.

Her hair was a haze of curls, but not the sort that ladies spent countless hours cultivating. Many had fallen free of her coiffure, and they were a riotous tangle that some might call titian to be kind but were, in fact, a garish orange. And though her figure was nice enough, her features were bland and forgettable, but that might have more to do with the attention her complexion commanded.

Finch had little experience with smallpox, as his family had been spared that scourge, but even his uneducated eyes recognized the signs its survivors bore. The state of her scars was such that he suspected it had been some years since she'd been afflicted, but there was no ignoring the uneven marks marring her face. The lady was not one to command a man's attention, let alone inspire love at first sight.

"I assure you, I have no designs on you no matter how highly you prize yourself," he said with narrowed eyes.

The lady had the gall to stare at him with wide eyes, her brows rising so high up her blasted forehead that they disappeared beneath the curls. Honestly, the gentlemen of Bristow must suffer from poor vision, but he had ample evidence of their odd proclivities: Simon called Mina beautiful at regular intervals.

Though the lady was a good, kindhearted sort of person, Mina was more than plump and her features were too bland to be anything but plain. Her hair was more a muddy brown than a lovely chestnut. And Finch was certain that Simon was the only gentleman in existence to find Mina Kingsley attractive.

Was it feigned, or did Simon truly see his wife in such a light? But that was not a quandary to dredge through when he was staring down a feisty lady in need.

Finch returned to his examination, feeling her lower legs through her skirts. Though it was difficult to tell with so many layers muting his touch, Finch doubted the lady was severely injured: she was complaining too vehemently.

But when she spoke again, the lady's tone was far more calm and sedate. "I apologize for being so beastly to you. I can only say that my fall has me out of sorts, and I fear I've unleashed my temper on you, which is monstrously unfair of me."

"I accept," he said, releasing her legs. "And you appear to be whole and unscathed."

"Except for my backside," she muttered in a low voice clearly not intended for him to hear, and so Finch ignored it.

Reaching forward, Finch assisted her to her feet, though she groaned like an octogenarian as she did so. Locks of her hair tumbled free, and she patted at it for a moment before giving up on the hopeless cause, but it drew Finch's attention to her missing bonnet. Glancing around the area, he spied a bit of brown and green resting amidst the white, and Finch fetched it for her. The lady looked at the snow-covered thing and grimaced, wiping at the flakes clinging to the fabric, before placing it on her head.

"Might I offer you my mount, Mrs…" Finch blinked at the lady, realizing he had no thought as to her surname.

"Miss Felicity Barrows," she said, brushing off her skirts. "And though I appreciate your generosity, I am not much of a rider."

Finch gave his name and a bow. "I thought every country lady was fond of horses."

Miss Barrows straightened. "I am a city dweller, Mr. Finch, and have spent little time on horseback."

"Then allow me to escort you," he said, offering his arm, though he had no idea why he was bothering to do so. Of course, a lifetime of training had taught him to never abandon a woman in distress, but he supposed it had more to do with the fact that it was something to fill his time.

Miss Barrows looked at his arm, her expression pinching in a manner that made him think she was unwilling, but the lady sloughed off her trepidation and took hold of it. The ground was not terribly slick, but there were enough worrisome patches that Finch had not allowed Sheba to gallop as they'd both longed to; he gave the beast a quick rub of her nose before retrieving her reins and leading her behind them.

"And where are we headed, Miss Barrows?" Finch was pleased to feel the lady holding tight to his arm, giving him more of her weight as she limped along.

She slanted him a glance. "Buxby Hall."

"You are staying with Lady Lovell?"

Mr. Finch's tone was warm and bright as he spoke that grand lady's name, but Felicity flinched at it. Playing it over in her head, she tried to discern some deeper meaning behind the question. Such things may seem innocent enough, but minor questions can lead to major annoyances.

"I am, sir," she said.

"Then you are a friend of the family?"

Surely she had no reason to be suspicious; she didn't even know if Mr. Finch was married or not. And until now, he had been pleasantly distant, showing the care and assistance any gentleman would offer. But if she admitted the connection, would he guess her situation? Assume more of her? Seek out a closer acquaintance?

However, there was little point in avoiding the truth, for too many knew her connection to Lady Lovell.

"She is my great-aunt." Then a thought struck like proverbial lightning from above, presenting Felicity with the perfect solution, and the words were out before she had time to think the better of it. "She's invited me to stay as her companion."

Chapter 7

No matter how little the lie seemed, it was impossible to speak it without her stomach giving a sour twist, but Felicity could not say she was sorry for the deception. It was near enough to the truth, as she would be serving as a companion of sorts during her stay; yet it made distinct inferences that shielded her from unwanted attention.

Only a poor relation lived as a companion, and Felicity was more than willing to embrace that role at present. Being free of proposals and feigned declarations of love was the precise reason she'd come to Bristow in the first place. A little lie was not such a terrible thing. Not if it brought her the solace she so desperately needed.

"Well, I am happy for that," said Mr. Finch. "Lady Lovell is delightful, and I've often worried about her living all alone. I gather her son and his family do not visit the estate often, and she ought to have company."

"I am glad for it, too. I have always enjoyed my time in Bristow, though I do not recall seeing you among the locals before."

"I am visiting my friend, Mr. Simon Kingsley, at present."

Felicity smiled at that. "Avebury Park is a fine estate."

And that statement led to questions about their respective homes, and though the conversation was hardly enlivening or interesting, it was familiar. Peaceful even. It was just the sort of discussion she'd had many a time before, full of the banalities one expected between strangers.

In her younger years, she'd despised such insipid subjects, but speaking with someone who had no designs on her was heaven-sent. Though Uncle George's money was a blessing in so many ways, it carried a slew of burdens, including an increased propensity for gentlemen to recite poetry at ridiculous moments. And Felicity reveled in her present anonymity.

As they walked, Felicity's twinges eased, attesting that she'd gained nothing more than a few bruises, but she was glad to see Buxby Hall appear in the distance. By the time they arrived, she was quite done with the outdoors and wanted a comfortable chair beside a blazing fire and a cup of something warm to drink.

A footman answered the door, and his eyes widened at the sight of Felicity hanging on Mr. Finch's arm. He called for servants to handle the gentleman's horse and led the pair into the entry, but her wet slippers touched the polished marble and struggled to find purchase. Before she added to her aches by crashing to the ground again, Mr. Finch swept her into his arms.

Felicity gasped and held onto his neck, and the fellow slanted a look in her direction.

"Are you attempting to impress me with your strength, Mr. Finch?" she teased.

"Only saving you from yourself, Miss Barrows. You are lucky I do not dump you right here, for you are quite heavy." Said in any other manner, Felicity might have believed him to be speaking in jest, but Mr. Finch's tone was all too serious to be mistaken. Perhaps she ought to have been offended by such an implication, but Felicity was no fool; she may be of average height and build, but that did not mean it was easy to haul her about.

"Then I am not the 'picture of feminine daintiness'?" she asked, repeating something one of her former swains had claimed.

Mr. Finch gave no vocal response, though his eyes spoke of his confusion and incredulity, further adding to Felicity's mirth.

"Why are you looking at me like that?" he asked.

"You are refreshingly honest," she said as Mr. Finch carried her into the parlor.

"Good heavens, what has happened to you?" said Aunt Imogene, rising from the sofa.

"I'm afraid your companion took a nasty tumble, though she is mostly unharmed," said Mr. Finch.

Aunt Imogene's brows rose at that, though it was more due to what he'd called Felicity. The older lady's gaze met Felicity's, and she gave her great-aunt a pleading look. Though Aunt Imogene's expression tightened, she did not correct Mr. Finch.

Mr. Finch set her on the sofa and bowed, giving a few words of farewell, but Aunt Imogene pounded her cane against the hardwood floor as Mr. Finch turned to leave.

"Lewis Finch, you cannot think to walk away without greeting me properly."

The gentleman glanced from Aunt Imogene to Felicity. "I thought you might wish to attend to Miss Barrows."

But Aunt Imogene, showing all the loving concern she was wont to do in such situations, waved the question away. "Bah, she is not going to die if we take a few moments. I haven't seen you in nearly a year, my dear boy."

A smile curled the edges of Mr. Finch's lips, and he turned back to the pair of ladies, giving Aunt Imogene a gallant bow befitting royalty.

"My dearest apologies, madam," he said, taking her hand in his and placing a kiss on her knuckles. "You must excuse my errant manners."

"I shall forgive you this time, but see that it does not happen again," she said with an imperious sniff. But her haughtiness melted away, and Aunt Imogene grinned at Mr. Finch, giving him a matronly pat on the cheek. "You are a good lad. I'm glad to see you've returned to us again. Are you enjoying your time at Avebury Park? Simon's new wife is a dear, and it does me good to see them so happy together."

"Yes, they are quite jubilant," said Mr. Finch, and Felicity caught a certain something that belied the warmth of his expression and words. She could not pinpoint what it was precisely, but she'd sensed a falseness beneath his earnest demeanor throughout his conversation. But that was not quite right, for he was not duplicitous. Felicity watched him as he and Aunt Imogene exchanged a few more pleasantries, and before long she recognized the truth for what it was—he held a tinge of sorrow beneath the placid exterior.

With another bow, Mr. Finch took his leave, and Felicity stared after him.

"What do you mean by misleading Mr. Finch?" asked Aunt Imogene, coming to stand before her great-niece with an imperious frown.

"It is nothing—"

But that prevarication was cut short by a snap of the lady's cane against the floor, and Aunt Imogene narrowed her eyes. "I do not care for falsehoods, Felicity Barrows."

A footman and maid entered at that moment, giving Felicity a reprieve as they readied a tray of tea and cakes for the pair of them. She ought to change out of her damp gown and slippers, but with the fire stoked, and a warm blanket provided by one of the servants, Felicity was in no hurry to vacate her position.

Once they left with a bow and a bob, Aunt Imogene turned on her great-niece, demanding answers.

"I didn't set out to deceive Mr. Finch," began Felicity, but she hung her head, rubbing at her temple. "That is not true. I did wish to deceive him."

Aunt Imogene opened her mouth, but Felicity spoke over her.

"I need some peace, Aunt, and this little fib will give it to me. Besides, it's not far from the truth. I am here to stay with you, I am your niece, and I do enjoy looking after you when I am around."

At that, Felicity readied a cup of tea for Aunt Imogene, which did wonders to erase the disapproving glint in the lady's eye.

"I simply do not wish to be known as the Heiress. Just for a little bit."

"I do not like deceptions, my girl. They rarely end well," said Aunt Imogene, though she set herself to enjoying her tea and cakes.

Tugging the blanket closer around her, Felicity stared at the flames in the fireplace. "Did Uncle George ever tell you of my failed elopement?"

With wide eyes, the older lady blinked at her great-niece.

Felicity took in a deep breath, letting it out with a pained expression. "I was a foolish girl of sixteen, who allowed herself to be swayed by a man with honeyed words and a calculating heart. He was the younger brother of one of Uncle's clerks, and I was convinced Alastair Dunn was everything I longed for in a gentleman. I knew how people view my scars—"

"Oh, Felicity—"

But she held up a staying hand. "I know, Aunt Imogene. I pay it no heed now, but I was not so self-assured at that age. He was the first person, outside my closest friends and family, who did not treat me as though I still carried the pox with me. Alastair convinced me I was the most gorgeous creature he'd ever seen."

The elderly lady abandoned her tea and cakes, coming to sit beside Felicity on the sofa and taking her hand in hers. "You are not the first to be swayed by such things."

Felicity squeezed her hand. "No, nor am I the first to be talked into an elopement. Alastair convinced me Uncle George was biased against his suit, and that Scotland was the only option for us. I hadn't spent much time in the company of gentlemen, so it never occurred to me that Uncle's money was the true enticement. Luckily, Uncle George discovered it before I boarded the coach."

Her heart gave a sad sigh, though Felicity did not know if it was because of the pain attached to the memory of that awful night or how much she missed her dear uncle. A year and a half of mourning had eased much of her sorrow, but at times like these, she missed his support and guidance.

"You should've seen Uncle," she said with a faint smile. "There I was, sitting in a coaching inn, awaiting Alastair's arrival, and Uncle George barreled in, leaping out of his carriage before it had come to a stop. I thought he'd be furious, but his only concern was my safety. I was such a simpleton and didn't consider what evil can befall an unaccompanied young lady at a coaching inn."

"I shudder to think of it," said Aunt Imogene.

"As do I, but providence smiled down upon me, and Uncle George discovered Alastair's plans. Once Uncle made it clear he would not give us a farthing if we eloped, Alastair disappeared, leaving behind a pathetic note of apology. The villain didn't even bother to give me the news in person or tell me before I spent hours sitting in the cold, waiting for him. He simply never showed."

And it truly was a pathetic note of apology, though Felicity was not about to share those brief words. She'd burned the missive long ago, but it could not erase their memory, as though the words were burned into her mind.

I cannot marry you, Felicity. Please forgive me. —A.

For a man with so many sweet words to say, he ought to have managed something more than that.

"I cannot imagine George cutting you off," said Aunt Imogene, drawing Felicity back to the present, and her observation drew a smile from her great-niece.

"Uncle George would never be so cruel, but my beaus believed it to be true, which ensured each petitioned for his approval, and not one received it. For a time, I was bitter over his interference, but I came to understand. And having seen the specimens that have lined up to claim my hand since Uncle George passed, it is no mystery as to why he sent them all packing."

Of course, there was more to the story than those few sentences could convey, but that was the heart of the matter. Felicity felt no need to expound at length over the pain Alastair and all the others had caused, for it was of no significance now. If anything, she silently thanked them for their part in her history. For good or ill, it had molded her, and Felicity was quite pleased with the end product.

"So, I am sorry for having misled Mr. Finch, but I could not bear the thought of yet another gentleman tripping over himself to earn my good opinion."

Aunt Imogene's lips pinched. "I cannot claim to be pleased with it, but I will not give away the truth. Nor will I lie."

"I am not here to socialize, and no one in the neighborhood knows of my inheritance. I doubt the truth will be discovered, and I cannot see how my financial affairs are anyone's business but my own. So, it should not matter if I am a companion or guest."

"Well, you may not be here to socialize, but I do hope Mr. Finch will keep his word and visit," said Aunt Imogene. "He is such a good fellow."

Felicity's brow furrowed. "Do you not think him the slightest bit…" She paused, hunting for the word until it came within her grasp. "…melancholic?"

Aunt Imogene's head cocked to the side, a smile on her lips. "Not at all."

"There is something in his expression that makes me think him unhappy," said Felicity.

Wrapping an arm around her great-niece, Aunt Imogene gave a start. "Oh, my dear. I have been terribly pudding-headed. You are wet and must change immediately."

"I am well enough." For all that the lady was correct, Felicity was not ready to relinquish her seat. The blanket and fire were doing their job to keep her warm, and the journey to her bedchamber would be far colder. But Aunt Imogene had inherited the Barrows family strength of will, and there was no standing against her.

Chapter 8

Having known that conditions were not conducive to a proper ride, Finch ought not to be disappointed about that lackluster turn about the countryside, but hearts are not logical things, and his was quite frustrated at present. Sheba's tail twitched, and she shook her head and neck, as though she wished to shake free of the reins holding her back, but there was nothing to be done about it. Better to end the ride in mutual irritation than risk injury to this fine beast.

He couldn't stand the thought of Sheba following in Miss Barrows' footsteps.

Handing the reins to the groom, Finch gave the horse one final rub along her neck, with a silent promise to do her proud once the ice was clear enough for a safe gallop. He watched the lad lead her away and wished he could follow.

During his time with the light dragoons, finances hadn't allowed him to turn the care of his horse over to others, and what had started as an unwanted necessity had grown into a delight. Whether it was brushing and feeding Ares or oiling and mending the tack, those many little tasks filled his days with something to do. Finch had adored the peace to be found in his horse's stall. But nowadays, he had few opportunities to ride and even fewer to care for a mount.

Turning away from the stables, Finch wandered to the house and amused himself by imagining what his father would have said if he'd seen his son mucking out the stall and giving Ares a scrub. That thought kept him smiling as he entered the front door.

"Is Mr. Kingsley at home?" he asked, as a footman took his jacket, hat, and gloves.

"In his study, sir."

Perhaps he ought to change out of his riding clothes, but Finch was all too pleased with the thought of catching his friend alone to allow a little thing like appropriate attire to rob him of the opportunity. With quick steps, Finch wove through the corridors, moving through those familiar passages until he arrived at Simon's study.

As he pushed the door open, his eyes fell to the sofa beside the fire; that piece of furniture was a new addition to the room, but it was clear why Simon had chosen to replace the matching armchairs. Mina and Simon were wrapped together, and Finch halted in his tracks, jerking backward as Mina flew upright with blazing cheeks, disentangling herself from Simon's hold.

Finch's jaw slackened, his hand affixed to the door handle. "I didn't mean to bother you."

"It is not a bother," said Simon, straightening his cravat. "I'd been wondering where you'd gotten yourself to."

But Finch's brows rose as he gave his friend a wicked smile. "I very much doubt that was on your mind, Simon."

Mina covered her eyes with one hand, though Simon took the other with a chuckle, placing a kiss on the back of it.

"Do not fret, my love. Finch merely derives much pleasure from teasing me."

"As every true friend ought," replied Finch, but his warm words were not met with a smile or a witty rejoinder. Instead, Mina watched him with wary eyes, and Finch felt the itch at the back of his neck that had become a constant companion whenever she was present.

"Had you a good ride?" asked Simon, leaning towards his wife. They were not so brazen as to cuddle together, but he kept her hand in his.

"Not particularly," Finch replied, as he turned the armchair facing Simon's desk towards the pair and took a seat.

Simon's brows rose. "You were gone for such a long time, I thought you must be enjoying yourself."

Finch huffed, shaking his head. "That was due to my impromptu rescue of a damsel in distress."

Cocking his head to the side, Simon gave a hint of a smile. "You rescued a fair damsel?"

"I wouldn't say fair, but I came across a lady who took a nasty tumble and needed a strong arm to assist her home," said Finch. "Lady Lovell has taken in some poor relation as her companion."

At that, Mina's gaze turned to Finch. "Not a companion, Mr. Finch. Her great-niece will be spending a few weeks with her. Lady Lovell spoke at great length about it the other day."

Finch waved an airy hand. "You must be mistaken, for I heard it from the lady herself that she is to be a companion."

He'd thought his comment innocuous enough, but for some reason, the lady's gaze dropped away from his once more as though dismissing him in the only manner available at present. Mina stared down at her hands as she smoothed her skirts, and Simon merely nodded at Finch.

"That is good news. Mina has grown quite close to Lady Lovell and visits her almost daily, but she is too often alone."

"Too true," said Finch with a nod. "Though I will be surprised if Miss Felicity Barrows lasts long in the position. She doesn't have the bearing of a servant and is excessively odd."

"Perhaps this is her first post," said Simon.

Finch shrugged. "Miss Barrows has quite the forceful personality, which will not serve her well as a companion."

At that, Mina huffed, though she remained mute, giving no further indication of the source behind the outburst. When Simon nudged her, she gave her husband a raised brow.

"I cannot think of a better companion for Lady Lovell than someone with a forceful personality. She is forever badgering me about my *mousy* ways."

The lady put a slight emphasis on "mousy," her eyes meeting Finch's for a moment before sliding away, and he knew there was some meaning behind it, though he could not fathom what it was.

"Lady Lovell is a force unto herself," said Simon with a laugh. "I suppose they are a good match, then."

Finch chuckled. "True, but I wish you had been there, Simon. Miss Barrows is an odd creature. There I was, attempting to be gallant, and she was fairly accusing me of being madly in love with her. And she is anything but the sort to inspire sudden bouts of romance."

And with that, he launched into a description of all that had happened while Mina watched him with hooded eyes.

"She seemed congenial enough after a few moments of conversation, but she behaved as though she was a great beauty destined to ensnare me with one glance," he said with a laugh. "It's not as though she is an unfortunate creature, but her complexion is the sort to raise eyebrows—and not in a good sense—and her hair is a most unsightly shade of orange and a tangled mess of wild curls—"

Mina rose to her feet, leveling a hard look at Finch before stalking out the door. Simon straightened and called after his wife, but she did not return.

"What have I done to offend her?" asked Finch. "Perhaps I was a tad harsh, but Miss Barrows' behavior was thoroughly strange—"

But Simon followed his wife's lead and rose to his feet. "I mean no disrespect, Finch, but I haven't the time to discuss that at present. I need to see to my wife."

And with that, Finch was left alone, staring at the books lining Simon's study. While he sat there, a thought crept up on him, whispering such maudlin things that he could not sit still. Getting to his feet, he straightened his jacket and cuffs as though that would right his off-kilter world.

Truly, it was a blessing to see his friend so happily situated, but this shift in Simon's life left him with no space for his aimless friend.

Casting that thought aside, Finch wandered to the drawing room, but when he poked his head inside, he saw the pianoforte was no longer in a forgotten corner of the chamber. Someone had shifted the instrument to sit beneath the windows at the center of the far wall, which afforded the instrument better light. Stacks of sheet music rested on the piano cover, but Finch gave them only a cursory glance, noting an excellent collection of Mozart, Clementi, and others before seating himself on the bench.

His fingers brushed the keys, and Finch smiled at the bright sound that came forth. It was a beautiful instrument, and it had long pained him to see it neglected by Simon and his family. At least its new mistress seemed to appreciate it.

The keys were smooth, their touch a silky joy to his fingertips, and with no more than a passing thought, his fingers climbed the keyboard, running through the crisp trills and runs the composers of the past century so adored. The bright, cheerful tune gave way to the more modern works that softened that precision, eschewing the rudimentary dynamics and giving the musician freedom to infuse his own emotions into the work. And Finch's heart did so, embracing the music as it swept him away from his present cares.

From the corner of his eye, Finch saw the drawing room door open.

"It is good to hear you playing," said Simon, coming to join his friend. Like many drawing rooms, the area was sparsely furnished with a few pieces of furniture edging the room, leaving the majority of the space free to be transformed into whatever was needed for evening entertainment. From the placement of the piano, Finch supposed Mina preferred music and dancing to cards.

"It seems your instrument is finally receiving the proper attention and maintenance it deserves," replied Finch in a dry tone. "How is Mina?"

Simon came to stand beside the pianoforte, his hand resting atop the wood cover as his fingers drummed along in pace with the notes. As Finch was quite familiar with this piece, his gaze drifted from the keyboard to his friend.

"She is well enough and just set off to pay a call to Mrs. Pratt concerning their new literary society," said Simon. The words were reassuring, though Simon's tone was not. Besides, Finch was hard-pressed to believe Mina's sudden departure was nothing. Her cool dismissal was easily understood, even if it was puzzling.

Finch glanced at his fingers. "It's hard to believe all is well when you look so fretful."

Sucking in a deep breath, Simon let it out in a great heaving puff of air. "We've not had a good go of it, Finch. Not three months ago, she left me."

The tune jerked to a halt, and Finch stared at his friend, but Simon hurried to add, "I hold all the blame. I was a fool and treated her shabbily. Mina had every reason for doing so, and I count myself eternally blessed that she forgave me after I prostrated myself before her. Things have been perfect ever since, but something has her at odds now, and I cannot discern what I've done this time."

Finch started to play where he'd left off, his thoughts gathering as the melody tripped along. "She seems displeased with me. Perhaps I ought to go—"

Shaking his head, Simon cut off that thought. "No, she assured me she wishes you to stay, so it has naught to do with you."

But Finch was not so certain of that. Surely, it was the truth as Simon saw it, but though the fellow was as good a friend as any could wish for, Simon Kingsley was not the most observant of men.

"If you are certain you wish me to stay, then I will." Finch kept his eyes trained on the keys, hiding away how much Simon's answer meant to him.

The thought of returning to London was enough to make his insides turn to lead. The city had its diversions, but too many were beyond his financial means, and those available to him were hardly enjoyable when Finch was forced to attend them alone. Simon would not return to London until the Season began—or perhaps he would not return at all, as Finch doubted the fellow's wife found much pleasure there.

"Of course I wish you to stay," said Simon, turning an incredulous look in Finch's direction. "If anything, your arrival is quite providential, for I require your advice."

Finch laughed. "What advice could I give you?"

Simon frowned at that. "You do not give yourself proper credit, sir. There are few whose opinions I value more than yours. If not for your input, I wouldn't have married Mina."

The music stumbled once more, coming to a stop, and Finch gaped at Simon. "I gave you a warning against marrying for convenience's sake, and you married against my advice, though I'm pleased to see it has fared well for you."

That soppy smile of Simon's grew, his eyes brightening. "It has fared more than 'well,' Finch. Mina is a treasure. I couldn't have found a better wife, and if not for you bringing her to my attention, I wouldn't have thought to pursue her."

Finch had no response to that, for he hadn't been in earnest in pointing Mina out at that fateful ball. True, he'd always harbored respect for the lady, but he'd never thought Simon would marry her.

"But we are drifting from the subject at hand," said Simon. "I have often found your opinions on finance and investments to be quite sound. As much as I value Mina's input on matters of the estate, she knows so little about the nuances of economy, and I am in desperate need of guidance."

Nodding towards a pair of chairs sitting beside the pianoforte, Finch abandoned the instrument while making plans to return and sift through Mina's music at a later time.

"My steward insists we invest some of our income into other ventures," said Simon. "And while his reasons are logical, I cannot help but feel as though it would be detrimental to siphon funds away from the estate. The weather has been so temperamental of late, and I fear we are bound for some difficult harvests ahead. With our financial reserves tied up in investments, there will be nothing to keep the estate afloat, and I cannot abide the thought of taking on debt."

Simon pinched his nose. "Mr. Thorne has been most vocal on the subject, but I cannot see my way to a solution."

This was a familiar subject and one that Finch did not understand. Why were those with money always seemingly so ignorant about it? But he supposed it was easy to take a fortune for granted when one had never known poverty. Simon was a good master, but the financial practices of the past were no longer viable in their modern world. And Finch told him so.

"It is not enough for estates to merely sit on their capital, Simon. While you ought to keep aside some funds for emergencies, take the rest and invest. That will give your estate other revenues during desperate times. You must expand but be prudent while doing so."

This was the sort of thing he would miss when Simon grew too busy with his new wife and the forthcoming brood of children. Even as they spoke about possible ventures to undertake, Finch found an odd sort of humor in the idea that a gentleman with a measly income was advising another with fifty times his fortune. Only Simon Kingsley would turn to Lewis Finch for advice on such matters.

But that was one of the many reasons Finch liked him. Unlike so many of his station, Simon Kingsley had no pretension, and though Finch could not understand why the fellow valued his opinion, he was glad to give it.

Chapter 9

Uncle George had preferred the city, and thus, Felicity had spent many of her thirty years surrounded by townhouses and buildings that were lovely but had not the splendor of their country cousins. Buxby Hall was a prime example of such estates. The Lovells had the wealth and status to own a very large and grand property, and it was a place of opulence, which existed to be a sign of wealth more than a true home.

Though appreciative of the refuge it offered from the toils and troubles of the city, Felicity did not feel wholly comfortable within it. She preferred simpler designs, which was no doubt a byproduct of Uncle George's influence.

Her newly inherited Farleigh Manor was a beautiful property, and Uncle George had purchased it for the estate's potential to turn a healthy profit, given the right management. Most of their class viewed the house as humble, which was laughable when compared to the truly humble dwellings of the poor, but Farleigh Manor favored economy over opulence, and Felicity loved it all the more for it.

Avebury Park, on the other hand, was a blend of the two. It shared Buxby Hall's grander scale, but eschewed the embellishments and focused on clean lines and economy of design. The building focused on space and light, giving an airiness to the interior that was too often lacking in many homes.

Standing in the entryway, Felicity clutched a basket in her hands and stared unabashedly at her surroundings. She couldn't recall ever stepping foot inside Avebury Park before (as she'd never had cause to visit), but she liked it and wondered if she might borrow the design for the staircase in Farleigh Manor. It would have to be scaled down, but the sweep of the banister drew the eye in such a delightful manner.

"Mr. Finch will see you in the library, miss." The footman's voice drew her from her musings, and Felicity followed the fellow as he led her through the building.

Felicity shifted the basket from one hand to the other and allowed her eyes to wander. The halls were darker, which was to be expected as they had less access to windows, but the doors to the adjacent rooms were all open, allowing a flood of afternoon light to chase away much of the shadows.

The footman stopped at one of the doors and motioned for her to enter, and Felicity found Mr. Finch standing in front of an armchair with his hands tucked behind him.

"Miss Barrows," Mr. Finch said with a bow, and Felicity wondered what she'd been thinking coming here.

This trip to Bristow was meant to be free of gentlemen, yet she was seeking one out. Had she taken leave of her senses? Felicity cast a glance at the bundle she carried and cursed herself doubly for the silly impulse. But there was nothing wrong with bestowing a kindness, and her status as a companion gave her the anonymity she craved.

"Am I interrupting you?" she asked, nodding towards the book he'd abandoned on the side table. "Were you reading anything of interest?"

"No." His expression held mild curiosity, glancing between her and the basket in her hands. "Are you feeling better today,

Miss Barrows? I didn't expect you to be walking the neighborhood yet."

"I am well enough," she replied, and apart from a few bruises, she was. Stepping forward, Felicity pulled back the fabric covering her bundle, and the scent of molasses, ginger, cinnamon, cloves, and nutmeg filled the room, drawing Mr. Finch closer. "I brought you a gift."

"Gingerbread cake?"

Felicity smiled. "Aunt Imogene assured me it was your favorite and that you pilfer her reserve whenever you are about."

Mr. Finch's brown eyes rose to meet hers, his fair brows drawing together. "And what have I done to deserve such a grand reward?"

Handing the basket to the gentleman, Felicity waved an airy hand. "After the service you rendered me yesterday, I would think it obvious."

"And I would think it obvious that such a service needs no reward," he replied, though it did not stop him from breaking off a small bit of cake and popping it into his mouth. "If I had left you there, I would've deserved a flogging."

Felicity gave another vague wave and smile. "Are Mr. and Mrs. Kingsley not around?"

"They keep to themselves in the morning," said Mr. Finch, his attention on the basket as he breathed in the spicy scent of the gingerbread.

"And you are left to yourself?" Felicity cast a glance at the empty room and wondered how often he was alone.

Mr. Finch shrugged. "They usually invite me to join them, but I prefer not being the awkward addition to their activities. Though I do not begrudge my friend's happiness, there is only so much romance one can stomach."

The gentleman smiled in a manner that was more of a good-natured grimace, and Felicity laughed, as she knew he meant her to, but it was as hollow as Mr. Finch's feigned humor. Casting her thoughts to the world around her, Felicity scoured for a way in which to bring a true smile to his face.

"Would you accompany me about the grounds, Mr. Finch?" The air was as brisk as ever, but it was better than allowing him to sit about in this great empty house alone.

Mr. Finch's head cocked to one side. "After our last stroll, I would say you are a glutton for punishment."

"Yes, but I met with disaster *before* you came across me in my prone state. I would love to explore some more, but I need a strong arm to keep me from ruin."

Mr. Finch's eyes brightened, and he watched her with a narrowed gaze. "Then you might wish to seek out someone with a stronger arm than mine, for you are exceptionally heavy, Miss Barrows."

"I suppose if I need assistance, you shall have to run and find me a more strapping gentleman to lend me his arm," she said with an innocent smile before turning to the library door.

The gentleman followed, and soon the pair were bundled up and on their way (though not before Mr. Finch pilfered another piece of gingerbread). He offered up a bit to Felicity, but she declined, and they made their way out into the world.

The sky was the clearest and lightest of blues she'd ever seen, and the sun shone bright, casting the world in a golden glow that was amplified by the ice crystals clinging to every still surface. The air was quiet, as though no one else stirred this glorious morning. Puffs of smoke curled upwards into the distance, marking the locations of the cottages in the area, and though the cold was already nipping at Felicity's cheeks, she could not think of a better way to pass a morning.

"I heard a lady say she was forty, and when it was questioned, she called upon another for his opinion on the matter," she said, infusing her tone with a casual air. "She asked him, 'Do you believe me when I say I am forty?' And he replied, 'I ought not to dispute it, madam, for I have heard you say so these ten years.'"

Mr. Finch's expression scrunched, and he cast her a side glance. Felicity pretended not to notice, simply walking along as though she'd said nothing out of the ordinary. And then the fellow began to chuckle. It was not a deep laugh, but he shook his head with a smile.

"My father adored publications like the *Covent Garden Jester*, and I was raised with an appreciation for wordplay and jests," Felicity said with a smile.

"You are a strange lady, Miss Barrows."

"I will take that as a compliment, Mr. Finch."

His smile quirked up to one side, his brown eyes lightening. "As you should. The world is overpopulated with normal ladies."

"And isn't it so much better to embrace the ridiculous?" she said, examining his profile. "I prefer to see people laughing."

If Finch wanted to lie to himself, he would claim ignorance as to why he'd accepted Miss Barrows' invitation. Or he may say it was his gentlemanly duty. But in the confines of his thoughts, he could admit the truth. Even though the lady at his side was decidedly odd, spending time with her was far preferable to spending another hour on his own at Avebury Park.

Another friend lost to matrimony.

His feet trudged along, each step plodding across the countryside as Miss Barrows regaled him with jokes and other silliness, and Finch couldn't say he was unhappy with the company. The lady's lightness of spirit radiated out of her and spread to those around her, and however fleeting, it was good to set aside his troubles and simply chat with someone who seemed keen for his company.

And that gave Finch pause. Slanting a glance in her direction, he mused over the possibility that she was pursuing him. The thought was so ridiculous that Finch felt like laughing out loud. Even if Miss Barrows were desperate for a husband to rescue her from servitude, Finch was not the fellow to for her: his income would leave her worse off than if she stayed in Lady Lovell's household.

But Miss Barrows was not flirtatious. Certainly, she was cheery and animated, and as their conversation evolved from the mundane into something more engaging, Finch was rather pleased to have been pressed into playing her escort.

"I do like to see you smile, Mr. Finch," said Miss Barrows, and Finch shot her a puzzled look.

"I smile quite often, Miss Barrows."

"My Aunt Imogene said the same thing of you, but..." The lady tucked her hands deep into her cloak and nibbled on her lip with a furrowed brow. "...but you seem to have a great many worries plaguing you."

Finch's brows rose at that, and he shifted from one foot to the other. His throat felt dry, but there was no relief to be found.

"I am surprised you feel that way. I wonder what gave you that impression."

Miss Barrows continued to nibble on her lip, her gaze traveling the landscape ahead of them. "Call it a preternatural ability to sense sadness."

Finch huffed, sending a puff of vapor out into the crisp air. "That sounds like a dreadful gift to have."

The lady gave him an assessing glance. "It is handy at times."

Though he did not turn to meet her gaze, Finch felt it. Miss Barrows watched him in a manner that made him shift his jacket and pull it closer, as though it might cover his exposed thoughts.

"I would think that someone in your position would have more to worry about than some random gentleman you met not twenty-four hours ago," he replied, giving her a hint of a smirk.

"My position?"

"A lady does not become a companion of her own volition."

The winter air had colored Miss Barrows cheeks to a bright pink, but there was a new hint of red that entered her complexion as she grasped his meaning, and Finch felt a twist of guilt at having pointed out her reduced circumstances.

"If you do not wish to speak of your troubles, I do not blame you," she said. "But there is some comfort to be had in speaking—even with a stranger."

"There is nothing to speak about."

Miss Barrows turned to give him an arched brow at that lie but did not press the matter.

"Why do you care so much about helping this stranger?" he asked.

Coming to a halt, Miss Barrows turned to him with a pensive smile. "I suppose if I am asking for honesty, I ought to give it."

Her bright brows pulled together, her gaze shifting to the side. With a swing, she turned back down the road, and the pair continued their journey.

"My mother named me Felicity because I was her felicity," she said.

"I see where you gained your love of wordplay."

Miss Barrows grinned at that. "My mother loved to laugh and took immense joy in making others do so. Though many of my memories of her have faded with time, I still recall the picnics where she would entertain us with stories that had us in stitches."

There was something in her tone and the way she described her mother that made Finch fear the worst. Of course, as the lady was destitute and living off the charity of her great-aunt, her story wasn't bound to have a happy resolution.

"She died bringing my brother into the world, and my father was never the same after that," she said. "It became my duty to bring laughter into his life as my mother had, and I embraced that role in the family. I learned to recognize his moods, no matter how much he tried to hide them from my brother and me."

Miss Barrows sent him a slanted grin. "I suppose it became a bit of a compulsion. I cannot stand to see someone unhappy when I have the power to make them smile."

Finch tucked his hands behind him, his gaze lowered to the ground ahead of them as his boots crunched against the snow and ice crystals.

"A father ought not to put such a burden on his child," he said, and Miss Barrows' smile grew.

"Do not think me hurt by it. I am no young miss and have learned in my thirty years of life that parents are as fallible as the rest of humanity," she replied. "Though I wish my efforts had mended my father's heart, I know he did the best he could. When his grief became too great, and he struggled to care for us and maintain his vocation, he surrendered his pride and brought us to live with my Uncle George. Many a man wouldn't have done so, and it would've been far worse for William and me. When smallpox struck Plymouth, he tried to fight through for us, but when it took my brother, his heart broke beyond repair."

"Is that when you received your scars?" he asked, nodding at her face.

Chapter 10

For a brief moment, Felicity could not form words. Her brain seized at hearing someone speak of the marks on her face so boldly. And even as her first instincts wanted to recoil at the bluntness with which he spoke, Felicity felt an odd lightness enter her heart.

No one ever referenced her scars. Not directly. Her wealth and position made few willing to insult her directly, so they feigned indifference to her complexion and whispered behind their fans, recoiling at the imperfections as though they still carried the dreaded disease.

But Mr. Finch spoke without judgment or fear. Felicity scoured his expression, looking for any hint of duplicity in his question, but instinct told her he was asking out of honest curiosity. Though his question was blunt, Felicity could not feel offended at his asking it. If anything, it was refreshing to face such an honest query.

"I was ten when the illness swept through our home. All three of us were struck down with it, and only I survived." Though her hand was gloved, Felicity brushed a touch against the bumpy edge of her cheek that stood as a testament to that time of her life.

"I am sorry for your loss," said Mr. Finch, his light brows pulled together. "That must have been quite the blow."

"I consider myself quite blessed, Mr. Finch. Uncle George was untouched by it, and my life was spared. Many were scarred far worse than I or left without any family. There was a time when I was bitter, but I have come to see the joys amidst the pain."

"Felicity, indeed," he mumbled.

She smiled and chuckled. "I cannot seem to help myself, sir."

Mr. Finch's gaze remained on the ground, and Felicity wished she could see more of his face. There was so much to be gleaned from a person's expression and eyes.

Turning her gaze to the distance, Felicity found her thoughts cast back to that past; there was little good to be had in bemoaning how her life had shifted and altered from those bright days of her youth, but at times, there was no ignoring the hole in her heart.

"That was a heavy sigh," said Mr. Finch.

Felicity's face warmed, despite the cold air, and she grimaced. "I suppose I was trapped in my memories and thinking of things best left alone. There are times when I miss my family. It is not the overpowering melancholy that gripped my father, but I do long for their support and love. I have learned to do things for myself, but it is exhausting always having to stand on one's own without aid or assistance."

Shifting her cloak, Felicity flexed her fingers beneath it. The gloves were helping to stave off the chill, but it was not enough. Mr. Finch stilled beside her, and Felicity cast a glance in his direction. Standing there with his hands behind him, he met her gaze with a furrowed brow.

"I don't know if I have ever had that sort of support," he murmured.

What possessed him to say such a thing? Finch wondered when he'd taken leave of his senses, but the words were spoken and sent out into the world before he thought the better of it. There was something about Miss Barrows that invited honesty.

Finch shifted from side to side before turning to continue down the path, but Miss Barrows stopped him with a touch.

"From what you've said of your family, it sounds as though you are quite close to them," she said.

Giving her a temperate smile, Finch continued down the path. "Forget what I said. It was a slip of the tongue."

"I would hazard a guess that it was entirely honest as well."

"That may be, however—careful," he said, holding out a hand to steady Miss Barrows as her feet slid beneath her. Eyes wide, she wobbled on the ice, but Finch held her firm, keeping her from taking another tumble.

Miss Barrows laughed, her breath swirling into vapor as a broad grin stretched across her face. "It is a good thing I brought your strong arm along, even if it can only carry a lady a few feet before fatiguing."

"It is a rum business to follow a compliment with a criticism after that very limb saved you from yet another disaster," said Finch, giving her a playful scowl.

"That is all it deserves when its owner complains like an old mule about his 'exceptionally heavy' burdens," said Miss Barrows, her voice dropping to a masculine register at those last words.

All reserve was lost at the haughty raise of her chin and the ridiculous attempt to mimic his voice, and Finch laughed.

"You truly are an odd lady," he said, turning to continue down the path while keeping a firm hand on Miss Barrows' arm as they crossed the icy way.

"And again, I take that as a compliment," she replied as they passed the danger. "Better to be viewed as ridiculous than dour."

Finch shook his head. "I doubt anyone has ever called you dour—"

His boot met the ground, and it took Finch half a heartbeat to recognize his foot had no purchase. Letting out a yelp, he released Miss Barrows and tried to shift his weight, but his balance was thrown faster than he could compensate, and gravity pulled him down. Pain shot from his side and hip at the impact, and it was only by pure luck that his head did not follow suit. With a groan, he rolled onto his back and rested against the frozen path, well aware that once the agony ebbed, his pride would be equally bruised by the display.

Miss Barrows appeared above him with wide eyes, her hands pressed to her mouth. And while there was a definite flash of worry in her gaze, it faded as her shoulders began to shake.

"You would laugh at an injured man?" he murmured.

"I suppose I ought to feel guilty about it, but your hat went flying in one direction and you, the other. And then there was this flapping motion you did..." Miss Barrows grimaced, though her gaze lost none of its mirth. "It was rather comical."

Miss Barrows disappeared from his field of vision, and Finch lay there for a moment before testing out his aching bones and getting to his feet. When he straightened, Miss Barrows held out his hat, brushing off the flakes of snow that clung to the brim. Finch tried to hold in a grin, but despite his aching joints, it was difficult to fight the humor when Miss Barrows gave him an innocent smile.

"A truly odd lady, indeed," said Finch, shoving his hat on his head.

"That I am," she said with a nod as the pair shuffled along, not risking full steps until they arrived at a clear path. "And now, I wish for you to regale me of the story behind your scar. No doubt you gained it during some heroic deed in the army."

Finch's brows rose. "Pardon?"

Miss Barrows motioned to the faint line that arced above his right eyebrow. "Your coiffure gives the ladies a peek at it from time to time, which makes it all the more enticing and simply begs them to ask after its origin."

Shaking his head, Finch chuckled. "That is a coincidence, nothing more, Miss Barrows. I have no need to entice ladies."

Miss Barrows waggled her brows at him. "You are so adept at stealing their hearts, you have no need of the tricks and traps others employ?"

"Hardly," he replied in a wry tone. "But to your question—yes, I received it while in the army."

Finch paused and debated what more to say on the matter. Certainly, there was the story he gave to the public, but it felt wrong to answer Miss Barrows' honest manner with fables.

"Come on, Mr. Finch," she said with narrowed eyes and a teasing smile. "I shared the story behind my scars, it is only fair you should do the same. Tit for tat, and all that."

He didn't know what possessed him to speak a truth that no one other than the witnesses and Simon knew. Perhaps it was Miss Barrows' frank discussion or the relative anonymity of speaking the truth to a stranger. Or simply that Finch wanted to give her a laugh.

"I spent the majority of my time far from any battles, but just after I purchased my commission, my regiment and I saw action at the Battle of Alkmaar." A knot in his stomach formed as he spoke. "Skirmishes" and "action" were mundane words that did not capture the horror of the battlefield, and he detested using them.

"And while I usually spin a poetic tale of my heroic deeds and how they led to my face being marked, the truth is not flattering," he said with a grimace. "I received it while my regiment was staying in Canterbury. When soldiers have too much time at their disposal, they resort to inventive ways in which to fill it."

Miss Barrows snickered. "I can imagine it, sir, for I am well aware of the idiocies men contrive when met with ennui."

"While riding, one of the lieutenants wagered I could not clear a particularly high fence, and I, filled with the folly of youth, agreed, and was promptly thrown from my mount. I was lucky it was only a gash and I did not crack my skull." Finch brushed a gloved finger across the scar. "Whenever I felt such a foolhardy urge, this reminded me to find something better to occupy my time."

"Well, I am pleased you did not do more serious damage and learned your lesson. Many never do."

Finch glanced in her direction, feeling rather grateful that he'd accepted her invitation today. Odd she may be, but Miss Barrows was proving to be quite entertaining, and as they strolled along, discussing an array of subjects, he was quite pleased to have someone with whom to pass the morning.

Chapter 11

With a start, Simon's eyes shot open. It was a dream. Just a dream. He told himself that several times, but the lingering panic in his heart would not believe it. Blinking at the darkness, Simon reached for Mina, wrapping an arm around her. She stirred but settled once more, curled against him. His Mina was there, but a shiver of worry still ran down his spine. Even in the midst of his dream, he'd known it wasn't real, but Simon needed to feel her in his arms to believe she was there beside him.

Simon's exhausted mind and body begged him to sleep, but to close his eyes would only send him back to his nightmares. Though each one was unique in the way it unraveled, each ended the same: Mina was gone.

A lock of Mina's hair fell across his hand, and he ran his fingers through it. Casting his eyes to the window, he saw the first rays of morning light peeking through the edges of the curtains. If it weren't for the residual fear niggling at his thoughts, Simon could think of no better way to pass the time than lying in bed with his beloved wife. But the dreams plagued him.

Without hesitation or qualification, Simon could say the last three months had been the happiest of his three and thirty years. Comparing his life before Mina to the life he now had was like comparing a child's drawing to a master artist's painting. The thought of losing her had his heart racing, a clammy chill sweeping over his skin as he clutched Mina closer.

Simon's dreams were merely telling him what he refused to acknowledge: one way or another, he would do something to drive Mina away again.

...

Light filtered into Mina's dreams, easing her into consciousness. Smiling, she rolled towards Simon but found his side of the bed empty. Cracking open her eyes, she was greeted by a lily on his pillow, and she smiled, picking up the blossom to breathe in its heavenly scent. Lying on her back with a sigh, Mina grinned at the ceiling, her heart swelling with a rush of joy. So many perfect days.

Something bumped against the bedchamber door, and Mina heard a grumble from the other side that sounded distinctly like her husband.

And then another.

The door handle moved and stopped. And another thump against the wood. But just as Mina was going to throw back the bedcovers, the door opened to reveal Simon with a massive breakfast tray balanced in his arms, the dishes sliding as he maneuvered it through the doorway.

"Breakfast, madam?" he said with a smile. Simon set the tray on the bed, and Mina's stomach rumbled at the array of treats and drinking chocolate. "I thought I might give the servants a rest this morning and bring you up a tray."

Simon presented each of his offerings with an adorable eagerness, giving Mina another reason to smile. Not that he would appreciate being "adorable," but he was so anxious to please that Mina couldn't help but find him thus.

"And I brought a special treat," he said, reaching into the pocket of his dressing gown to retrieve a box wrapped in a ribbon.

Mina straightened, sitting up in bed to stare at the gift and wonder what her husband was up to. Simon pushed aside the breakfast tray so that he might sit beside her as she tugged the ribbon free and pulled open the lid.

"Oh, Simon," she whispered.

Inside the box rested a hair comb wrought in silver; it was not bedecked with gems or pearls as so many of them often were. The design was simple, naught but a series of filigree orbs running along the spine of the comb. Each one was intricate and unique from the others while still looking as though they all belonged together. It was unlike anything Mina had seen before and absolutely perfect.

"It is gorgeous," she said, lifting it from the box to run her fingers over the twisted, twine-like prongs and up along the bubbled spine.

"Then you like it?"

There was something in his voice that drew Mina's attention, and she met his eyes. Simon had a broad smile and happy glint to his eyes, but there was a tightening at the corners of his lips and a subtle tension in his brow. Though Mina could not decipher it, she sensed something was amiss.

"Of course," she said, reaching over to run a thumb across his cheek. "I adore it."

Simon placed a kiss on her palm, and whatever Mina had thought she'd seen disappeared. Twisting a handful of her hair, Mina took the comb and slid it into place. It would never hold without hair pins to assist in anchoring her tresses, but she couldn't wait.

"How does it look?" she said, glancing at the vanity, though it was too far away to get a proper look.

"Positively lovely," Simon murmured, sitting on the bed beside her.

Mina turned to him, and words flew from her mind at the look on her husband's face. His gaze perused her face and figure in a manner that made her blush. For all her belief that attraction could grow from friendship, it still astonished Mina to see desire glowing in Simon's eyes. Three months ago, she had been little more than a chum and partner. Mina Kingsley, his helpmeet. Yet now, he behaved as though she was his Aphrodite.

If she allowed herself to think on it, the change wrought in Simon was rather startling.

Leaning in, Simon whispered, "I love you," before pressing a sweet kiss to her lips.

"It is comforting to know I am not the only one afflicted," she teased, but Simon did not laugh.

"I do love you," he insisted, a hint of his previous tension returning, and Mina wished her words unsaid. "I am sorry I was a fool not to see how precious you were from the start, but you mean everything to me—"

"Hush." Mina pressed a kiss to his lips, silencing any further castigations. When she had him distracted enough, she continued, "You have apologized aplenty, Simon. Mistakes were made, but it does no good to wallow in them."

Simon nodded, though his eyes held a hint of disbelief that broke her heart. However, there were no more assurances to be made, and time would simply show him the truth. Curling into his embrace, Mina rested her head against his shoulder. Her new comb poked him in the cheek, and Mina leaned back as Simon rubbed at the place with a chuckle. But as she spouted apologies, Simon merely smiled and removed the comb, placing it on the bedside table.

Shifting, Simon moved them to rest against the headboard, and she wrapped an arm around him. It was sad that their morning outing was so often curtailed by the winter weather, but in moments like these, Mina was not terribly upset about it.

"You're not regretting Finch's visit, are you?"

Simon's question had Mina lifting her head to meet his gaze.

"Why would you ask that?"

"I…" His words faltered, and Simon's gaze drifted away from Mina. "No reason in particular. I simply worry you are unhappy."

That gave Mina pause. She had thought she hid her feelings better than that. There was something so vexing about Mr. Finch, and Mina did not care for his presence, but she did not wish to chase Simon's friend away; he enjoyed the fellow's company for some odd reason.

"…she is too mousy to cause you much bother, too unattractive to have a wandering eye, and so firmly on the shelf that she'd likely accept any offer she got…" Mr. Finch's words had made an impression on Mina—as well they should. No woman wanted to hear herself described in such a manner, and Mr. Finch's unfiltered opinion had served as a sound reminder of how the world viewed Mina.

That ball.

All things considered, Mina was grateful for Mr. Finch's stark assessment: it was the reason Simon first took note of her. Or rather, the embarrassment that she'd overheard Finch's harsh critique had driven Simon to approach her. Mina had long ago given Simon the forgiveness he'd sought, but to date, Mr. Finch had not acknowledged his part in it, and he'd been the main instigator. Perhaps Mina could overlook it as a bit of brutally honest conversation between gentlemen, but Mr. Finch continued to spout harsh critiques of the ladies around him. His words about Miss Barrows were enough to show that the fellow was callous and prideful.

Mina adored her husband, but he had terrible taste in friends, and she wanted nothing more than to chase away yet another who'd invaded her home. However, Simon was happy his friend was visiting. Mina didn't know why her husband trusted Mr. Finch's input on estate matters, but he did. And Mr. Finch wasn't as terrible as their last visitors; he may be apathetic towards Mina, but he made no move to chase her out of Avebury Park or force a wedge between her and Simon.

A squeeze of her husband's arms drew Mina from her thoughts.

"Are you unhappy?" he asked.

"Of course not, Simon." Perhaps not the entire truth, but it was true enough that she felt no twinge of guilt for speaking it. Simon was happy with Mr. Finch around, which made Mina happy in turn. She simply needed to recall that when Mr. Finch was near.

"You would tell me if you were?"

"Of course," she said, pressing a kiss to Simon's jaw. He turned and met her lips, and Mina reveled in that touch, for it spoke more than his words.

"I love you, Mina. Body and soul." His words echoed the sentiments he'd given her that first time he declared his love, and Mina clung to them.

"I know, Simon, and I love you, too." But before Mina could say another word, he kissed her so soundly that she could not form another coherent thought.

Chapter 12

There were few greater joys in this world than passing a few hours with a friend. Refreshment, a plush armchair, and a blazing fire on a cold winter's day added exponentially to that felicity, and Finch found himself in possession of all four.

Legs outstretched, Finch picked at the remnant sweets and found himself wishing for a bit of Lady Lovell's gingerbread. He'd rationed out Miss Barrows' gift over the past fortnight, but now he'd be forced to go begging from Buxby Hall when he wanted more. The cook outright refused to share her recipe with the Kingsleys'; some nonsense about demanding a biscuit recipe in return, which was soundly rejected despite his attempts to broker a negotiation.

The fire sent out a wave of heat, chasing away the chill seeping in from the windows, and though Finch would like to take off his boots and change into a dressing gown, his present situation was near perfect.

Finch glanced at his companion. One of Simon's hands rested against the arm of the chair, his fingers tapping a rhythm against the leather, while his other propped up his chin as he watched the flickering light in silence. As they'd not been afforded many opportunities to pass a few hours together, Finch wished his friend was in a chattier mood, but Simon had been reticent of late.

"Are you going to tell me what has you at odds or are you going to keep brooding?" asked Finch.

Simon straightened, his gaze shooting to his friend. "Brooding?"

Finch smirked. "Definitely brooding."

Letting out a huff, Simon dropped his head against the back of the chair. "Don't mock me."

"I'm not." He paused, gave that statement some consideration, and amended, "Not much, at any rate. But you leave me no choice but to poke and prod if you refuse to tell me what has you tied in knots."

"My wife."

Finch slanted a look towards Simon, but the fellow was already shaking his head.

"That is not fair of me. Mina is not the problem. She never was..." And with that, Simon began to unravel the tale of the first months of his marriage. Setting aside the food, Finch crossed his arms, watching as Simon flushed red at parts, smiled at others, and even looked close to weeping at various intervals.

It seemed love was for fools because Finch could hardly countenance Simon's tale and the absolute muck he'd made of his life. While he claimed no skill with the ladies, even the eternal bachelor Lewis Finch recognized how foolhardy his friend's behavior had been.

"Don't just sit there like a lump, Finch. I don't know what to do."

Finch stared at his friend for a long moment before speaking.

"Let me see if I grasp the situation. You, proving yourself an utter halfwit—" Simon scowled at that, but Finch continued, "—you allowed your harpy of a mother to invade your home, towing along your equally wretched sisters *and* the repugnant lady you'd courted and pined for, even though she threw you over in favor of a man with higher social status. And don't try to defend your decision to allow them entrance to Avebury Park, Simon, for even I know that was especially idiotic."

The angry pull to Simon's expression eased, and he gave Finch a sad nod. Only once he conceded the point did Finch continue.

"Then, they spent weeks tormenting and brow-beating your wife, while you stood by and did nothing—"

"I did not understand the extent of their actions. Had I known, I would've tossed them out far sooner than I did."

Finch nodded. "But that does not excuse the fact that you fawned over your former love *in front of your wife*. Good heavens, man! You are lucky Mina forgave you! She'd have been within her rights to run you through."

"I know!" Simon pounded the arm of his chair and straightened. "Do you think I don't know that, Finch? The only defense I can give for my action is that I did not intentionally flirt with *that woman...*" Simon paused, his brows pulling tight together. "Or, I don't believe it was intentional. I am no longer certain if it was an accident or simply self-delusion."

"Likely both."

"But that is neither here nor there. The fact is that something is at odds with my wife again. Since we reconciled, my life has been as close to perfect as one can find in this imperfect world, but something is shifting. I felt it in the weeks leading up to her leaving me, and I feel an echo of it now..."

Simon's voice faded into nothing, and he sat limply in his chair as though that confession had robbed him of his strength. His eyes bleakly stared off into the distance as though seeing the future he feared was unfolding before him.

"I've tried asking her about it, but she claims nothing is the matter." Simon paused, his brow furrowing. "Perhaps I ought to be more direct."

"That is a terrible idea. Neither of you wishes to discuss the matter, so why subject yourself to a drawn-out and painful conversation? Besides, the issue is easy enough to remedy without such discomfort," said Finch, and Simon's gaze snapped to his.

"How so?"

"The problem in the past was that you neglected your wife. So, shower her with affection. Gifts, outings, whatever you like." Finch was not particularly pleased with that course of action, but even if it left him abandoned even more often, he would not let the selfish impulse keep him from advising his friend.

Simon collapsed back into his dejected posture. "I have, but it's not doing any good."

"Then do more."

Head tilting to the side, Simon tapped the chair arm. "I've been thinking about a jaunt to Ainsley. There's a novel Mina is desperate to get her hands on, and their bookstore is far better stocked than Bristow's. It's a bit of a journey there, but we could make an afternoon of it." As the fellow pondered the idea, a smile crept across his lips. "That may be just the thing. But I would hate to abandon you to yourself yet again. Unless you would like to come along—"

But Finch snorted. "You cannot think to invite me on your lovers' outing. A grand gesture is hardly romantic if your chum is seated in the boot. Besides, I was planning on going into the village to do some shopping."

That was a lie, of course, but it was a good enough excuse to ease his friend's conscience. And with the way this visit was going, it was unlikely that Finch would be returning to Bristow much in the future; Simon's life was only going to get busier with children and family, after all. So, he ought to pass an afternoon giving his goodbyes to the place.

...

Another missive, another issue. Why was it that most letters carried unhappy news? Felicity supposed her business contacts had no reason to write unless there was some dire item needing her attention, but the sheer amount of time spent on those negative aspects of her finances far outweighed the positive. From their correspondence, one could be forgiven for thinking her on the brink of ruin. The doomsayers.

"You are sighing again," said Aunt Imogene from her sofa.

"Until they send me better news, it will be a common occurrence," said Felicity, tossing aside a letter.

Looking up from her novel, the elder lady gave her niece an arched brow. "I thought you came to Bristow to get away from such megrims."

Giving her a tart look back, Felicity replied, "Then I should have chosen some other relative to visit."

Aunt Imogene mumbled about "ungrateful children" with a spark of mirth in her eyes before returning to her story.

Retrieving the next missive, Felicity broke the seal and perused the contents.

With a snap, Aunt Imogene shut the book and set it aside. "You are sighing again, child."

"It is these wretched business partners of Uncle's." Felicity wanted to launch the letter into the fireplace, but as she still had need of the information inside it, balling it up was the best she could do to show her displeasure.

"I hate to point out the obvious, but as that dear man has been gone for some time now, I believe it is safe to call them *your* business partners."

"For all that they treat me as such." Felicity scowled at the paper, as though that conveyed her displeasure to its scribe. "I may control the majority of capital, but they vacillate between ignoring my existence and treating me like a child incapable of comprehending matters of business. When they are forced to seek my approval for investments, they harp and hound. They write again to beg me to reconsider Mr. Merdle's venture."

Aunt Imogene's expression softened, her gaze filling with concern. "I am certain you will sort it out."

Shoving aside the fact that she had no interest in sorting it out, Felicity focused on the matter that haunted her restless nights. "Mr. Merdle's scheme goes against everything Uncle George taught me about sound investments, and I cannot shake the feeling that giving my money to the venture would be a fool's errand. Yet all of Uncle's trusted advisors and partners agree it would be foolish not to. My heart will not let me follow their advice, yet I fear that with so many against me, I am in the wrong and too stubborn to see it."

Lifting a hand to Felicity, Aunt Imogene beckoned for her, and the young lady gladly came to her great-aunt's side. The elder lady wrapped her soft and gentle fingers around the younger's.

"I wish I could give you some advice on the matter, but I fear I know little about such things," said Aunt Imogene. "However, you are an intelligent young lady. You will sort things out with time."

The words brought a flush of comfort, wrapping around Felicity to chase away the chill, but they did not soothe her troubled heart. As horrid as it was to wade through the issue, Felicity had no doubt she'd solve the problem eventually on her own.

But that was the true frustration. Though plenty loved and supported her, not a one gave her any sound advice or guidance, leaving Felicity to handle the whole business by herself. Neither accepted by the gentlemen nor understood by the ladies. With no husband or family of her own, Felicity's life was a solitary existence, but this left her feeling all the more alone. Isolated. Lonely.

Which made her hate the whole business all the more because it robbed Felicity of the happiness she'd gathered in her life. Investments, accounts, demanding partners, and condescending men of business chipped away at her contentment, leaving her dreading every knock at the door that heralded more concerns she'd be forced to sort through alone.

"Thank you, Aunt Imogene. I am certain you are right, of course." Felicity smiled and squeezed that dear lady's hands. Then casting her thoughts to another issue at hand, she added, "But there is a matter in which you might assist me."

Rising to her feet, Felicity crossed back to the writing desk and retrieved one of the letters that had been set aside for further perusal.

"Mr. Lipman's figures for Farleigh Manor are disconcerting," said Felicity, scanning the page for the proper section. "I am not as familiar with the requirements of a country estate as you are, so I am uncertain as to whether I am being ridiculous or if there is something more sinister involved."

Pointing out the part of the letter, Felicity turned it to Aunt Imogene, whose brows rose as she read it.

"As servants are residing there, coals, candles, food, and the like still need to be purchased, but this is more than I would expect," she murmured, passing her eyes over the passage again. "Not enough to raise significant concerns, but I fear your steward may be derelict in his duties."

"Or simply dishonest," said Felicity, her shoulders dropping. "I had feared as much."

"I would think that any property purchased by my nephew would be more profitable than this," added Great-Aunt Imogene with a frown. "Its expenditures are less than its income, but not as much as one would wish to see."

Felicity sighed. "I suppose I can no longer pretend that everything is well with Farleigh Manor."

Glancing from the letter, Aunt Imogene patted her great-niece's knee. "Do not despair, my dear. If you would like, I can write to my son and ask his advice on your behalf."

With a wan smile, Felicity shook her head. "My thanks, but as you said before, I shall sort this out."

Yet another issue that needed addressing, and though she tried to give all the proper assurances to her aunt, Felicity couldn't feel them herself. Of course, that was mopey nonsense, for despite the despair of the moment, Felicity knew she would find a solution. She only wished she found some joy in the hunt.

"Perhaps you ought to go for a drive, my dear," said Aunt Imogene. "I find that some time in the country air does wonders to clear one's head."

Felicity bit on her lip, considering the possibility.

"You may take my phaeton. It has been an age since it got any proper use, and it would do both you and it some good." Aunt Imogene fairly beamed, patting Felicity's knee once more. "I'll have the grooms harness Duchess. She's such a sweet-tempered creature that you'll hardly have to steer."

Turning her thoughts to that possibility, a smile crept across Felicity's face. "I think I may just do that."

Chapter 13

"I love what you've done with this cuff," said Finch, leaning closer to inspect the tailor's work.

Mr. Abbott maintained a dignified air, but pleasure gleamed in his eyes at the compliment. "I doubt my skill measures up to the quality you are used to finding in London, sir."

Holding back a smile at the blatant lure the tailor set out, Finch ignored the comment and turned his attention to the cuff. It was a shame he didn't have all his tools with him, for seeing the stitches and tucks of fabric made him long to know if he could mimic it. Mr. Abbott had a way of interpreting trends, and though Finch had little interest in chasing after them, the fellow's work presented a new challenge.

The pair stood together, discussing all the work Mr. Abbott had done since Finch's last visit. In London, so many of the shops worth visiting were too busy to allow the owners to pass a half-hour chatting about the nuances of their trade, especially with a gentleman who never spent a farthing.

Finch would miss this.

Glancing around the shop, Finch sized up his options. It had been years since he'd worn anything he hadn't made himself, but it didn't feel right to leave without purchasing something. Mr. Abbott had shown far too much patience with him over the years, and Finch owed the fellow.

The shirt they were admiring was beyond his reach, but Finch settled on a few cravats. Sewing them was his least favorite task, so it was an expense worth shouldering. With a few words of farewell, he took his package and wandered out of the shop.

His boots squeaked in the snow, and a flash of wet on his toes told him they were in need of repair, but they would have to wait until he was home again. His cobbling skills were minimal, but he knew enough to get another year out of this pair with the right tools, which were back in London. Perhaps it was finally time to dedicate himself to the art of boot-making. With the cost of supplies, it would be a pricey undertaking at first, but it would save him funds in the end.

And it would give him something to do once he returned to London.

So, cobbling it was.

A dusting of snow skittered across the road, and Finch looked around at the various shops and cottages that formed Bristow's heart. So much of the world was changing at a breakneck speed, but this village looked much the same as it had two hundred years ago. While it was invigorating to see London grow and to witness the new commerce and inventions driving it forward, it was comforting to know that some places remained constant. He wondered if Bristow would still look this way in another hundred years.

Calling out to the lad who was walking Sheba up and down the lane, Finch tossed the boy a coin and patted the mare on the neck. Checking the harness and cinch, he mounted and pointed her towards Avebury Park.

No doubt Simon and Mina would still be on their adventure to Ainsley, but Finch had wasted enough time here, and shopping was a bore when one did not have the funds to indulge. Tucking his solitary parcel into his jacket, he meandered away from the heart of the village and saw the lane splitting between the path that would take him to Avebury Park and that which would take him to Buxby Hall.

Perhaps he ought to pay a call on Lady Lovell. She was an engaging conversationalist and always welcomed a visit. What more could he ask for than to pass an hour or two in good conversation? That and some more delectable gingerbread cake.

Pointing his mount down that lane, Finch was willing to admit that he wasn't wholly disappointed at the thought of occupying more of Miss Barrows' time. The lady may be odd—exceptionally so—but she'd proven to be quite entertaining on more than one occasion. Even if she did enjoy prying into his business.

Finch's lips curled into a half-smile as he stared off in the distance, his eyes tracking the curving lines of the rolling hillside all covered in a dusting of snow. Casting his thoughts back, he was caught by a sudden thought. He wasn't certain he'd ever seen Bristow in summer. Or any other season for that matter. The world expected him in London during the Season even though he had neither the funds nor standing to do much with that social whirl. Heaven forfend that he should spend those months elsewhere.

Rounding a bend, Finch jerked Sheba to a stop before they collided with an abandoned phaeton. Turning in his saddle, he scoured the area for any sign of the imbecile who'd left it blocking the narrow lane at a blind corner. Finch guided Sheba around the vehicle and noticed footsteps continuing down the road, and he followed after them to see a lady cutting across a nearby field.

"Hello, there!" Sheba trotted forward, following after the figure. The lady did not pause in her trek, her footsteps cutting determinedly across the landscape. Even with her hair mostly hidden beneath a bonnet, he recognized the unruly curls peeking out the back and realized that her path was the most direct route to Buxby Hall.

"Miss Barrows!"

At her name, she turned, squinting against the sun at Finch's back, and as he came up beside her, rather than her usual smile or greeting, Miss Barrows scowled.

"Wretched beast," she grumbled. Or so Finch thought. It was such a strange exclamation to make that he wasn't entirely certain.

"Pardon?" Finch slid from his saddle, but Miss Barrows swung around and continued her march to Buxby Hall.

"Stupid creature that refuses to follow a simple command!" she barked, jabbing a thumb back towards the phaeton.

Finch took Miss Barrows by the arm, pulling her to a stop, and turned her to face him. "Now, why did you leave your carriage—"

"That infuriating horse refuses to go another step!" Her brown eyes blazed as she threw another furious point in the phaeton's general direction. "It was supposed to be a relaxing drive, but the worthless thing won't move more than a few steps before stopping again, so now I am left to walk several miles in the snow and cold!"

Finch's eyes widened as her voice rose, her temper snapping and hissing like a snake. He held up his hands, and Miss Barrows kicked at the ground, sending up a flurry of flakes with a grunt. The lady's muscles tensed and she sucked in a deep breath, but as she let it out in a hiss, her body relaxed once more, deflating her posture as she rubbed at her forehead.

"I apologize," she murmured. "I didn't mean to lose my temper, but it has been a trying day, and this has sapped me of my last bit of patience. But, if you'll excuse me, I must be on my way. It will take some time to make my way back on foot."

Finch frowned and stopped her when she moved to leave. "Allow me to take a look at it. I may be no groom, but I know a few things about horses and carriages."

A smile crept across Miss Barrows' face as though he'd offered her the moon and stars. "Would you? That would be divine."

Motioning for her to return to the phaeton, Finch stared at her with a scrunched brow. "I only offered my assistance, Miss Barrows. I hardly think that is deserving of such praise."

Giving a faltering chuckle, the lady patted his arm and followed his lead. "You underestimate the assistance you are offering, Mr. Finch. Today has been trying, and a helping hand is heaven-sent."

Finch slanted a look in her direction as he guided her and Sheba back to the carriage. "I'm growing rather used to rescuing you. This is the second time I've done so."

Miss Barrows gave him a haughty sniff, straightening as she replied, "I've rescued you as well."

"I recall you standing over me and laughing without a hand up or even an offer to carry me."

"Yes, but I rescued your hat."

Finch chuckled. "That you did, and my hat thanks you for it."

Arriving at the road, he tied Sheba to the carriage and gave the other poor creature stuck in its harness a rub on her neck and a few words of comfort. Working his hands along the straps, he examined the tack.

"We were driving along, and one of the reins slackened," said Miss Barrows. "I tried to get Duchess to move, but she would not follow my commands and started listing towards the edge of the road. I stopped to get a better grip, but she refused to move another inch."

It took no more than a moment or two before he discovered the issue. "Lady Lovell's groom has been derelict in his duty. The leather hasn't been properly maintained, and the tack has broken in a couple of places."

Miss Barrows' shoulders drooped, her expression falling once more. "Then might I ask you to send word to Buxby Hall—"

"No need," he said, nodding at the tack. "I should be able to rig it together enough to get us there."

Before Felicity could protest (if she'd even intended to), Mr. Finch herded her into the phaeton, handing her the blanket she'd abandoned. Tugging off his gloves, he shoved them in his pocket and set to work. The gentleman moved around Duchess, soothing her with a rub and soft words, and took the straps in hand.

Smoothing out the blanket and tucking it around her, Felicity snuggled into the warmth as she watched Mr. Finch move with impressive skill and ease. She bit on her lips, turning her gaze to the side as she blinked away the first signs of tears. It was utter foolishness to be overwrought by such a simple thing, but it had been such a long time since someone had taken matters in hand on her behalf. The weight in her heart lifted as she faced one catastrophe she needn't resolve on her own.

It was rare enough for her to be on the receiving end of such honest kindness. Most of her days were filled with those making demands on her time and attention, many of whom put forth an amiable mask to hide their forthcoming petitions (which often revolved around her money). Yes, she had her friends, and Aunt Imogene was a dear, but so much of her world was filled with those more intent on taking than giving.

And when faced with Mr. Finch's genuine care, Felicity's heart couldn't help but warm towards the capable man who assisted without making her feel incompetent or weak. Helping because he simply wished to.

"You are looking at me quite strangely," he mumbled, glancing between his work and her.

Felicity sent out a silent prayer of gratitude that the air had a nip, for her cheeks were already rosy enough that her blush would not show. Reining in her ridiculous thoughts, she shook off that odd turn and smiled as though nothing were amiss. Romantic musings were best left alone; Felicity had not come to

Bristow to fall madly in love with the first gentleman to show her kindness.

"I am admiring your skill with Duchess," she said, which was true enough. "Even gentlemen who adore horses do not show such ability with the creatures and their equipment. If it does not involve them sitting majestically atop their steed, they think it an insignificant detail best left to stable masters."

Mr. Finch leveled a wry smile at her. "I would hardly call it skill; it is something any groom can manage—even if Lady Lovell's seems incapable. As a member of the light dragoons, I learned a thing or two about caring for horses."

"Or three," she added, but the gentleman shrugged, turning his gaze back to his work.

"The army may seem thrilling, but it is mostly monotonous with little to occupy one's time. With a horse on hand that needed tending, I chose to spend my time in better pursuits than wagering and drinking."

"And if I recall correctly, you weren't terribly good at wagers." Felicity scratched at her face in the exact place his scar rested and gave him a saucy smile, to which he replied with a good-natured scowl.

With a tug of the straps and another rub of Duchess's neck, Mr. Finch came round to climb in beside her. "It should hold until Buxby Hall."

Checking that his mount's reins were still tied to the back of the phaeton, Mr. Finch took Duchess's in hand, and they set off down the road. Felicity felt like gaping at the miracle that was a functional carriage and the wonderful Mr. Finch who'd brought it about.

Chapter 14

"So, Miss Barrows, what is it that has you in such a tizzy?" asked Mr. Finch. Felicity glanced at him, and he slanted her a look, adding, "You said it had been a trying day before I rescued you so heroically once again."

Yet another reason to be grateful for Mr. Finch's assistance, as she no longer needed to focus on steering Duchess and could enjoy the winter scene before her. Felicity cast her gaze out to the landscape as she pondered his question. Here may be a solution. Mr. Finch might have the answers she sought if she trod lightly.

For a brief moment, Felicity wondered if she ought to simply admit the truth of her situation. Mr. Finch had proven himself to be far more trustworthy than the others who had courted her affection. But even as she contemplated it, the past reared up to warn her to keep on her guard. Alastair Dunn had seemed honest; even now, Felicity struggled to see his duplicity in her memories of him. Yet he had turned out to be as false as all the rest. More so in some ways.

But no. Felicity could not imagine Mr. Finch behaving in such a manner. He was far too blunt and honest a person to maintain a facade. And yet, many of her newly acquired beaus were equally amiable when they hadn't known she was in possession of a fortune. Only when they thought to snare her did they become wholly unbearable.

Better not risk it.

"I am concerned about a friend of mine who is struggling with her finances." The lie burned in her stomach, but there was no good to be had in telling the truth at this juncture. Besides, the subject arose so infrequently that she hardly had to reinforce the falsehood regarding her finances.

Clearing her throat, Felicity continued, "She inherited a fortune, but she has been struggling to know what to do with it. I long to give her some guidance that might ease her burden, but I fear I have none. Might I ask your opinion on the matter?"

Finch held back a snort, though he did chuckle to himself. If Miss Barrows only knew she was seeking the advice of someone with little funds to his name and no experience with fortunes. Except if one were speaking of metaphorical fortunes, in which his expertise leaned towards ill rather than good.

"Might I suggest speaking with Mr. Kingsley? He is a good fellow who would love to assist your friend in any manner."

"Though I've met his wife, I fear I do not know the gentleman," she said.

"I can give an introduction." With a gentle hand, he steered Duchess around a particularly nasty bump, saving them all from being rattled.

"While I am grateful for that Mr. Finch, I would like your opinion. You seem a sensible fellow with a good head on his shoulders, even if you require the occasional assistance in rescuing wayward hats."

Turning an eye towards his companion, Finch sat there, mute. Casting his thoughts to their previous conversations, he could not recall any instance in which the lady might come to such a startling revelation, and he didn't know whether to laugh at her misjudgment of his abilities or blush at the implication.

It was one thing for Simon to ask his opinion. They'd been friends for years, and Simon generally knew his mind and merely needed a listening ear and a few proddings.

"If you think I can be of assistance, then I will do what I can," said Finch, keeping his tone even. There was no need to broadcast just how doubtful he thought his help would be, especially when Miss Barrows looked so terribly pleased by his answer.

"You see, my friend inherited a fortune, including control of the capital invested in a bank..."

There was an odd quality to Miss Barrows' tone when she spoke of this friend, and Finch wondered if there wasn't a hint of jealousy or discomfort on the lady's part. Though that didn't seem in line with what he knew of Miss Barrows, it was natural to feel something of the sort when faced with one's own reduced state. As much as Finch adored Simon, there were moments when he was plagued by such dark sentiments. Not that he resented his friend's good fortune. Finch was pleased his friend was so well situated, but there were times when Simon's life made Finch's feel all the starker.

But as Miss Barrows continued to speak of her friend's dilemma, Finch turned his attention away from those thoughts and focused on the subject at hand. Outlining the scheme in great detail, Miss Barrows showed incredible insight into the issue, and Finch found himself rather impressed at her grasp of finances. Many gentlemen struggled to gain such an understanding.

Her brows pinched tight, her expression scrunching as she spoke. Miss Barrows gestured from time to time, punctuating her words with more and more force.

"As she controls much of the capital invested in the institution, my friend has a say over whether or not to invest in such a risky scheme, but everyone is certain it will be a boon to the bank. They say it is not much of a risk at all—"

"There is always a risk. Anyone who tells you differently is either a fool or a thief."

With a smile, Miss Barrows turned bright eyes towards him. There was a quirk to her lips that told him the next words would be one of her jokes. "I've heard it said that a great financier is a thief who succeeds, and a thief is a great financier who fails."

With a shrug, he chuckled. "That is all too true. I've yet to hear tell of a scheme promising great returns that hasn't ended in ruined fortunes for everyone except for the men behind it."

Miss Barrows paused, examining his profile. "Then you would not invest in it?"

"I cannot say for certain without knowing more particulars but not likely. No businessman of sense would guarantee such grand promises as Mr. Merdle, and I wouldn't entrust that amount of funds to anyone without good sense. It is better to invest in sound ventures with lower yields than risk it all like some foolhardy youth wagering on a card game."

Silence followed that pronouncement, and Finch shot a glance at Miss Barrows to find her staring at him, a hint of a smile tugging at her lips.

"What is it?" he asked.

"You reminded me of my uncle just then, Mr. Finch. He was fond of saying 'a fool and his gold are easily parted.' In truth, I felt the scheme was unsound, but so many were for it that I couldn't help but feel as though I had the wrong end of the stick."

Finch turned his attention back to Duchess, though the horse knew her way well enough to need little guidance on his part. "It's easy to feel that way, but why doesn't your friend have a man of business to assist her in such matters?"

Miss Barrows sighed, sending out a whirl of vapor into the air. "She's had several, but they were either incompetent, unwilling to follow her direction, or seeking to make their position a more permanent one." When Finch sent her a puzzled look, Miss Barrows added, "As her husband."

"And she doesn't wish to marry?"

"What woman wishes to marry someone who only loves her money?"

"True," he said with a shrug. "So she wishes for a man of business who will aid and assist but not dictate and has been unable to locate one?"

Sadness tinged Miss Barrows' eyes as her shoulders drooped. "I am beginning to think she shall never find such a person."

"Only because she is going about her search all wrong," Finch mumbled.

Miss Barrows straightened. "Pardon?"

Finch shrugged again. "What she needs is someone with ability who has yet to climb the ranks. Too many professions and businesses reward connections over talent, ensuring that some of their best assets are left to languish in obscurity for years. Gentlemen stuck in such circumstances would be grateful and eager to manage her assets in any manner she chooses."

"Even if it means listening to a lady's counsel in matters of business?" she asked in a derisive tone.

"Even then," he said with a smile. "There are plenty of young men desperate for the opportunity to prove themselves."

Miss Barrows made a noncommittal noise, her gaze turning to the landscape.

"If you wish, I could make a few suggestions. I know several gentlemen who would fit the bill nicely." In truth, he wished he could add his name to the list, but that was such a useless thought that he banished it in a trice. He could only imagine what Father would say if he found out his son longed to be a man of business; if being a banker was not good enough for a son of Darius Finch, something lower down the social ladder would hardly suffice.

Then Finch gave her a wry smile. "And most of them are either married or otherwise engaged, so she needn't worry on that account."

"And what of stewards?"

Finch gave her a puzzled look. "What sort of employer is she that she cannot keep a man of business or steward?"

Miss Barrows shook her head with a laugh. "A good one, I assure you. She's simply terrible at finding the right employees. Do you have suggestions for a steward as well?"

"Certainly. If you wish me to, I could supply a list of candidates for both."

The phaeton shifted and before Finch could do a thing about it, arms wrapped around him, squeezing him tight.

"You are a gem, Mr. Finch!" said Miss Barrows before she released him and returned to her seat. "You are a godsend, truly!"

Finch's cheeks warmed, though it wouldn't show beneath his chill-reddened skin, and he was grateful that he was dealing with the horse, as it gave him a reason not to look at his companion. The lady gushed about his brilliance, and Finch had no idea how to respond to such glowing and undeserved praise.

It was nothing but a recommendation. Anyone could've easily given Miss Barrows' friend such guidance, yet the lady was acting as though Finch was a paragon among gentlemen and the only source of truth and light available in this dark world.

And though he wished she would desist, Finch couldn't help but feel an inkling of pride warming his heart. But that was likely due to the thought that he would be giving a few friends some much-needed assistance in their professions. Nothing more.

Mr. Finch was such an odd fellow. At first glance, he had the look of a society fribble who was more likely to be flippant than earnest. Yet he lacked the social grace to fare well with that crowd, as speaking one's mind in such a blunt fashion was not tolerated unless done with a biting wit that required more cruelty than Mr. Finch was capable of.

Then there was the ennui, which might seem affected if not for the way it resonated in his eyes. Felicity's efforts to lighten that shadow were only temporarily successful and though Mr. Finch proved himself capable of enjoying a jest (even at his expense), the sentiment always returned. At this point, Felicity couldn't decide if it was melancholy or boredom. Perhaps it was both.

And now he shifted in his seat, tensing at her praise and casting her a look steeped in disbelief, and Felicity swore his cheeks had a touch pinker than before. But even as she wished to reinforce her praise and gratitude, instinct held her tongue. That little voice whispered that it was best to leave it be for now.

The men in Felicity's life were arrogant to the core, surveying their world with an unshakable confidence that rarely aligned with reality. Men who thought themselves capable of winning her heart with a few trite compliments. Men who believed themselves the expert on all things—even Felicity's own life. They dominated and demanded, driving her to distraction until she was forced to flee her home.

Yet here was a fellow who looked at her with a question in his gaze. Vulnerability, even. As though dismissing her praise, yet hoping it was true. And Felicity felt an urge to hold him close and assure him.

"You mentioned you've worked with investments and finances," said Felicity. "Yet I have also heard you say you studied medicine and served in the army, and now you are a gentleman of leisure. You've had quite the varied past, Mr. Finch."

The gentleman's jaw tightened, and he shifted in his seat once again, but with his gaze fixed on Duchess, Felicity could not see enough of his expression to surmise anything more than a faint feeling that he was uncomfortable again.

"I've tried my hand at a few professions, but none of them suited me or my family," he said. Felicity opened her mouth to ask after that, but before she could, he added, "As I have given you a bit of assistance, might I ask you a question as well?"

Shifting the blanket around her, she smiled. "You've been most helpful, so it would only be fair for me to attempt the same for you."

Mr. Finch nodded, though his brow furrowed as he considered his question. "What might I do to make my friend's wife warm to me?"

Finch groaned at himself. That was not something he wished to discuss, but it was the first subject that formed in his thoughts, and it was better than continuing with the previous one. Besides, Miss Barrows was a lady, and she might have better insight into his mess with Mina.

"I was anticipating a fond visit with my friend, but it was clear from the first moment that his wife wishes me to Hades." Frowning at the road ahead, he recounted a few of their interactions, each ending with cold dismissal or silent hostility. Shaking his head, Finch shifted his grip on the reins. "For the life of me, I cannot fathom what it is she dislikes so. Her reaction is inexplicable—"

But his ramblings were cut short by a strong snort from his companion. Turning his gaze to Miss Barrows, he found her fairly laughing in his face.

"I doubt her reaction is inexplicable," said Miss Barrows.

Finch nearly yanked on the reins, but he kept himself from upsetting Duchess; it would do neither of them any good if he were to send their carriage into the ditch.

"I have been unobtrusive and friendly," he said with a scowl. "What possible offense could she fashion from that?"

"Oh, you are a dear," replied Miss Barrows with a faint smile. "I've only spoken to the lady a few times when she's called on my great-aunt, but anyone who spends more than a few minutes in her company knows she is a tender soul."

When Miss Barrows did not continue, Finch prodded her. "And?"

"And you are blunt. You likely said something—however unintentional—to offend her."

Finch gaped. "I've hardly spoken to her."

"Need I remind you that during our first conversation, you criticized my weight and called me very heavy?"

"I was carrying you! Even the most petite of ladies would be heavy in such circumstances."

"And you made pointed remarks about my plain appearance."

With a scowl, Finch muttered, "You were fairly accusing me of accosting you, and I needed to dispel you of that assumption."

Miss Barrows nodded but did not look the slightest bit repentant. "But you could have done so in a more kindhearted manner, Mr. Finch."

Shoulders slumping, Finch sent another scowl inward. Perhaps Miss Barrows had a point, though acknowledging that did not make him feel any better.

"I apologize if I offended you."

"Think nothing of it," she said with a wave. "I knew you meant no offense, and your blunt manner suits me. But I do not think Mrs. Kingsley cares for it."

Finch's lips pinched together, and he felt an urge to let loose some of the more colorful epitaphs he'd learned during his time in the army. "And how is one to speak to a person who finds offense when none is meant?"

Miss Barrows' expression filled with such sweet innocence that Finch prepared himself for a witty rejoinder as the lady smiled and said, "Carefully, of course."

Finch gave her a narrowed look, though his lips curled into a smile. "Might I say that I gave you far more assistance than you gave me?"

"I only promised to offer my advice. I did not say it would be helpful," she said with a spark of humor in her eyes. "But I might add that you must be patient with the lady. Whatever blunder you've committed can be overcome with time and kindness. She doesn't seem the type to nurse a grudge."

The lane split ahead, signaling the entrance to Buxby Hall approaching, and Finch felt weighed down at the sight of it.

"I once heard of a most extraordinary sermon," said Miss Barrows, gazing out at the passing trees and shrubs. Again, Finch sensed some mischief about, for the lady's tone always altered when she thought she was being especially clever or witty, and she couldn't hide the mirth in her expression—no matter how she tried.

"Oh? Do tell," he said in a dry tone.

"The vicar was giving a blistering sermon," she said, swinging her bright gaze to meet Finch. "Full of fire and brimstone, he chastised his flock for all the sins of humanity until he reduced the congregation to weeping and gnashing of teeth. But there was one fellow who looked not the slightest bit perturbed. When the vicar questioned why he did not weep with the rest, he replied, 'Oh, I belong to another parish.'"

Finch's brows pulled together as he cast her a questioning glance before giving her the expected chuckle.

"Not my best?" she asked with a sniff, turning her nose up as though disdaining his sense of humor. "I stumbled across that jest a few weeks ago, and I rather like it."

That brought a genuine smile to Finch's lips as he shook his head. Despite the chill in the air and the breezes blowing past them, Finch felt warmed through, as though the glow of Miss Barrows' heart was a hearth.

"You are an odd lady, Miss Barrows."

"My thanks for the compliment, sir," came the tart reply, spoken with all the regality of a queen.

Chapter 15

Usually, Mr. Thorne was an engaging fellow. His exceptional conversation was one of the reasons Simon had hired him to act as steward of Avebury Park; if they were to work side by side, Simon had wanted someone enjoyable. Though he entrusted most of the minutiae to Mr. Thorne, Simon would not concede complete control like so many of his class did, which meant he spent a good deal of time in his steward's company.

But today, Simon couldn't follow Mr. Thorne's monotonous ramblings about the tenants, the upcoming renovations, income and expenditure, and the like. There was so much to do in the coming months that he needed to concentrate, but Simon's thoughts were decidedly elsewhere.

"Is anything amiss?" asked Mr. Thorne, pausing amidst a discourse on crop rotations. "I get the distinct impression you haven't heard a word I've said in the last several minutes."

Or the entire conversation, more like.

Rubbing the bump of his nose, Simon gave the fellow an apologetic smile. "I fear my thoughts have strayed. Perhaps you could write down your thoughts about the more important issues, and I can peruse them at my leisure."

Mr. Thorne gave him an assessing glance. "Is there anything I might do to be of assistance? I haven't seen you this distracted in months." The fellow gave his statement a thought and amended, "Or irritated, rather. You've been plenty distracted since you and Mrs. Kingsley returned from your trip to Rosewood Cottage."

Simon narrowed his eyes at the impudent fellow, but that was the most he felt he could do. He'd hired Mr. Thorne knowing he was an outspoken sort, and Simon couldn't punish him for being precisely what he was. Besides, such candor was usually refreshing.

"It is nothing of consequence. Just a few things on my mind," replied Simon, as he was in no mood to discuss the very significant issue plaguing him at present.

Mr. Thorne gathered his things with a nod and left Simon to himself, though there was no point in remaining in his study. There was nothing here with which to distract himself. No book or letter could hold his attention. Even Finch had abandoned him, as his friend spent more time at Buxby Hall than at Avebury Park of late.

Getting to his feet, Simon went in search of the person who was both the source of his discomfort and his solace. He wandered the halls of his home, and it struck him just how much his life had altered from the previous year and how much vitality and joy she'd brought to Avebury Park. Simon couldn't recall there ever being such contentment within these walls. Certainly not during his childhood; even at their best, his parents weren't the contented sort.

But what would his home become if its mistress were absent? That was not such a difficult hypothetical to sort through, for Simon's life before Mina had not been terribly happy. The Simon of those days had believed himself to be, but the Simon of now knew better.

Simon's feet led him to the place he knew he'd find her. Kingsleys of the past had preferred the formal parlor, as was evidenced by the additional care and attention given to its decoration, but from the beginning, Mina had made the morning room her preferred place. The space was smaller but the windows overlooked the garden, and in summer, the scent of the blossoms filled the room with their heavenly bouquet.

Mina stood at that window. It was shut tight against the winter's bite, and her eyes were fixed on the frosty panes of glass. Creeping up behind her, Simon slid his arms over hers, enveloping her and placing a kiss on her neck. But Mina did not soften at his touch and gave only a vague sound of acknowledgment that was something of a greeting but with no life to it. The pair of them stood together like that, watching the snow fly across the window as the wind filled the silence, and Simon wondered what he'd done to inspire such a lukewarm reception.

Or was it Finch? Had that fool done something to annoy her?

Then Simon recalled what she'd been up to today and knew the appointment with her charity group was the culprit. Of course, he shouldered some of that blame as well; the neighborhood was still rampant with whispers concerning his alleged infidelities.

Plenty of ladies nipped at his wife. Whether it was those who hated her for being the lady who'd stolen the eligible Simon Kingsley from their daughters or those who found delight in bruising her fragile ego, he'd witnessed enough little moments to recognize that there was vitriol aplenty pointed towards Mrs. Simon Kingsley.

And then he'd added the rumors. With time, they would die down, but there were far too many who found glee in stirring up trouble and teasing the newly married lady about her husband's wandering eye was prime fodder.

The thought of it twisted his stomach in knots. Flashes of his nightmares came to mind, and Simon's heart quickened. He had to do more to cement their relationship. Strengthen it somehow. Ensure that Mina would have no reason to leave again.

Tracking the flakes slithering through the sky, Simon cursed the weather. A picnic would be the perfect thing: an afternoon in which he could lavish attention on his dear wife. But the seasons refused to cooperate.

There were plenty in her acquaintance who thought Mina Kingsley incapable of anger, as though her quiet nature made it impossible for her to feel such a roaring emotion, but the truth was that she felt her fair share; she simply chose to keep it a private matter. Until it wasn't.

Mina didn't let it loose often, but neither was it unheard of, and she felt precariously close to releasing her anger in all its glory. Those wretched, spiteful she-demons!

Her fury wasn't a blazing fire burning through her; it was a chill that froze the blood in her veins until she was as icy and cool as winter's touch. She stood there, staring out the window, consumed by thoughts of those harpies and what she wished she had the gumption to do. Mrs. Baxter deserved a thorough setting down.

It was a school. Something of benefit not just to the poor of Bristow but the village as a whole. To educate and lift their lowest members would bless the entire community, yet Mrs. Baxter was determined to hinder the project.

"I am certain you think you know best, Mrs. Kingsley, but you've been in Bristow such a short time..." Mrs. Baxter's voice had an infuriating nasal quality that made her condescension all the more vexing. She feigned concern for the children and their families, for Mina's own ability to helm the school, and for anything else that might wrestle control away from Mina.

And all because Mrs. Baxter was bitter over the Bristow Literary Society's success. In truth, Mina was still surprised at how well-received it had been, as neither she nor Mrs. Pratt was among the social epicenter of the village, but Mrs. Baxter's reaction to it was nothing short of vexed. And more than a little appalled. Heaven forfend that anything in Bristow happens without her seal of approval, and now the village children would be punished for it.

That odious creature...

Mina's thoughts jerked back to the present and she realized Simon had left again. Her shoulders drooped, and she puffed out her cheeks. Glancing over her shoulder, she wondered when he'd disappeared, for Mina desperately wanted Simon to hold her and assure her that all would be well. His touch was a balm she needed at present.

And like he'd been summoned from her desires, her husband strode back into the room. Mina reached for him but stopped as he held up a thin wooden box.

"It's for you," he said when she stood there blinking at it.

Such words may inspire fits of rapture in other women, but they made Mina's heart sink like a stone. "Another gift?"

"Of course. And there's plenty more where it came from. I had planned on giving it to you in a more romantic setting, but I couldn't wait another minute."

She ought to be grateful (didn't every wife long for such grand gestures?), but a shiver tickled Mina's spine, scurrying along her skin as she stared at the offering, not daring to touch it. Hardly a day passed without some token, and the initial excitement upon receiving them had faded as the desperation in Simon's gaze grew.

The box rested in his hands, whispering that something was amiss with her husband, echoing the worries tickling the back of her thoughts—ones she'd refused to give voice to before. But it was difficult to deny the determined nature of his generosity. Almost as though Simon wished to convince himself of his feelings.

With a hand at her back, he guided her to the sofa, and Mina tried to shake away that thought. Simon loved her. He showed it in so many different manners that she couldn't doubt his heart. But his heart had changed once without warning; could it not change again?

Mina dropped onto the sofa beside him. After the day she'd had, she was in no state to handle such turmoil. She wanted no presents. She simply needed her husband to talk to her. Hold her.

Carefully, he placed the gift on her lap, and Mina sent him a questioning glance. He merely smiled in return and sat down beside her.

"Open it," he prompted.

Mina looked into his eyes and saw all the good things she hoped to find, but buried beneath them was that strain. Worry, perhaps? And it only grew as she watched him. Turning her attention to the box, Mina pulled open the lid and gasped.

Lying inside the velvet interior was a rivière necklace made of amethyst. The rosy purple stones were the loveliest shade she'd ever seen in such gems. Each one was clear and sparkling, making it the most gorgeous and by far the most expensive piece of jewelry she owned. It was fit for a queen.

"Simon," she whispered his name, uncertain as to what more she could say.

"Do you like it?"

"Like it?" Mina gaped at the question, turning to meet his eyes, and there it was. Though Simon beamed at her, there was a tension to the edges of his lips. A strain in his gaze. It was a smile tinged with unease.

"I found it among the family jewels a few weeks back. It made me think of you."

Mina blinked at him, and he continued, his words coming at a clipped pace, "If it doesn't suit you, you needn't keep it. I thought you liked that shade..."

Simon babbled on, and Mina was speechless. She should ignore it, but the unease kept niggling at her. Something was amiss, and Mina could not decipher the source. Dropping her gaze to the necklace on her lap, she fiddled with the string of stones and hoped Simon could not see her cheeks blazing pink.

A tremulous voice inside her begged her to ignore it. Leave it be. No good would come from dredging up that which Simon wished hidden. She mustn't forget the time when *that woman* had haunted the halls of Avebury Park, both figuratively and literally; Mrs. Susannah Banfield had been a presence in the Kingsleys' marriage long before she'd appeared on their doorstep. It had been the right thing to confront Simon then, but it had ended with Mina fleeing the county with a shattered heart.

Did she truly wish to know if Simon's feelings had changed once more? His behavior would settle before long, and then Mina could pretend that all was well. But to know with certainty that his feelings had dwindled, or had fled altogether, would crush her.

Just as Mina was about to affix a smile on her face, she realized that they were following that same terrible pattern from before. Denying. Ignoring. Excusing. Fearing. Mina had been a coward before, and she was returning to that all too familiar behavior.

Before she could rethink her course of action or scuttle away back into silent acceptance of their situation, Mina blurted out the question she needed to ask.

"What is wrong, Simon?"

Chapter 16

Sweat gathered on his neck as his blasted cravat strangled him. Simon tugged at the bit of cloth, wishing his valet would learn to tie a proper knot without asphyxiating his master. With a cough and swallow, he cleared his throat.

"You do not like it?"

"It is one of the most beautiful necklaces I've ever seen, and I cannot wait to wear it, but that is immaterial," said Mina, closing the lid and placing it to the side without a second look. "What is the matter?"

Simon shifted in his seat, tugging at his jacket and wishing he could rip the wretched cravat from his neck.

"I don't know what you mean—" But Simon stopped when Mina put her hand over his mouth. Squeezing her eyes shut, she shook her head, and Simon couldn't help but notice how red her complexion had grown.

"Please don't," she whispered. "Don't tell me that nothing is the matter or that all is well or any other lie. I know something is amiss. I have seen it building for the last few weeks. I know you are not sleeping, and that something is bothering you."

Mina's body tightened, and she refused to meet his gaze. Simon's lungs seized at the sight of her bracing herself as though expecting a blow. It was a posture he'd not seen in some months, and seeing it once more made his heart twist in half.

With a wince, Simon's shoulders dropped, and he removed her hand so he could mumble, "You forgave me too freely."

Eyes popping open, Mina stared at him. "Pardon?"

Mina's fingers were so soft. Not delicate, as the lady herself was no fragile, tiny thing. No, they were elegant. Graceful. Simon ran his own along them, allowing the feel of her skin to anchor him. His gaze fixed on their hands as they entwined.

"I behaved abominably, and I do not understand how you forgave me so readily or why you love me now," he murmured, his eyes tracing the lines of her fingers.

Tugging on their joined hands, Mina drew his gaze to hers. "That is ridiculous, darling. You have more than made up for what has passed—"

"No, I haven't," he said, fighting to keep his voice from rising. Adding to his sins by losing his temper now would hardly help. "I behaved like a cad, and I cannot help but be angry at my behavior, so how can you possibly be at peace with it?"

"But Simon, you didn't act maliciously then. You were blind and foolish," she said with a half-smile, "but not purposefully cruel. That makes a world of difference."

Simon sighed, turning his gaze back to their hands. "And are you going to say that your mood of late has nothing to do with it? I see you are unhappy, Mina. Have I done something to deserve that cold reception?"

Mina straightened, staring at her husband like a landed trout. "Just now? That was nothing, Simon."

His jaw tensed, and he slanted a look in her direction. "Do not think me a fool, Mina. That was not nothing. You were practically growling when I approached. What have I done?"

Pressing a hand to her stomach, Mina felt like slouching back onto the sofa as the pressure in her chest eased. "You've done nothing, dearest."

Simon's expression fell, and she shunted aside the gift, scooting closer so that she could wrap her arms around him and burrow into his hold.

"Nothing, Simon," she whispered. "You had not a thing to do with my foul mood, except for abandoning me when I needed your embrace."

Leaning back, her husband gave her a pair of raised brows, his gaze desperate to believe her, and Mina closed the distance between them, pressing her lips to his with a reassurance that spoke better than words. Her heart lightened as he met her touch with eagerness, meeting her earnestness with a matching fervor.

Thank the stars above. Mina's heart was able to beat its regular pace once more. She had been in such a foul mood of late and hadn't realized how much of it had seeped into her marriage. Rubbing her hand along the curve of his jaw, Mina slowed the kiss and met her husband's gaze.

"I apologize if I've hurt you, my love," she murmured, pressing another touch of her lips to the corner of his. They quirked up in such a pleased manner as he relaxed into her embrace that she couldn't stop herself from kissing them.

Simon relaxed into the sofa, bringing Mina with him and wrapping an arm around her as she rested her head against his shoulder.

"It is not you who has been vexing me," she murmured, bringing her hand to rest on his chest. "Mrs. Baxter has been in fine form the last few weeks, subtly undermining my efforts with the village school and wrestling away control."

"You make it sound as though she is staging a coup." Simon's chest rumbled with a silent chuckle, and he pressed a kiss to her head.

"We would easily quell France and dispatch Bonaparte if our soldiers had her at their head," she mumbled.

Mina had intended to give only the barest of details when she began recounting their latest interlude, but the more she spoke, the more came out, and soon she was scowling and recalling all the additional times Mrs. Baxter had lashed out.

"And the most infuriating thing is that I do not care who leads our efforts. But if I leave it to Mrs. Baxter and her coven, they will abandon the school at the first opportunity, leaving the poor children without an education."

Simon's arms drew her close, and Mina felt another kiss on her head. "Only you would subject yourself to such ill-treatment and then lament that the true tragedy is the children's suffering."

Mina leaned up to meet his eyes as her brows pulled tight together. "I will survive Mrs. Baxter's venom, but the children need this—"

Another kiss stole away her words, and when Simon released her again, he remained close, his words a whisper. "You humble me, Mina."

She breathed in Simon's natural scent and the strong herbs from his cologne and contemplated whether or not they could simply bolt the bedchamber doors and remain here together, away from the world.

"My beautiful wife," he murmured.

Mina flinched at the words, but she rested her head back down again so he would not see the doubt in her eyes. Beautiful was not a familiar description when applied to her. Papa and her brothers were known to use it at times, but even they tended towards "pretty" or "fetching."

Susannah Banfield was beautiful. Though Mina thought the woman hideous in all other aspects, even she could admit Mrs. Banfield was a gorgeous creature. Her features were unparalleled, with sparkling eyes of brightest blue and golden tresses that never failed to hold the perfect curl. To say nothing of her figure, which was called divine more often than not.

Mina Kingsley was Mrs. Banfield's antithesis. She did not despair over her looks, but "beautiful" denoted something extraordinary, unique, and better than others; not everyone could achieve such lofty expectations. Mina had long ago accepted her limitations, and there was nothing demeaning about embracing her plain features and unattractive figure. There was little to be done about her outward appearance, and whether it was lovely had no bearing on who she was as a person nor her happiness with the lady she'd become.

Yet Simon adored using that descriptor. Ever since that...moment? Interlude? Mina was never quite certain how to describe those horrid days when she'd thought her marriage was ruined beyond repair. But since that time, Simon peppered such compliments into his conversations with a liberality that would get him banned from a kitchen—though he'd thought her quite plain before.

Did that mean something?

Simon held her gaze, and Mina shoved those thoughts aside. They were of no value at present, and they'd dredged up enough drama today; she had no desire to stir from this peaceful moment.

"Do you wish me to call her out? I'm not a good shot, but I'm bound to be better than Mrs. Baxter." Simon affected a serious air, his words spoken with such dry humor that Mina laughed out loud at the thought of it.

"She would likely choose swords, so she could run you through for not choosing her daughter over 'that dreadful wife of yours,'" she said, affecting a passable impression of Mrs. Baxter's imperious tone.

Simon chuckled, his chest bouncing her as she rested against it. Leaning close, Mina laughed at the ridiculous image Simon had conjured with his offer and snuggled into him.

"I am joking, but only slightly. I cannot stand the awful things they say about you," he murmured, his arms clinging to her as tightly as she was to him.

Mina smiled, head nestling into his shoulder. "I know, love, but it is of no consequence. They are only bitter at having lost such an unparalleled prospective son-in-law."

"I am a fine specimen of manhood."

Mina poked him in the ribs, and Simon chuckled, but his tone softened as he added, "I know you do not wish to make a scene or stir up more trouble, but I shan't stand by and watch them abuse you. Not ever again."

"She is an irritant and nothing more, Simon. With time, things will settle in the neighborhood if we simply let things lie. But should I need any assistance in disposing of my enemy, I know who to call upon."

"Too right."

Simon couldn't decide if he felt like giving a bellowing shout of victory or letting out a long, bone-deep sigh. If not for the fact that either would disrupt his wife, who was so cozily snuggled up against him, Simon would've likely done both.

All was well. Or as well as it could be while ladies like Mrs. Baxter attacked his dear Mina. Though calling that harpy a "lady" was a generous use of the term. Simon had always believed that the terms gentleman and lady required an attitude of generosity towards one's fellow man. *Noblesse oblige* may be a foreign phrase but not a foreign concept.

Some feral part of him wished to shove aside his gentlemanly strictures and hunt Mrs. Baxter and all the rest down, but again, that would require relinquishing his current position. And angering his wife. Mina was too kind, and though he didn't deserve her, Simon wished to at least feign that he was worthy of her.

So, he let that anger die to a flickering flame and reveled in the contentment of being so warmly situated with his wife. Mina hadn't been upset with him; that was good. Of course, it didn't dispel the shadows lingering in his heart, which warned that he would ruin it eventually, but for now, Simon was willing to embrace the joy of the moment. Tomorrow would be soon enough to continue his campaign of trustworthiness.

Mina ran a hand across his chest, tracing a pattern into his waistcoat, and Simon breathed in the scent of lilies that had become synonymous with his wife. He didn't know if he'd ever noticed that fragrance before, but now it permeated the house, bringing a smile to his lips.

But that smile fled as he recalled Mina's earlier reaction. With the conversation shifting quickly from that moment, Simon hadn't given it much thought then, but his mind drifted back to that little comment he'd made.

"My beautiful wife..." Simon had said it in all sincerity, yet Mina had flinched. Though she'd tried to hide it, he'd seen the doubt. Even after months of honest affection, Mina shied away from such compliments; she did not go so far as to fight him on it, but neither did she accept it.

Simon's fingers twitched, tapping a gentle rhythm against Mina's arm as he held her close. One way or another, he would rebuild the trust he'd damaged.

Chapter 17

Sunlight poured through Finch's bedchamber window, filling the room with a golden hue. The crystalline dusting of snow sparkled outside, begging him to abandon the warmth and comfort of Avebury Park. Perhaps he might persuade Miss Barrows to join him on another excursion. The lady seemed keen to traipse through the snowscape, but Finch wondered if it might cause her trouble; Lady Lovell was the picture of generosity, so he hoped she did not mind losing her companion so frequently.

But then, he reminded himself that Lady Lovell was also the picture of blunt conversation and would have no qualms about telling him if he'd made a nuisance of himself.

Taking one final perusal in the mirror, Finch straightened his jacket and cuffs and turned to the door in search of breakfast. And found trouble instead. Not that Mina was trouble in and of herself. She was an amiable lady, but Finch thought it better if Simon served as a facilitator between them. Unfortunately, the man in question was taking his leave.

Like so often, the couple seemed unaware of Finch standing in the doorway. Their heads were together with a few smiles and whispers. Finch wondered if he ought to back away, but his stomach gave a treacherous gurgle, drawing Simon and Mina's attention.

"Had you a pleasant morning, Finch?" asked Simon, getting to his feet.

"Quite." And that was true enough. His mornings at Avebury Park were neither extraordinary nor unbearable despite his friend's noticeable absence.

"I wish I had time to chat, but I am to meet Mr. Thorne about some improvements we are planning to begin as soon as the ground thaws."

And kissing his wife's cheek, Simon swept from the room, off to do terribly important things. At present, the most pressing matter Finch had to decide upon was whether to finish the book he'd begun last night or go on yet another walk; he'd prefer a ride, but the ground was just treacherous enough that he didn't care to go too often and risk injury to his borrowed mount.

Mina watched her husband leave and spared Finch a passing glance before returning to her toast, giving it far more attention than any food ever warranted. Finch stood by the edge of the table and stared at the empty seats, his lagging wits finally urging him to move as it was too late to escape now.

Loading up his plate from the array of foods on the side table, Finch took a seat beside his hostess. The crunch of toast and the clink of silverware against china broke the silence as the pair munched. Slanting a glance at Mina, he tried to know what to say to her.

If Miss Barrows was correct (and Finch's stomach gave an unhappy lurch that told him she was), then Mina had reason to be wary of him. Whether he'd earned it or not, he ought to do something to ease her worries. This was his closest friend's wife, and it was time Finch did something to secure her good opinion.

"I understand you are building a school in the village," he said.

Mina's brows climbed upwards as she froze mid-bite.

"Simon often talks about it," added Finch. "He is rather proud of your efforts."

The lady's cheeks pinked, her lips curling into a smile, and Finch was quite amazed at how quickly her expression had gone from apprehensive to pleased. He didn't know if she'd ever looked so happy at something he'd said before.

With a quick chew and swallow, she took a sip from her teacup and cleared her throat. "I am attempting it, though my detractors are determined to see it fail."

Finch gave a low chuckle and spread a napkin across his lap. "I can imagine many of the ladies in Bristow are quite livid at you stealing away their prize. They've been vying for Simon since their daughters were born. If nothing else, I will be forever grateful you've secured him so I will no longer have to suffer through their machinations. My visits often revolved around assisting Simon in avoiding their lures."

Mina did not laugh as he'd intended, but neither did she recoil or flee as she was wont to do when he said something outrageous like that. Slanting a look in his direction, she studied him while pretending not to study him, and Finch took a bite of cold ham as he pondered what to say next.

"I am pleased to see your pianoforte is finally receiving the love and attention it deserves," said Finch. "Simon always neglected it terribly unless I pressed him to tune it."

Her gaze held his for a silent moment before she replied, "I understand you are quite the musician."

A smile crept upwards, and Finch nodded. "Not enough to be useful but enough to appreciate the sight of a well-used instrument and sheet music."

"It is a shame that we haven't had a musical evening in which to display your talents."

Finch huffed. "Talent is too grand a word for my musical abilities. My love of it outweighs my skill."

Mina's gaze did not waver from his as she spoke in a pointed, though quiet, tone. "I could invite Lady Lovell and Miss Barrows to join us."

Refusing to flinch at that insinuation, Finch held her gaze, taking a bite of kippers before answering. "I am certain they would enjoy that."

Making a vague sound of agreement, Mina took a sip of her drinking chocolate and added, "You've been spending a fair amount of time at Buxby Hall."

"It has beautiful grounds," he said, slanting another curious look at Mina. Her meaning was clear enough, though Finch didn't know what her intentions were. And for all his desire to heal the fracture between them, he wasn't about to allow her free rein to muck about in his life. There was already one lady determined to do so, and he wouldn't suffer the interference of another.

"And Miss Barrows?" asked Mina, dropping all pretense.

"She is a fine lady whose company I enjoy." Finch turned his gaze to his meal, digging into it with determination. Once finished, he could flee Mina's piercing gaze and pointed questions. If this was what came from furthering his acquaintance with her, perhaps it was best if he kept his distance.

"Such a shame she's so unattractive," murmured Mina, seeming far more interested in her toast and drinking chocolate than the inflammatory words she'd spouted.

"Pardon?" asked Finch, setting down his silverware with a thud against the table.

"An unsightly complexion and shocking hair..." Mina's voice drifted off before murmuring, "Or was it a shocking complexion and unsightly hair? I cannot remember the precise manner in which you phrased it."

As Finch didn't dare scowl at his friend's wife, he turned his face to his plate. "I admit I did not have the highest opinion of her looks, but I was not as harsh as all that."

"True," said Mina in a tone that was drier than her toast. "You conceded that her figure was 'fine enough.'"

Finch took another bite of food. With his mouth otherwise occupied, perhaps the conversation would lapse back into awkward silence. But it was not to be.

"Your opinion seems to have altered somewhat since that harsh assessment," said Mina, her dark eyes studying him with too much interest, and when a footman arrived with a stack of letters atop a salver, Finch felt like embracing the lad as his savior.

"It looks as though you've received a letter from home," said Mina, sifting through the missives and handing one to Finch.

"Would you forgive me if I read it now?" In truth, his sister-in-law's letters rarely needed immediate attention, but it provided him an excuse to avoid returning to the previous conversation.

"Think nothing of it," said Mina with a wave, though she placed her own correspondence to the side.

Breaking the seal, Finch unfolded the paper and wondered if Miss Barrows had sent her friend his recommendations for her steward and man of business. The list hadn't been lengthy, but he felt quite certain there were perfect candidates among the selection; certainly, Finch wouldn't hesitate to hire a single one to manage his affairs—if he had any.

Would Miss Barrows tell him if his suggestions were successful? It seemed logical that her friend would continue to confide in the lady, and hopefully, that would eventually make its way to Finch. His assistance may not have amounted to much, but it would be pleasing to know it had done some good.

Finch's mind wandered from that thought to his sister-in-law's elegant script. Annette was a stellar correspondent, who sent him a steady stream of missives detailing her family's daily life, and even when Finch was on the other side of the country, he knew precisely what dishes the Gardiners had served at their dinner the previous evening, his nieces' newly found disdain for geography, and even a daily account of the weather since her last letter.

No doubt, she wrote to each of her brothers-in-law to relay them similar information, and though her letters were tedious at times, Finch appreciated Annette's efforts to maintain the familial ties. It was a tradition Mother had begun when the eldest first stepped out into the wide world, and her daughter-in-law strived to maintain it.

Yet Finch's brows furrowed as he scanned the lines, searching for anything of substance. Not that he didn't enjoy hearing of Ginny and Barbara's antics, but there was a quality to her letters that left Finch feeling empty. Annette's words were a flood of information, but never once did they touch on anything of personal interest to Finch.

There was a passing mention of his trip and wishing him well, but no questions about his affairs. Not even asking after his health. The letter was little more than a lecture on their lives, asking nothing of him but to sit and listen as she expounded on the greatness of the Finch family.

The other brothers' illustrious careers were outlined in detail. Phineas's effective negotiation with the tenants to raise rents. Solomon and Arnold's victory in a case that had languished in the courts for some years. Julian's advancement from commander to captain was all but done. Even remembrances of Wesley's heroic exploits were given a passing mention, though he'd been gone from this world nearly fifteen years.

Finch wondered what she wrote to his brothers on his behalf.

"Finch still lives." What more could she say? There was a reason he rarely replied to Annette's letters, and it wasn't just a matter of the cost.

"Is it bad news?"

Mina's question jerked him from his thoughts, and Finch looked up to see her staring at him with a furrowed brow.

Tucking the letter back into the envelope, he smiled and waved away the question. "My sister-in-law enjoys writing novels about the goings-on of the Finch family. I hardly need to visit them, for she paints such a vivid picture of their lives."

But the words didn't mollify Simon's wife, and she stared at him with those warm brown eyes of hers; something in them made him feel as though she was not as easily fooled as her husband, nor would she be put off by false claims of apathy. Yet what advice or sympathy could Mina Kingsley give?

There was only one person who might understand his plight.

"Please excuse me, but the morning has gotten away from me." Tossing his napkin aside, Finch rose to his feet, gave Mina a bow, and made a hasty retreat.

Chapter 18

Felicity hadn't thought herself particularly fond of winter. She held no hatred towards the season but neither did she think it a fine time of year. As a child, Felicity had enjoyed all the trappings of the season, but then, youth held more possibilities for such cold months, and it had been some years since she'd enjoyed skating or frolicking in the snow.

The city in winter was a cold, dark thing. The occasional snow lent some beauty to the buildings for fleeting moments, but that pristine white was quickly tinged brown and grey by the press of humanity. And to Felicity's thinking, there was nothing uglier than a city street filled with melting snow and mud, painting the world in dull colors.

But a country winter was a different beast. Stretches of snow lay undisturbed, covering the countryside in pristine white. The world looked clean and pure in the country. Staring out the parlor window, Felicity took in the sight, certain she would never tire of gazing upon it. Where a city winter demanded sequestering oneself by a warm hearth until spring arrived, the countryside begged her to explore.

"Staring out that window won't make him arrive any faster."

Felicity gave a start and then sent Aunt Imogene a narrowed look from over her shoulder. "You are speaking gibberish again, Aunt. Should I send for the apothecary? He might have some medicine to heal your troubled mind."

Aunt Imogene gave a halting chuckle, shaking her head at that impudence.

"You can pretend all you like, but I am no fool, and even a fool could see how often you and Mr. Finch spend your days together," she said, turning her attention back to her sewing. "He was a regular visitor to Buxby Hall before, but now he is a fixture. And if he is not here, you are guaranteed to disappear to Avebury Park before long."

"This has been a beautiful winter," said Felicity, not bothering to hide her shift in subject. She turned her attention to the window, and her gaze followed the bending swirls of frost edging the window. Even that was prettier in Bristow. "I don't know if I've ever enjoyed a winter so much."

Aunt Imogene was quiet for a moment or two, but Felicity felt the lady smile and braced herself for whatever mischief her great-aunt would spout next.

"I imagine it's the company that makes it so remarkable." Aunt Imogene's tone was so laden with significance that it was a wonder her words did not fall to the floor.

Turning from the window, Felicity raised her nose to the air with a sniff and said, "If you are going to be ridiculous, I will leave."

"And visit Avebury Park?"

The reply was too quick and too on the nose for Felicity to do anything other than laugh. Though Aunt Imogene had delivered the retort with utter nonchalance, her eyes glittered with silent mirth as she regarded her great-niece, and Felicity finally cried surrender and dropped onto the sofa opposite her.

"I will not pretend I do not grasp your meaning; you've been as subtle as a herd of stampeding cattle," said Felicity, which earned her a smile. "And yes, I do find Mr. Finch's company enjoyable, and yes, it has added to my appreciation of the season, the country, and everything else I've prattled on about. But that doesn't mean I'm ready to set my cap at him."

"I think it fair to say you set that some time ago," murmured her great-aunt, placing another stitch in her embroidery.

Felicity leveled a narrowed look at Aunt Imogene, but the lady remained unrepentant. "I am fond of Mr. Finch. I am. He is a lively conversationalist with a broad knowledge of so many things, and more talents than I can lay claim to. He's traveled abroad, fought in battles, and experienced so much of the world. I cannot help but seek out his company when it is so delightful."

And even as she meant to dispel Aunt Imogene's wild fantasies, each reason led to more, and Felicity's heart stirred, telling her that which she wasn't ready to admit to herself, let alone Aunt Imogene.

"But he is a friend, nothing more." The words sounded hollow, even to Felicity's reckoning, but they ought to be true. She was nearing one and thirty, and well past the age of flirtations and fancies. Her matrimonial goals had been dispelled long ago, and Felicity had fled to Bristow for the very purpose of avoiding such entanglements.

Or rather, *false* entanglements, and there was nothing about Mr. Finch that rang false.

Aunt Imogene was wise enough to ignore Felicity's denial and instead said, "You ought to tell him the truth of your circumstances."

"I ought to do a great many things." The older lady leveled a narrowed look at her niece, and Felicity sighed. "I hadn't intended to mislead Mr. Finch."

"Lie," corrected Aunt Imogene. "You didn't 'mislead.'"

Feeling like a young girl a quarter of her age, Felicity gave another sigh and nodded. "I lied to him, and I had every intention of doing so, but I hadn't expected our acquaintance to develop into a friendship. And now it is difficult to admit the truth."

Aunt Imogene met that with a raised brow. "That is the nature of falsehoods. Like a small debt incurred, the interest builds, and when collection is due, the burden is much greater than the original lie was worth."

There was wisdom in that, though it did Felicity little good, as bemoaning what she ought to have done did not alter her present situation. "But so many of my friendships shifted when I inherited, and admitting the truth might ruin—"

Felicity fell silent at a knock on the door, and when the footman entered to announce that the gentleman in question was there to call on them, Felicity's face burned red, and she bit her lips until they ached.

"Calm yourself, my dear," said Aunt Imogene, putting aside her sewing as the footman moved to fetch Mr. Finch. "But this might be providence telling you it is time to speak the truth."

Any other objection Felicity might have mounted was cut off when Mr. Finch swept in with a bow.

"I found my morning quite empty and thought I ought to bother you instead of wandering around Avebury Park." Mr. Finch's words were light and seemingly carefree, but that underlying sadness was out in force today, and Felicity longed to ask what was troubling him. But that question would yield no answers in mixed company.

"And we are always grateful when you do," said Aunt Imogene, motioning for him to sit. Felicity ignored the happy little flutter of her heart when he chose the seat beside her.

"What have you got yourselves up to this morning?" he asked.

"I was working on some embroidery while my niece was philosophizing." Aunt Imogene slanted a wry look at Felicity, and she pretended to ignore it.

Mr. Finch's blonde brows rose at that, and he turned a bright eye to Felicity. "I hadn't thought you a philosopher."

"My aunt gives me too much credit," said Felicity, forcing herself not to speak through gritted teeth.

Great-Aunt Imogene gave her niece a faint smile, and Felicity braced herself for the forthcoming mischief.

"Felicity, dear, fetch me my shawl," she said, waving a hand towards the item, which was draped across a chair on the other side of the parlor.

The request was not odd on its own, but the pointed tone and innocent look she gave her niece spoke of trouble afoot, and Felicity was quick to ascertain it even as Aunt Imogene reinforced it by mouthing, "You are my companion."

Getting to her feet—and causing Mr. Finch to do the same—Felicity quickly fetched the shawl and handed it to Aunt Imogene.

"Drape it properly," she said with another sweet smile, and Felicity complied. It was one thing to speak the truth to Mr. Finch when they were alone, but she wasn't about to reveal her ruse in front of an audience. With a few quick adjustments, Felicity had the shawl placed precisely as Aunt Imogene directed and returned to her seat.

With a smile, Felicity turned her attention to the gentleman at her side. "And what else—"

"Felicity, dear," said Aunt Imogene. "My sewing box is in the way."

Felicity held Aunt Imogene's gaze, which sparked with a combination of humor and challenge. Then, rising to her feet once more—and forcing Mr. Finch to do the same—Felicity lifted the box from the cushion beside Aunt Imogene and walked it to the table on the other side of the room. It was only when she returned to the sofa that Aunt Imogene spoke up again.

"Not over there. I wish it to be out of the way but within reach. I might wish to do a little more sewing while we chat." Though Aunt Imogene maintained a careful facade for Mr. Finch's sake, Felicity felt the older lady's laughter begging to burst out.

Going back to the table, Felicity lifted the sewing box and walked it to the sofa. It took several attempts to find a proper place before Aunt Imogene patted Felicity on the head and gave her a sickly sweet, "Good girl."

Felicity wondered if the lady was going to scratch her behind the ear and give her a treat.

Mr. Finch stared at the pair, and Felicity feigned a smile, though she sent her great-aunt a glance that promised retribution; it inspired not an ounce of remorse in the lady. Taking her seat beside Mr. Finch once more, Felicity opened her mouth but found herself interrupted by Aunt Imogene. Again.

"This shawl just won't do. Besides clashing terribly with my gown, it is not the proper thickness. Felicity, dear, fetch me my grey shawl from my bedchamber."

Felicity didn't know how the lady managed to say all that without bursting out into laughter, for Aunt Imogene's gaze was ablaze with it.

"I could call a maid to stoke the fire if you are cold, Aunt," said Felicity.

"No, I need my grey shawl."

With a huff, Felicity rose to her feet again, gave her aunt one more narrowed look, and left the parlor.

Tucking his hands behind him, Finch stared at the empty doorway, wondering if he ought to take a seat once more or simply await Miss Barrows' return as he was. Casting a glance at Lady Lovell, Finch wondered what she was up to, for there was no mistaking the unspoken conversation playing between the two ladies even if he couldn't interpret it.

"Have I overstepped my welcome?" asked Finch.

"Don't be a goose," said Lady Lovell, motioning for him to sit. "You are always welcome here."

Finch examined the lady, and though her expression was impassive, her eyes sparkled with mirth. "Are you intentionally annoying your companion?"

Lady Lovell broke into a beaming smile, and she chuckled. "Your forthright nature is why I adore you, Mr. Finch. My niece ought to follow your example."

"I've always found her quite forthright."

The lady gave no response to that, merely grinning at him with a sad shake of her head. "And how are you faring today, Mr. Finch?"

Annette's letter burned in his pocket, but Finch gave a lazy grin. "Have you ever known me to be anything but well?"

Lady Lovell met that with a narrowed look, her smile fading into contemplation. "Perhaps Felicity is not the only one in need of some honesty."

A movement at the door drew Finch's attention away from that enigmatic response, and Miss Barrows appeared, her lungs heaving (though she feigned nonchalance).

"I have—" Miss Barrows took in a breath, smiling at the pair as she attempted to recover from her hurried trip. "—your shawl."

Coming to Lady Lovell's side, Miss Barrows moved with precise and overly courteous movements, removing the previous shawl and replacing it with a formality and care that was due a queen. Before Miss Barrows could take another seat, Lady Lovell spoke again.

"I would like some marzipan."

Miss Barrows' solicitous smile faltered, and she stared at the lady for several quiet seconds. "Do you not recall that you ate the last of it yesterday?"

Turning to Finch, the young lady added in a whisper (though not one quiet enough to keep Lady Lovell from overhearing), "I fear her faculties are failing her, Mr. Finch. Perhaps we ought to call for the apothecary to see if he has some means of restoring her wits."

Lady Lovell coughed, though Finch swore it had been a snorting chuckle. He stared at the pair.

"Felicity, dear," said Lady Lovell, not hiding the humor in her tone, "I had thought you might go into the village and fetch me some."

Miss Barrows' smile tightened, but loosened when Lady Lovell added, "Perhaps Mr. Finch might accompany you."

Not waiting for another invitation (or for Finch to agree), Miss Barrows leaned down to bestow a kiss on her aunt's cheek and herded him out of the parlor. She had the pair of them bundled up and out the front door before Finch could question what insanity was rife in Lady Lovell's household.

Chapter 19

"Are you happy in your situation?" asked Finch.

Miss Barrows sent him a puzzled look, the wide rim of her bonnet framing her face. Tucking her cloak's hood more securely around her hat, she shook her head before adding with a smile, "You sound so terribly ominous."

"Lady Lovell seemed intent on torturing you. She does love a good jest, but I hadn't thought her cruel."

Miss Barrows let out a barking laugh. "Yes, she was torturing me, but it was not malicious. She has been exceptionally kind and generous to me."

Finch tucked his hands behind him. "Good."

People often said that snow crunched beneath one's boot, but that was not the proper descriptor at all. There was a hint of a scrunch, true, but the snow squeaked and squealed, as though protesting the abuse. The sound followed them as their lazy steps meandered around the gardens and in the vague direction of the stables.

Miss Barrows turned her gaze to him, examining his profile. "You seem out of sorts today."

Tapping his fingers against his clasped hands, Finch wondered if he were truly going to confess the truth. He'd longed to do for some years, but one did not speak of such matters. Certainly not to a person whom he'd met only a few short weeks ago—even if it felt as though he'd known Miss Barrows much longer.

But even as he thought to toss out a flippant reply, Finch recalled all the reasons he'd escaped to Buxby Hall. Perhaps more than anyone else among his acquaintance, this lady knew the struggles of straddling the great divide between the lower and upper classes. Raised in comfort, yet reduced to low circumstances. Having neither wealth nor the capacity to earn it. Miss Barrows could do more than merely sympathize. She would understand.

Not allowing himself another thought, Finch snatched Annette's letter from his breast pocket and shoved it into Miss Barrows' hands.

"Do you ever feel hopeless about your life, Miss Barrows? Seeing the years stretching before you in a vast string of nothing? Trapped in a position you didn't choose and cannot change?"

Speaking those words aloud was like taking a particularly difficult jump atop a horse. Positioning himself in just the right place as the beast's muscles bunched and launched them into the air. And then that exhilarating moment when rider and horse were in flight, their fates set as hope, glee, and fear all battled together, promising that this would be magnificent or a disaster.

Thrilling and terrifying all at once.

Felicity smoothed the crumpled letter and glanced between it and the gentleman at her side. He continued to stare down the path, his profile showing none of the turmoil rife in the words he'd spoken. As she turned her attention to the missive, Felicity's breath caught in preparation for whatever terrible news it contained. Her eyes flew through the lines, never wavering until she reached the end.

And then she straightened.

"It sounds as though your family are doing well," she said, slanting a glance in his direction while struggling to see the connection between this innocuous letter and his current state of agitation.

"They are doing perfectly well," he mumbled.

Felicity's brows furrowed. There was no mistaking the discontent and agitation growing in the fellow. His footsteps came quicker as they marched the length of the garden, and she struggled to keep pace with him.

"Finding utter success in their professions, wives, and children. Perfectly content as they conquer the world and claim the glory for the great house of Finch," he added, his tone growing more heated with each word.

Fairly puffing to keep up with Mr. Finch and at a loss to understand what was happening when all she had were a few cryptic words and his profile, Felicity grabbed his arm and yanked Mr. Finch to a stop. Standing before him so she could properly read his expression, she waited for him to arrive at the point.

"My family are perfectly content with themselves and with relegating me to be the family ornament," he said. "A useless thing that sits on the shelf, gathering dust."

"I'm afraid I do not understand, Mr. Finch. You may think you're being direct, but without context, I cannot decipher your meaning."

Mr. Finch thrummed with energy wishing to be unleashed. Though he stood with hands clasped behind him and a tilt to his shoulders and hips that spoke of a relaxed, calm soul, his muscles were tight, as though begging for something more than a sedate walk about the countryside.

Glancing around the garden, Felicity saw the raised edge of a fountain. The feature was not operating during the winter, but it provided a passable seat.

"Pace," she ordered as she made herself comfortable. Mr. Finch stared at her, and she repeated herself and added, "You need to move, but I cannot keep up. There is plenty of space here for you to walk to your heart's content without wearing me to shreds. Now, pace."

Laying the letter on her lap, she rested her clasped hands atop it, and he stared at her for a silent moment before doing as told. A stone seat was not ideal in the winter, and the cold seeped into her backside, but Felicity wasn't about to move from this spot when Mr. Finch was in such desperate need of a listening ear.

"You have brothers," she prompted.

Mr. Finch glanced in her direction and nodded, his feet taking him back and forth before her. "Five. All older. I was an unexpected addition to the family, and by the time I was of an age to begin planning for my education and future, the family's resources had been drained establishing their professions."

His boots thumped against the ground as he moved back and forth. It reminded Felicity of a traveling menagerie she'd visited, which had a leopard that prowled the edges of his bars, as though searching for any weakness in his cage.

"Funds and connections are paramount to a gentleman's profession, and my father had expended all the latter on my brothers and was determined not to spend more of the former."

He came to a stop before Felicity, his brown eyes blazing and his chest heaving.

"You once remarked upon my 'varied past,' but the truth is far more varied than you realize. I was thrust into the Royal Naval Academy at the age of twelve because it was an inexpensive education. Father hoped I would excel there as my brothers Wesley and Julian had, but it didn't suit. When I graduated, my father decided against wasting blunt on a university education and handed me to my barrister brothers, Solomon and Arnold. The law didn't suit, either."

Turning on his heel, Mr. Finch returned to his marching. "Father finally realized I wasn't going to succeed without him investing something, so he purchased me a commission and packed me off into the army, hoping that would be the end of it. Little did he know I would bungle that as brilliantly as the rest."

Felicity's brows pinched, her heart chilling at his words. "I highly doubt that."

Mr. Finch huffed, shooting out a puff of vapor into the air, and slanted her a half-smile. With an economy of detail, he told her of the day his father had surrendered all hope of his son's future, and though he feigned indifference, Felicity felt his pain. What son wouldn't be crushed by his father discarding him in such a manner?

Nodding at the letter lying on her lap, Mr. Finch said, "My sister-in-law is an avid correspondent, keeping me abreast of every detail of my brothers' lives, but it only serves to remind me of the vast difference in our positions. As I said, I am the family ornament. Forced to sit about and bear witness to all the goings-on in the family while having nothing of my own. Trapped by my father's demands. Living on their charity and the pittance I've scraped together. Longing for more yet denied any opportunity to pursue it."

The fire that burned inside him flickered and died, and Mr. Finch wandered to her side, dropping onto the stone beside her.

"So, Miss Barrows, as one who is likewise forced to beg scraps from your family, trapped in a situation not of your making and which you cannot change, do you ever feel hopeless? Like your life has no meaning or purpose? And you are merely existing day to day, each hour stretching into unending emptiness?"

His tone was hollow and devoid of any sentiment, as though he was merely reciting the multiplication tables or describing the weather and state of the roads. But more than that, Mr. Finch's gaze lacked any feeling. It wasn't uncommon for him to appear apathetic or bored with the world around him, but this was the bone-deep resignation of one who had surrendered to his misery.

Felicity had seen such an expression before, and the sight of it now threw her back to her childhood when her father had viewed the world with all the warmth and joy of a corpse; those days after her mother's passing and before they'd gone to live with Uncle George, when Father had spent hours staring off at nothing, ignoring his daughter's pleas.

"But surely there is some course of action you might take, Mr. Finch. Some gentlemen find success without their family's assistance."

Giving a humorless chuckle, he shook his head. "I have some skill with finances, but my father doesn't approve of banking as a profession for a gentleman, and to go against his wishes or those of my eldest brother would be tantamount to exile from the family. Their honor wouldn't support one of theirs being in trade."

Instinct had her reaching to wrap her arms around him, but propriety won out, and Felicity compromised by leaning closer to Mr. Finch, resting her shoulder against him as though that touch might heal some of the hurt his family had caused.

"So, your choice is to forge your own path and lose your family or to be their ornament." With a faint smile, she added with a touch of humor, "You could always marry an heiress."

Mr. Finch laughed at that, though it was not a happy thing. "Do you think I have the lures to attract one? An average fellow has no hope of standing out among the extraordinary gentlemen available. I am neither handsome nor witty enough to make up for my empty coffers. And I cannot afford a wife without a hefty dowry."

Felicity stared at the fellow, wondering if he had any idea just how appealing he could be. Perhaps not overtly handsome, but his features were fine enough, and he was terribly pleasant to be around. Many a lady would welcome such a match.

"But even if I caught an heiress's eye, I couldn't bring myself to marry for money. It would only exchange my current prison for another. My complaints aren't that I lack money or position, for the life I desire needn't have an abundance of either."

When he didn't speak further, Felicity prompted him, needing to hear the thoughts he kept silent. "What sort of life do you desire?"

A light entered his gaze as he looked out at the frozen world, a hint of a smile tugging at his lips. "One with a purpose. I've accepted that my life is not one destined for greatness, but I wish to feel as though I have a place in this world. That I am not merely existing."

These were perhaps the most honest words Felicity had ever heard. There was no dissembling or half-truths. Watching him, she knew Mr. Finch had shared a bit of his heart that had not seen the light of day before. And that knowledge humbled her.

And shamed her.

Here sat a man burdened with pains foreign to her own, opening his soul to her because of the lie she'd spoken. What comfort could she give to someone so belittled by his family? Perhaps they did not mean to treat him so shabbily, as elder children were always given precedence over the younger, but that did not lessen the damage they'd done.

Filling her heart with silent pleas for guidance, Felicity wished there was something she could say to heal her friend's heartache.

Chapter 20

Finch had never understood the power of silence until he'd broken his. The details of his life hadn't changed one jot, yet it felt as though the world around him brightened. Like a layer of gauze, his secrets had covered him, dulling his senses and leaving a thin barrier between him and everyone else. Pretending nothing was amiss had only added to his heartache.

Misery compounded.

The cold seeped from the stone, and Finch rose to his feet, offering his hand to Miss Barrows. "Come. I promise not to run you ragged again, but it is too frigid to sit about."

Finch tucked Miss Barrows' arm through his, as much to remind himself to keep pace with her as to assist her on the slippery ground; but though the action had begun as a gentlemanly overture, it felt natural to hold her thusly. Turning them towards the stables, he knew it was time for them to be on their way, but Miss Barrows nudged him towards a more circuitous path that led them through a copse.

"I cannot pretend to understand your situation in its entirety, but I am quite familiar with feeling trapped in circumstances not of one's own making." Her words hung in the winter air, swirling around them as the snow squeaked beneath their shoes.

Finch glanced at her, and even in profile, he could see the tension pulling at her brow as she nibbled on the edge of her lip.

"But I have tried hard to let go of my expectations and embrace the joy to be found in any circumstance," she added.

Lips twisting into a half-smile, he replied, "I admire that about you, Miss Barrows. You are an optimist through and through. I try to be content with what I have, but it is not so easy for me."

Miss Barrows sniggered, her eyes sparkling as she met his. "Whatever makes you think it is easy for me?"

Pulling him to a halt beneath a tree, Miss Barrows faced him with her brows pulled tight together, concern aglow in her eyes. "My father's world was defined by what he lacked, rather than the joys he had in my brother and me. He withered and faded, surrendering to the darkness. But Uncle George lost his wife at an early age as well. He loved her as dearly as any man could, yet he threw himself into the role of uncle and brother, supporting our little family in our time of need, and he found joy in that calling."

She paused, taking in a deep breath, dropping her gaze from Finch's as she added, "I long for a great many things, Mr. Finch. For my family to be alive. For a husband and children of my own. Reality is never as grand as our imaginings, but that doesn't make life worthless."

Miss Barrows' lips twitched, and she shook her head at nothing in particular. "Misery is easy. There's always a reason to wallow, for no life is perfect. It takes work to smile and laugh and be happy despite the world telling you to surrender. Happiness isn't about circumstances, and it doesn't happen by chance."

Her eyes rose to his once more, and Finch found his heart lightening. Her beliefs were so strong and woven through every facet of her, and it lent him a vitality of his own, as though merely being with her made it easier to see the world as she saw it.

A spark of laughter brightened her eyes, and Miss Barrows smiled that impish grin of hers. "But it helps to have friends around to make you laugh when you need it."

With a kick of her foot, Miss Barrows struck at the tree just behind Finch, leaping backward before the snow and ice crystals cascaded from the branches. He yelped and sputtered as cold flakes flew into his face. Muffled giggles filled the air, and Finch scraped his face clean enough to see Miss Barrows standing there with her hands covering her mouth, her eyes dancing.

Finch's gaze narrowed, though it was impossible to remain grumpy in the face of her mirth.

"I apologize, but it was too perfect to resist," she said, stepping closer. "I do hope you are not too messy."

"I don't know if an apology is enough for that assault on my person—" But Finch's teasing drifted off when Miss Barrows plucked the hat from his head, brushing it off with gentle care while murmuring more apologies to it.

A chuckle began, deep and low, growing as he watched her tend to his abused hat with all the care and affection a mother gives her child. His mirth grew at the serious nature in which she gave her performance, giving no heed to the ludicrous behavior she was exhibiting. It was only when he was well and truly laughing that Miss Barrows gave up her charade, her beaming smile matching his.

"You are truly ridiculous, Miss Barrows," he said.

"Thank you for your kind words, Mr. Finch," she replied, accepting his statement as the compliment he'd intended. Stepping closer, Miss Barrows brushed off the remnant snow from his shoulders and placed the hat on his head.

The innocent movement drew them close, her skirts brushing across the tips of his boots. What had begun in jest shifted, the world quieting around them as Finch held her brown eyes. They were quite magnificent and shone with the brightness of her loving heart. The finest eyes he'd ever seen.

Miss Barrows was like the winter sun. That joy and laughter glowed from within, chasing away the gloom of the world and casting it in a golden hue. Even her hair was fiery and bright, matching the lady in a manner that no brunette or blonde could manage. Her curls fought against the pins and ribbons adorning them, and Finch's fingers itched to twist one of those unruly locks and see if it was as soft as its mistress.

Where had his friend gone? And when had this lovely creature replaced her?

Finch's gaze dropped to her lips, and they tugged at him like a magnet, drawing him in with blissful promises as though one touch might fill him with the same brightness. His breath caught in his lungs, and Finch stared at her, realizing how desperately he longed to kiss her. His heart whispered to him that the joy Miss Barrows spoke of would be found there. With her.

Shifting closer, Finch drew near enough to feel her breath tickling his cheeks; her eyes widened, but the curl of her lips told him it was not from fear. Her lids slid closed, and she stilled, waiting for him to close the distance. To...claim her as his own?

Finch's stomach wrenched, his heartbeat stilling as frost stole across his skin. His throat closed on him, and though he ought to move away, his feet were fixed to the ground. Finch's lungs screamed as he realized he wasn't breathing.

Lewis Finch could not afford to marry and never would. He'd known that from the moment his father had sentenced him to this life of eternal bachelorhood, and yet here he'd raised the hopes of a dear lady. Giving her reason to believe him free to court her.

Thoughts racing, Finch tried to calculate some manner in which he could pursue this. But even if they moved to the country, his meager funds would not support them. His professional options had only dwindled with time, and even if he were to begin again tomorrow, it would take years for him to gain enough of a position to afford a family, assuming he could; many younger sons remained unmarried for just such a reason.

Finch knew this. He'd spent years thinking this through, and he'd known that truth. Accepted it. Until Miss Barrows had appeared. And now, both of their hearts were at risk because he'd been too selfish to keep his distance.

"I must return to Avebury Park," he said, forcing his feet away from her.

Miss Barrows' eyes snapped open, her brows raising as she stared at him. "Pardon?"

"I promised Mr. Kingsley I would assist him with some business this afternoon, and it slipped my mind." The lie came quickly to his lips, and Finch moved back the way they'd come.

"Oh," she murmured, drawing her hands beneath her cloak and casting her gaze to the ground.

Finch's chest squeezed at the sight of her dejected posture, and his feet nearly carried him back to her side. But distance was best.

"I do apologize..." he whispered, his throat seizing against the words. Finch stared at her, warring between the need to flee and the need to comfort her. To make her smile once more as she had done for him. "I..."

But what could he do? Better to break her heart a little now than ruin her future, and the best he had to offer her was a clean break. So, like a coward, he turned heel and fled. Finch felt her gaze on his back, burning holes through his jacket, and he pled for absolution.

Chapter 21

Standing on the cobblestones, Felicity gazed up at the church that stood center stage in Bristow. The spires pointed upwards, as though silently pleading for mankind to turn their thoughts heavenward. With a sky choked with clouds, there was not light enough to catch the stained glass, but candles lit inside the nave gave flickering hints of color.

The bell rang out from above, announcing the passing of another hour, and Felicity wondered why time was determined to march so slowly. Aunt Imogene's orders were quite explicit, and Felicity would not risk irritating the lady further by returning to Buxby Hall a moment sooner. But there was so little for her to do.

Felicity meandered along, passing by the village square, which sat silent, waiting for spring and the sellers' stalls to return. Even the inn was quiet at present, as the locals were still toiling and no coaches had stopped. The world itself seemed to be waiting.

Two days. A full forty-eight hours had passed since Mr. Finch's hasty departure, and Felicity was no more at peace with what had happened than when he'd fled from her. And there was no other way to describe how he'd stumbled and slid in his need to distance himself after that almost-kiss.

Yet again, Felicity replayed that moment, scrutinizing every detail as she tried to understand. Her feelings were in no doubt, for she had nearly leapt into his arms. She shifted the basket, which held the items Aunt Imogene had asked her to retrieve (including the marzipan they'd forgotten during that fateful outing), and Felicity sighed at her foolishness.

Had she truly closed her eyes and leaned into him? That had been as subtle as hanging a sign around her neck, begging him to kiss her. But even now, she didn't think she'd been wrong. The look in Mr. Finch's eyes had spurred her to do so. Even with flocks of suitors, no one had ever gazed upon her with such admiration and warmth. Or rather, such a genuine display of the emotions.

Surely he had felt the same pull towards her, the same desire. Felicity couldn't have been the only one to feel the promise of something wonderful thrumming between them.

Kicking a foot out, she scattered the snow ahead of her, wishing her thoughts could leave it be. For Aunt Imogene's sake, if not Felicity's own, she ought to turn her thoughts to something else.

It did not help matters that the first of her replies had arrived today. Though the job of choosing her steward and man of business was far from done, Felicity was quite pleased with the first applicant. It was hard to tell much from a few lines, but Mr. Baldwin had already shown himself superior to her previous staff. And while such news ought to drive her thoughts to finances, Felicity's thoughts were fixed on the gentleman who'd recommended him. Which led her back to the conundrum at hand.

"Miss Barrows," said a gentleman, giving her a deep bow, and Felicity gave him a vague smile and nod without bothering to stop. She was in no mind to be conversational at present unless the other wished to discuss Mr. Lewis Finch. But as Aunt Imogene had already proven by barring Felicity from Buxby

Hall for the afternoon, even those who loved her most had limited patience on that subject.

Felicity continued on her way, but paused as the fellow called out again, "Miss Barrows?"

Taking in a steadying breath, she turned and smiled at the gentleman. There was no need to make him bear the brunt of her bruised heart. "Good afternoon, sir."

But the gentleman merely stood there, staring at her as though he were lost in a desert and she was an oasis.

"Have I altered that much?" he murmured, a smile creeping across his face. "You have not changed one jot. Still the beautiful creature who haunts my dreams."

The basket dropped from Felicity's hands, but he scooped it up before it crashed to the frozen cobblestones. The cold seeped through her skin, wrapping around her like a blanket of ice, and Felicity was unable to do anything but blink. Her thoughts seized, holding her in place as though time itself had stopped at the sight of him.

Alastair Dunn.

"I know this must be a shock to you." Alastair shifted in place, his smile sliding into his slanted grin that always set her heart aflutter. Once her slow wits decided to believe he was not a phantasm, Felicity was amazed at how little he'd changed since he'd broken her sixteen-year-old heart.

Alastair was like a Gothic character come to life. Broad shoulders and a ready smile with a wicked gleam in his eyes. His dark locks were gathered in that windswept fashion that highlighted the carefree manner of its master. His nose had a new, unnatural bend to it, and time had drawn a few lines around his eyes and lips, but those imperfections only emphasized his handsome features.

"I've waited so long for this day," he murmured, taking a step closer to her.

The movement snapped her free of her astonishment, forcing Felicity to scurry backward, shoving a hand out to ward him away. Words fled her as her thoughts scattered in every direction like down erupting from a ripped pillow. Her brows pulled low and she shook her head back and forth as she turned and stalked away.

"Felicity!"

Whipping around, she held up a rigid finger, jabbing it at him. "Do not speak to me so informally, sir. You haven't the right."

Alastair's expression grew taut as though her words gave him physical pain, but he did not retreat. "There are not words enough to apologize for what happened—"

"You left me in a coaching inn!" Felicity paused, reining in the fire that drove her voice to shrill levels. Sucking in a breath through her nose, she fought to relax her muscles, but they were pulled tighter than violin strings. Casting wild glances around, Felicity saw a few others moving about the street, but none paid her any heed, giving all their focus to their labors. "I spent hours waiting for you to arrive, unable to believe my beau would abandon me in such a callous manner."

"I am so very sorry—"

"No," she said, shaking her finger in his face. "You have no right to reappear now. If you want forgiveness, I give it freely. I hold no ill will towards you, but neither do I wish to renew an acquaintance with someone who only loved my money."

"You do not know the whole of it," he whispered, his eyes begging her to believe him, but Felicity turned away. Her path would take her in the opposite direction of her carriage, but she'd rather take a circuitous route than turn back to see that snake gaping at her. But then he was there at her elbow, guiding her down the street.

A pair of ladies passed them, and Felicity gave them a passing nod, hoping (though not believing) that they would see nothing amiss in her countenance. Rumors were not what she needed at present. But then, neither was Alastair Dunn.

It was a few more steps before Felicity realized that the fellow had herded her towards the churchyard, away from prying eyes. His voice lowered, a gentle whisper in her ear.

"Please, allow me a few minutes to explain: I did not abandon you."

Chapter 22

Felicity's gaze snapped to his, and his eyes gave strength to his words, pleading for her to believe him. Perhaps it was foolish to do so, but Felicity's feet were not as reasonable as the rest of her, and they followed him, drawing her deeper into the churchyard. They stopped, and Alastair stood before her; his gaze was a caress, taking in each feature as his smile softened. He set her basket beside her and brushed a finger across her cheek.

"I have missed you, my darling."

Stepping away, Felicity narrowed her eyes. "I did not come here for that nonsense."

And yet, her heart fluttered, and her breath caught as they stood in the snow. Time reversed, flying backward with alarming speed, and Felicity felt as though she was sixteen once more, stealing away a private moment with the man she loved. Her first love.

Dropping his eyes, he released her from his hold and sighed. "My greatest regret is that I was unable to speak to you before I left Plymouth, but I had no choice in the matter. I tried to send word, but he did everything he could to separate us."

Alastair's head lowered, his shoulders slumping. "I have practiced this speech so many times over the years, and yet my words are muddled."

"Then start at the beginning, and we will go from there," she said, crossing her arms. "I gather Uncle George confronted you about our elopement."

He snorted with a wry smile, though his gaze held no mirth. "Confronted would be a mild term for it. That wretched night, dear old Uncle George discovered our plans and thought my love could be purchased for a couple of thousand pounds. When his bribe didn't win my loyalty, he came after me with a few of his dockworkers and left me a bloodied mess."

Felicity's gaze moved to the unnatural bump in his nose, and the fellow nodded. "It took me weeks before I was able to leave my bed, but I went in search of you the moment I could."

His words were like a song, lulling her fears and worries. Alastair inched closer, his gaze holding hers, and though Felicity searched for any sign of deception, she found none. And she could well imagine Uncle George resorting to violent means if he thought it necessary; he was not one to bother with words when action was required.

"He was always watching you. Always aware of what you were doing, who you were with. I tried to write you, but I can only assume you never received my letters."

Felicity shook her head, her fingers twisting the edge of her cloak. "Only your farewell note, which Uncle gave me himself."

Alastair's brows rose, and he shook his head. "I didn't write it. I was in no state to hold a quill. And even if I had been, I would never have agreed to it."

Eyes widening, Felicity cast her thoughts back to that scrap of paper Uncle had given her. She'd read it enough times to know its contents by heart, but the words were too few to know if Alastair's hand had written it. Though, in her heart, Felicity wouldn't be surprised if Uncle had forged it in an attempt to give his niece some semblance of a farewell.

"I went to our place," he whispered. "That little spot near the Barbican where we'd stroll by the sea."

Felicity nodded, and his expression lightened.

"For weeks, I went there, hoping you would appear and I would have the opportunity to explain myself. To tell you that my heart was still faithful. That I would love you—and only you—to the end of my days."

Sometime in his speech, his hand entwined with hers, and Felicity peered down at it, but before she could think what it meant or what she wanted, Alastair continued in a frantic whisper.

"When he discovered what I was doing, your uncle came after me again. But this time, he threatened my family, saying he would sack my brother and make certain no one else hired him. Then he would go after my father's debts and see my family turned out into the streets if I did not leave Plymouth immediately. I know I promised never to forsake you, but I couldn't risk my family's well-being. I had no choice but to leave."

A whisper of uncertainty skittered across Felicity's spine, but she couldn't focus on it when Alastair stood so close to her. It was there and gone before she could give it a voice.

Goodness, she was a spinster who had long ago relinquished such silly notions as swooning, but with Alastair so near, his voice speaking the things she'd longed to hear all those years ago, Felicity found it impossible to remain aloof. This was her first love, and perhaps—just perhaps—he hadn't been as false as the rest.

Reaching into his waistcoat pocket, Alastair retrieved a lock of fiery red hair, tied up with the green ribbon she'd worn the first time they'd met. He lifted it to his lips and kissed it before tucking it back away.

"So, I moved across the country and built a new life for myself, but I never forgot you. No other woman could compare, for they were only pale, lifeless imitations. Years passed, and I waited for the day we could have a life together." His head dropped, and Alastair let out a heavy sigh tinged with a self-deprecating laugh. "I even took to writing you. Even when I knew I couldn't send them, pretending gave me some peace."

Without meeting her gaze, he withdrew a bundle of letters tied together with twine and handed them to her. "Forgive the late delivery, but these are yours."

Clutching them, Felicity stared at the stack, uncertain what to say or think or even feel at their appearance. And her confusion only grew when Alastair raised his gaze and she found his eyes steeped in unshed tears.

"I only just heard of your uncle's passing and rushed to Plymouth. When I found you gone, I couldn't rest until I saw you again," he murmured, that hand of his drifting to her cheek once more. "I did not come here demanding or expecting anything. I came with the desperate hope that you'll allow me the opportunity to win your heart again."

Alastair Dunn had the most expressive eyes Felicity had ever seen; that much had not changed. And though she had long since believed her memory of his affection to be false or flawed, his eyes burned with an adoration that was as warm and devoted as she remembered.

A heavy silence filled the churchyard, though unspoken declarations rang in the air.

Alastair drew closer, his foot bumped hers, and she looked up into his eyes as he leaned down to meet her. But when his lips drew close, Felicity straightened and jerked away.

"Alastair, please," she murmured, clutching his letters in one arm while pressing her other hand to her stomach, as though that touch might calm the flutters that were less butterflies and more like a swarm of angry hornets.

His smile tightened, but Alastair nodded, putting a minor distance between them. "I apologize. I cannot seem to help myself around you, Felicity. You are intoxicating, and when I look into your eyes, my good sense is lost."

Felicity gave him a tremulous smile, though she had no idea if she was pleased or irritated by his sentiment. Too much had happened in the past few days for her to think straight, and

Alastair's reappearance and confession were enough of an upheaval.

Holding her gaze, Alastair gave her a low bow. "I do not wish to add to your heartache. Please read my letters and see that my heart has always been true."

Alastair straightened, the movement drawing him close once more, and he raised her hand to his lips. Though her hand was encased in leather, Felicity felt his warmth as he kissed her knuckles with a smile and a sigh as though her touch eased a pain in his soul.

Turning on his heels, he marched away without a backward glance, though Felicity watched him until he disappeared from view. She cast a look around her and fled to a bench someone had placed beneath a nearby tree. Her legs trembled, struggling to keep her upright in the ice and snow before she dropped to the stone, not caring how frigid it was. She clutched Alastair's letters, her gaze unfocused as she stared into the distance.

Uncle George had always been careful to behave with the utmost decorum around Felicity, but he was not a perfect man, and a few of his more colorful phrases sprang to her mind as she tried to unravel the tangled mess that was her life. She had come to Bristow to escape such entanglements. Her time here was intended to be a solace from such overtures, yet two gentlemen had attempted to kiss her in the last few days.

Felicity Barrows was no young miss unaware of the machinations of fortune hunters. She was well used to spotting their lures and traps, but none of her experience gave her an ounce of clarity when it came to these two.

Mr. Finch wasn't aware of her fortune, so it was a moot point. But Alastair?

Her first love. The man whom all others had been compared to, even if Felicity hadn't recognized the bias. Alastair had left his mark, leaving her forever altered. And even with Uncle George's claims of his unfaithful heart, some part of her had always longed for a moment exactly like the one he'd just given her. One filled with regret, apologies, and longing. An explanation.

Felicity glanced at the bundle in her arms that contained fifteen years of unspoken sentiments. She couldn't believe he'd written so much without hope of delivering them. To carry them with him for so long surely meant something significant. Didn't it?

Sliding out the topmost letter, Felicity unfolded the paper. The script was splotchy and hurried, as though Alastair could hardly get his words out fast enough. But then, he'd written it in the coach on his way to Plymouth.

My dearest love,

I can hardly breathe. Is it true? Are you free of him at last? I hardly know what to think and dare not hope that no other has captured your heart and hand. I find myself hanging from the coach window, shouting at the driver to lay on the whip, for every passing minute without you is an agony...

Goodness. The page was filled with his undying devotion and his dreams for their future. And Felicity was willing to admit that they called to her. Though her present life was beautiful in its own right, the letters promised a future filled with love, tenderness, and a family of her own.

Though the cold nipped at her nose, Felicity ignored it, setting aside the letters to stare out at the churchyard. Her breath spiraled and swirled into the chill air, and the world was silent and still. If only her heart could find such peace.

Had Uncle George been wrong about him?

Freed from the fog of attraction that clouded her thoughts whenever Alastair spoke, Felicity picked through the past few minutes, trying to see the truth. The stack of letters beside her was a strong testament in Alastair's favor, yet as her mind cleared, Felicity struggled to accept the accusations against her kin.

The picture Alastair painted was not favorable to Uncle George. Felicity could well imagine her uncle going to great lengths to protect her—it was in his nature to defend those he loved—but she couldn't reconcile the uncle she knew with the malevolent fellow who'd threatened the Dunn family. Uncle George was more likely to send Felicity to the country and out of Alastair's influence than destroy the livelihood and well-being of innocents.

Uncle George may have been gruff at times and far from what anyone would call "refined," but he'd been a good man. Though often uncertain how to comfort a brokenhearted young girl, he'd done his best. That brusque man had held her as she wept and watched over her as fiercely as any father. Better than Felicity's own, who had hardly comforted his child after the loss of her mother.

Leaning forward, Felicity rubbed her forehead, hoping the faint pain pulsing there wouldn't grow. It was unlikely, but she still hoped.

Truth was a fickle thing. Though called immutable, one's perspective colored it. Altering it. Twisting it. Even if one believed themselves impartial or a defender of it, so much of what was deemed "true" was merely the world as one perceived it.

Had Uncle George been truthful then? Or was Alastair now? Or was reality merely bits and pieces of both cobbled together like a chimera?

Chapter 23

Gathering the stack of letters, Felicity deposited them in the basket and made her way out of the churchyard. The overcast sky and short days always made it difficult to tell the time, but she hoped it was time to return to Buxby Hall. Unfortunately for Aunt Imogene, Felicity's afternoon away had only provided her with more questions, concerns, and conundrums with which to pester the old biddy.

Alastair. Mr. Finch. Uncle George. Bristow was proving to be as irksome as Plymouth.

Within minutes she arrived at the inn and her groom had the carriage readied. Once seated inside and pointed home, Felicity tried to puzzle out the truth. The letters called to her from the basket. She rather wished to get some distance and perspective before rushing through them, but her mind would not give her peace. Perhaps they might hold some answers. Untying the twine, she turned to the bottom of the stack and unfolded the letter.

My dearest Felicity,

It breaks my heart that we are apart. If fate had been kinder, we would be married now. Irreparably bound as husband and wife and beyond your uncle's power. I wish I had been stronger or faster. I wish I had set out sooner. But there is no undoing the past, and I only hope we do not suffer long for my weakness.

Do not fret, my love. I will be whole again soon, and we can try again...

Alastair's words flowed across the page, recounting each pain and agony he'd suffered and the treachery of her uncle and his men. And while it stirred Felicity's heart to sympathy, a tickle at the back of her neck grew more pronounced. Without Alastair standing before her to cloud her judgment, she could feel it there, pricking at her peace of mind and warning that not all was right.

The gentleman was so enticing. More than his looks, his personality drew her in, enchanting her through his passion and zeal; with naught but a few words and a look, he ensorcelled her. But away from his influence, she studied his letters, acknowledging just how wrong Alastair's accusations against Uncle George felt.

Picking up the next letter, she read more of the same. Recounting his injuries and cursing her uncle. Pleading for a swift recovery in order to return to her side once more.

Felicity understood why he held Uncle George in contempt, but the more Alastair darkened her uncle's name, the more ill at ease she felt. No one could ever accuse George Barrows of being a gentleman, but that did not mean he lacked honor or kindness. Such virtues were not exclusive to those who clung to social niceties and etiquette. And the man Alastair described in his letters was not her uncle.

...The sun is setting outside my window, and it brings to mind the afternoons we spend together, wandering along the Barbican. The afternoon light caught your hair, and it blazed

like a sunset. Golden, fiery hues that lit my world with your loveliness...

Words like these had filled Felicity's dreams for years after Alastair's disappearance. It was the precise thing he'd whisper to her before stealing a kiss. The gentleman was so adept at surrounding her with such lovely compliments and declarations, but seeing them written in black and white drained them of much of their power.

Flipping through the letters, Felicity scanned one after the other, hardly giving more than a passing glance. Each was much the same. Frustrations at their separation. Declarations of undying love. Recounting her beauty. Promises to remain true to her.

The carriage rocked, and Felicity turned her attention to the window. Buxby Hall was fast approaching, and she was grateful for a chance to speak to someone about this turn of events. Perhaps Aunt Imogene had some insight into Alastair and what she ought to do next.

Ought she to welcome his attention? Uncle George might've been wrong about Alastair, but he might've been correct. Yet here, before her, was evidence that her former beau's heart had been true. The dates in the letters spanned years, each showing that she was never far from his thoughts. With such a sign of his devotion, it was difficult to believe Alastair's motives to be sinister.

But even as she contemplated that possibility, her stomach turned. Not only because something felt amiss, but because even with the hope of rekindling that long-lost love, Felicity couldn't rid herself of another gentleman who'd taken up residence in her thoughts.

Felicity chuckled to herself. Was she truly debating whether to welcome the courtship of a gentleman who seemed intent on distancing himself or the gentleman who had broken her heart so many years ago? It was laughable.

Only she could find herself embroiled in such chaos during a holiday—

Her gaze fell back to the stack of letters strewn across her lap, and clarity took hold of her, allowing Felicity to see the truth. Lined up as they were, there was no mistaking the uniformity of their appearance. They were worn and smudged, spattered with mud and showing clear signs of wear, yet the oldest had fifteen supposed years to its name and looked no more yellowed or aged than that which had been written a few days ago.

The letters did serve as evidence, but not to Mr. Dunn's credit.

Closing her eyes, Felicity said silent words of gratitude to Uncle George, thanking him for saving her all those years ago, and she hoped Mr. Dunn's recovery from that night had been as long and painful as he claimed.

Felicity's lungs heaved, sucking in and out as she glared at the letters. With a sweeping motion, she gathered them up and crushed the wretched things. Her teeth ground together as her mind filled with every vile thing she could think of to describe Alastair Dunn. Stuffing the bits into the basket, Felicity felt like throwing the entire thing out the window, but the only safe place to dispose of them would be a fireplace: the last thing she wanted was for someone to find the evidence of her foolishness.

Her heart shuddered, and Felicity shriveled in on herself, her strength waning as she collapsed against the seatback. The world around her blurred, and her chin trembled as the full understanding of her foolishness struck. With little effort, he'd turned her head once more; it may have been for a short time, but that did not lessen her shame.

Felicity's throat tightened as tears gathered in her eyes, and she sucked in a breath through her nose, letting it out in a shaking gust. In and out.

How had she allowed this to happen? Felicity's heart had long ago healed from his first betrayal, but with a few words and a callous lie, Mr. Dunn had exploited that weakness, fracturing it anew.

A weight settled on her, and her mind drifted to the future. Was this to be her life? Forever guarding herself against skilled manipulators? To be viewed as easy prey by fortune hunters? Even going to ground hadn't deterred them from their quarry.

The thought of returning to Buxby Hall had her stomach churning. As uplifting as Aunt Imogene's conversation could be, Felicity couldn't bear the thought of speaking to her aunt. Not yet. Even as her insides rebelled at the thought of admitting what had passed to anyone, there was one person with whom Felicity wanted to speak. One who understood her as readily as she did him. One who gave her peace and sound advice. One who was blunt and forthright, devoid of falsehood and flattery.

Knocking against the roof, Felicity opened the carriage window, calling out the new destination to the coachman when he slowed enough to hear her. Though they were near Buxby Hall, the coachman didn't question the order, merely guiding the carriage along as they wound their way to Avebury Park.

The carriage rocked and bumped along the frozen road, and Felicity yearned for it to move faster. Though her bedchamber called for her to find solace there, she longed for comforting words. Support and friendship. Someone who would assure her that not all feelings were fickle and false. That she had value beyond her bank account.

Felicity's gaze was fixed to the window as the minutes passed with agonizing slowness until she was certain she could've walked to Avebury Park in less time. The road curved and drew her towards the building, her anticipation growing with each turn of the carriage wheel, and she bounded out before the vehicle was fully stopped.

Smoothing her skirt and straightening her cloak and bonnet, Felicity forced in a calming breath. She wasn't going to burst into the Kingsleys' home, demanding to see Mr. Finch like some Bedlamite. Though it felt like an eternity before her knock was answered, Felicity drew her decorum close and met the opening door with a calm facade.

"Is Mr. Finch at home? I have a matter of some urgency I need to discuss with him," she said, forcing her lips closed as her wayward tongue seemed determined to say far too much to the servants.

The footman ushered her in, and then came more waiting as he went in search of her quarry.

Felicity forced herself not to fidget. She was a grown woman capable of standing still and waiting—even if she felt like a foolish young girl of sixteen once more. Turning her gaze to the foyer, Felicity tried to distract herself by admiring Avebury Park's entry, but she'd seen it too many times for it to serve as a distraction.

"Miss Barrows?"

Turning her gaze from the staircase, Felicity saw Mrs. Mina Kingsley gliding towards her with a book clutched in her hands.

"Good afternoon, Mrs. Kingsley," said Felicity, giving a curtsy. "I have sent your footman to hunt for Mr. Finch. I had hoped he would join me on a stroll. The weather is too fine to remain indoors."

Mrs. Kingsley cocked her head to the side, her gaze straying to the windows that framed the front door, which showed a fairly gloomy, overcast day. Felicity held onto her smile, refusing to betray her mistake.

"I see," murmured Mrs. Kingsley, her brows furrowed, but otherwise accepting the oddity. "Mr. Finch has seemed out of sorts the last few days. I am certain he will welcome the opportunity to do something other than mope about the library, which is how he is currently occupying his time."

Felicity smiled. "Aunt Imogene was hoping you might visit the two of us tomorrow. We haven't anything particular planned, but I do think she is looking for an excuse to lure you to Buxby Hall."

"As if she needs it," replied Mrs. Kingsley with a grin. "I would be honored to call on you. I have been so busy of late that

I haven't seen dear Imogene as much as I would like. I have much to tell her concerning my battles to organize the charity school."

With a grimace, Felicity nodded. "She has told me much of it, and I wish you good luck. Nothing is as infuriating as having good intentions thwarted by shrews intent on stopping you for no better reason than to make you look the fool."

Mrs. Kingsley's brows shot upwards as she chuckled. "You sound as though you have experience with such things."

"A little—"

But the sound of footsteps stopped Felicity, her gaze shooting in the direction from which it came. The footman appeared at the end of the hallway, coming towards them with a bow.

"My apologies, Miss Barrows, but Mr. Finch is not at home."

Though being "not at home" was often a euphemism for turning a guest away, those words were innocuous enough that Felicity couldn't immediately assume the worst. However, Mrs. Kingsley's eyes widened a fraction, her brows tensing, and there was no hiding the discomfort in her posture. According to her, Mr. Finch had been in the library. Perhaps he had truly disappeared and was unavailable, but Felicity felt it in her heart—the same one Mr. Dunn had fractured today—that Mr. Finch was avoiding her.

"I will tell Aunt Imogene to expect you tomorrow," she said, proud that her voice remained steady.

"Perhaps you would like to join me for some refreshment?" asked Mrs. Kingsley, motioning for her to follow. "You look frozen through, and some tea and cake would be just the thing."

But Felicity shook her head, stepping towards the door. "My thanks, but I ought to be on my way."

More like she needed to be on her way before her strength gave out and she turned into a weeping mess. It was one thing to have such a vulnerable moment in front of a friend, but Felicity could not handle doing so in front of a mere acquaintance.

Besides, if Mr. Finch did not wish her company, she would not force it upon him.

Before allowing Mrs. Kingsley to make any further protests, Felicity hurried out the front door and into her waiting carriage. The door latch snapped shut, breaking the last of her composure. Tears flooded her eyes, and Felicity embraced the agony that flowed through her veins and made her heart burn.

She would conquer this. It was not the first nor last time she would be forced to bear such burdens, and Felicity would face them as she always did. Tears were a necessary part of life, and they would flow for now, but tomorrow, she would square her shoulders, face the pain, and find a way through it.

Even if the heartache was all the more acute because she'd hoped that for once, she'd not have to bear it alone.

Chapter 24

Standing at the threshold of Avebury Park's stables, Mina breathed in the mix of horse and hay. Not that the stench of horseflesh and muck were pleasant on their own, but so many happy thoughts, feelings, and memories were associated with it. Her marriage had first blossomed here. Those morning rides with her husband had been the flint with which they'd lit the embers that now burned bright in both of them.

Her dear Simon.

Even with the nip in the air warning her that this afternoon would be a bracing ride, Mina was thrilled at the prospect of going out once more. The fields were still icy enough that they did not wish to risk their mounts (or their necks), but the roads had cleared in the past few days.

Footsteps sounded behind her, and Mina knew who it was before Simon threaded her arm through his. They meandered together through the stables, visiting each of the animals in their stalls as the grooms prepared their mounts.

"Are you certain you are not put out by Finch accompanying us?" he asked in a low voice.

Mina glanced at Simon. "I will always prefer to ride with you alone, but I do not begrudge his presence."

"You would tell me if you felt otherwise?"

"Certainly." Though Mina had spoken with utter honesty, Simon's brows remained furrowed, his expression not relaxing until he noticed her watching him.

"I promise this won't be a regular occurrence," he said, reaching up with a gloved hand to rub at the bump on his nose. "Finch has been so out of sorts the last few days, and he needs something to lighten his spirits. I fear I've abandoned him too many times during his visit."

Mina clutched his arm, reveling in the faint warmth that leached through the layers of cloth and wool. Even if she despised Mr. Finch, she would welcome his presence for Simon's sake. Besides, his behavior seemed more amenable and courteous of late, and his flippant remarks had grown fewer, which made him a far more pleasant houseguest.

Yet there was something in his demeanor that made Mina uneasy. As though his ready smiles and wit were hiding something. During one of their visits, Imogene had mentioned Miss Barrows' theory that Mr. Finch's demeanor was nothing but a thin facade, hiding some sadness beneath it, and the more time she passed with him, the more she thought Miss Barrows might be correct.

They stopped before one of the occupied stalls, and Banshee stuck her head out to greet them, so Mina released Simon to rub the horse's nose.

"I think he and Miss Barrows have quarreled," said Mina. "She came for a visit yesterday, but Mr. Finch wouldn't see her. And she was seen in the company of another gentleman yesterday in the churchyard."

"Miss Barrows spends quite a lot of time away from her duties at Buxby Hall," said Simon with a frown. "It is a wonder Lady Lovell allows it."

"I've told you, she isn't a companion. I don't know why Mr. Finch believes differently, but she is simply visiting her great-aunt," said Mina, but when Simon's frown deepened, she waved it away. "It doesn't matter anyhow. What ails him is likely the same thing that was ailing her yesterday. Miss Barrows made a good show of being at ease, but she was distraught over something. It broke my heart to see him turn her away."

Simon puffed out his cheeks, his gaze drifting to the side. "It's a shame. I've never seen Finch show interest in any woman before, and Miss Barrows seems a good sort. She would make him a fine wife."

Stepping back from the stall, Mina took Simon's arm once again, and he cast a glance in her direction, his smile tightening.

"Not that I find her remarkable," he said.

Mina wrinkled her nose. "That is an odd thing to say, Simon."

He swallowed, his lips pinching together as his gaze darted towards her and away again. "I only mean to say that though I admire her, I do not hold her in special regard. She seems a good sort for Finch. That is all."

"I knew exactly what you were saying before, but I am at a loss now." Mina gave her husband a puzzled look to match her tone.

Simon drew her to a stop and turned to face her. "You are lovely, my darling."

Mina's brows pinched together, and she stared at her husband and the determined manner in which he complimented her. Yet again. While his incessant gift-giving had faded some, honeyed words now filled that void.

"That is the sixth time you've said that today, Simon, and it is not yet noon," she said.

"I cannot help but say it often, for it is always true." He gave her a sparkling smile, but that tinge of worry colored his gaze, making Mina's stomach sink yet again. She had thought this foolishness was over, yet here they were again.

But then Simon drew her close, capturing her lips in a kiss that was tender and heartfelt, sweeping all other thoughts away as Mina wrapped her arms around him. Bundled up as they were, she missed the feel of his hands brushing her skin, but even as muted as it was, Mina's heart swelled in the euphoria her husband's love elicited.

A loud, pointed clearing of a throat had the pair leaping apart, and Mina's face blazed as they turned to see Mr. Finch standing there with his gaze fixed on the ground, but with a bemused smile that said he'd witnessed more than enough of their display.

"It is ill-mannered of you to carry on like that," said Mr. Finch, the laughter in his tone muting any bite his words might've had. "The time is long past when you two should be merely tolerating each other's company."

Simon narrowed his eyes with a smirk. "Not at all, though it is long past the time when you should return to London."

Finch chuckled at that, but as Mina watched him, she saw little hints of something more beneath the jovial expression. A melancholy in his gaze. Resignation in his shoulders. Perhaps Miss Barrows was correct about the fellow, and between that revelation and seeing how happy he made Simon, a hint of guilt tickled her stomach as she thought back on her behavior towards Mr. Finch: she had not been a very kind or attentive hostess.

Though Finch had spoken in jest, there was some truth to his earlier statement. Having witnessed many marriages, he was familiar with the sad decay that followed the first heady months. Even the love matches often ended in cold silence and resignation, and Finch was more pleased than he could say to see that Simon had lucked into a marriage that grew stronger with each month.

In quick order, the grooms had their mounts readied, and Finch pretended not to watch as Simon fussed and fluttered over his wife. Anyone seeing Mina atop her horse would know she was a capable rider, yet Simon assisted her up the mounting block and straightened her skirts, making certain she was comfortable before mounting his own.

It was a little moment and something clearly commonplace (since the grooms relinquished their duties to their master without a questioning glance). Small yet so tender that Finch was undeniably moved by it, and he wondered if they understood just how important such moments were. They must on some level, for this was not the first of such tenderness he'd witnessed from both sides. Mina and Simon were true partners; helping for the joy of it, even if the other was capable of handling it on their own.

Getting atop his borrowed mount, he followed the pair out of the yard and down the road, feeling grateful that Simon had found his happiness. Though Finch's own life seemed a bleak thing, it was comforting to know that such joys existed.

The sky was clear above, and the roads were clear below. The day was as fine as anyone could wish for, despite the frigid weather, yet Finch's mind struggled to lay hold of happiness. Not that he deserved any peace of mind at present while Miss Barrows haunted his every thought.

What had he been thinking? For years, Finch had remained aloof from females. There was no good to be found tempting himself with a life he could not have. Marriage was not in his future, yet he had allowed Miss Barrows to slip into his heart. How and when she'd done so was a mystery to him, but that did not absolve him of his culpability.

The look in Miss Barrows' eyes when he'd stepped away pricked at his conscience, layering guilt upon guilt. Intentionally or not, he had raised her expectations while unable to fulfill them. Her heartache was his doing and his sin to bear.

Good heavens. It had been a mistake to visit Bristow.

And then, as though Simon had a window into Finch's thoughts, he asked, "I understand you and Miss Barrows have quarreled."

"Simon!" Mina hissed, glowering at her husband.

But the fellow shrugged. "I only wish to ask—"

"Mr. Finch," said Mina with a bright and brittle smile. "As you are a musician, who is your favorite composer?"

Finch stared at her. Not so much because of the awkward shift in subject, but because she was engaging him in conversation. Turning his gaze back to the road ahead, Finch gave her question some thought.

"To play or to listen to?" he asked. "I find my answer varies greatly depending on whether I am the musician or someone more skilled is. And there is a vast difference between my favorite composers of opera compared to concertos."

Mina blinked for a quiet moment before her grin grew into a genuine expression of pleasure. "I see you are of my mind on the subject. It is impossible to choose just one, for each shines in different situations. I, for one, do not care to play Mozart, but I adore his operas."

"I gather from your music selection that you enjoy Clementi."

She laughed in reply. "Not particularly, but I have not the skill to play those I truly adore. His pieces are simple and enjoyable enough. I find myself drawn to this new style that focuses on dynamics and passion—like Johann Hummel and Ludwig van Beethoven."

Finch's brows furrowed, and he stared at her for a long moment before she blushed and added, "My tastes shock you?"

"Only because they are so similar to mine. I do not know many who are familiar with Hummel, but his pieces are so dramatic and engaging to play."

"And now I am to be subjected to endless discourses about music," grumbled Simon, though his pleased expression belied his irritated tone.

His wife gave that comment all the attention it deserved and proceeded to discuss and debate the finer points of compositions and music. Mina seemed different. Warm and welcoming as she hadn't been before. It was refreshing to converse without any awkwardness or discomfort as though the past weeks had been all that was amicable and pleasant between the pair of them.

As they rode, they shifted until Mina was between Simon and Finch, and from time to time, his friend gazed around his wife to give Finch a smile that spoke of a bone-deep contentedness that Finch was all too grateful to see.

"You are an excellent rider," he said, casting out the first compliment that came to mind. It couldn't hurt to sweeten her disposition with a bit of flattery.

Mina reached down to rub her mount's neck. "It is easy to look capable when riding Beau."

Finch expected nothing less than the finest mounts to be housed in the Avebury Park stables, as both master and mistress were avid riders, but Mina's horse could hardly be called such. Streaks and spots of white marred the beast's otherwise perfect coat of darkest brown. While the occasional odd marking might make a horse unique, these were too large to be overlooked and too misshapen to be anything but unsightly.

"Bow? For a gelding?" he asked with a touch of humor to his voice. Odd name that.

"*Beau* as in the French word for handsome," said Mina with a smile, giving her horse another pat.

Finch let out a burst of laughter. "That is perfect."

Shaking his head, he wondered at the wicked sense of humor some breeders had when it came to naming their horses. It was a second or two before he felt the shift in the air and glanced at his companions to see them both staring at him. Simon's eyes were wide, his brows pinching together as he vehemently shook his head, but it was Mina's blazing glare that held Finch's attention.

Finch cleared his throat. "You must admit it is quite witty."

Eyes narrowing, Mina's expression hardened. "Beau is the finest horse I've ever owned and worth more than all your perfect mounts combined. Appearances are not everything, sir!"

And before Finch could give a word in defense, Beau took off at a gallop, leaving the gentlemen far behind.

Chapter 25

Simon turned his mount, rounding on Finch as he scowled. "What were you thinking? You two were getting along until you opened your foolish gob and mocked her horse."

Finch pointed at the flurries of snow kicked up in Beau's wake. "You must admit that the breeders were having a good laugh when they named that creature 'Handsome.' I wasn't trying to be cruel. I was simply appreciating wit."

Jaw clenched, Simon's gaze darkened. "It was Mina who named him, and I assure you it was not in jest. Beau is among the finest horses I've ever ridden, yet he would've been bound for the butcher's simply because of his markings."

Above the searing reproach in Simon's tone, Finch heard Miss Barrows' voice echoing in his thoughts, chiding him for his blunt words and the harm they'd done to Mina's tender heart.

"Well, get out of the way, Simon," said Finch, waving an arm at his friend. But when the fellow didn't budge, he added, "It appears I have some groveling to do."

Simon remained where he was, watching Finch with a wary eye, as though debating whether or not to run him out of Bristow. But after a moment of reflection, Simon moved his horse out of the way with a silent challenge in his gaze, warning Finch of all the dire things that would happen if he didn't make it right with Mina.

Holding in a sigh, Finch took off after her, hoping to catch her before she had too much time to brood about his inadvertent faux pas. However, Beau was proving to be as fine an animal as Mina and Simon claimed and outpaced him with ease, and Finch only caught up once the beast had stopped back at the stables.

By the time his mount came blustering up, Mina was already unsaddled and showering Beau with affection. Finch didn't hear her words, but the kind tone and warm meaning behind them filled the air as Beau's mistress brushed his coat.

"I don't know many ladies who give their horses such personal care." Finch had hoped a compliment might ease his arrival, but Mina stepped between him and the horse, as though shielding the creature.

"If you've come to spout more of your cruelty—"

Finch held up his hands. "I hadn't meant to be cruel. I've come with an apology and truce."

Mina huffed, turning her back to him to continue her ministrations. "You needn't give me false assurances that Beau is handsome, sir. I am well aware of your disdain for ugly things. You made such opinions clear when you first pointed me out to Simon."

Straightening, Finch blinked at the lady, his thoughts grinding to a halt as thoroughly as though a Luddite had taken a hammer to one of the dreaded machines. "Pardon?"

"I heard you, Mr. Finch, at the ball last year when you and Simon discussed his plan to marry for convenience. It was you who drew me to his attention."

Finch nodded. He remembered that conversation, for it had been an infuriating moment: Simon had been especially bullheaded.

But Mina didn't look at him as she continued, "What better wife for a marriage of convenience than a mousy spinster, who would do his bidding, give no fuss, and gratefully accept any marriage offer, no matter how revolting and insulting it is?"

Her movements grew jerky as she spat the words, but Mina stopped herself, apologizing to Beau and calling for a groom to finish the work. Shoving past Finch, she marched out of the stable without a backward glance, leaving him to wince and groan. Miss Barrows had been kind when she'd said Mina was right to be upset with him. Though he didn't recall what he'd said that evening, Finch could well imagine he hadn't been gentle.

"Mina, please. I apologize for my blunt and cruel words. The truth is I've long admired you."

Halting just outside the stable doors, Mina turned and crossed her arms with a narrowed look. This man thought he could give some empty compliments and all would be well? Did he think her so simple and trusting as to accept such a false apology?

To think that she'd been feeling a kinship with Mr. Finch!

The fellow held up his hands, approaching her with the care and timidity of one standing before a slathering beast. And heaven help her, Mina liked seeing the wariness in his eyes.

"I find that impossible to believe, Mr. Finch."

Stopping just before her, he shifted from foot to foot and tugged at his greatcoat. "In all honesty, I do not recall what I said, but I can well imagine they were as heartless as you claim. I've discovered recently that my words are often harsh."

Mina scoffed, sending tendrils of vapor into the air. "Your words were more than 'harsh,' sir. They were cruel, and though you hadn't intended for me to hear them, it doesn't change the fact that you think such horrid things about me."

"But that is not true," he said with a shake of his head, his expression tightening as he shifted once more. "What I said was due to my frustration with my closest friend, who—despite having the fortune and prospects to marry for more than convenience—was determined to snatch up some random young lady.

And all because he was mooning over a horrid woman who didn't deserve him. If he was going to marry for convenience, I wanted him to choose a good lady."

Straightening, Mina dropped her arms and stared at him. "You didn't care for Mrs. Banfield?"

Mr. Finch snorted and shook his head. "How could I? She didn't care for Simon, except as a devotee willing to do whatever she requested. She was pretty enough, I suppose, but she was conniving, selfish, and bound to make any man she ensnared miserable."

Mina blinked, for that was all she could manage. Mrs. Susannah Banfield was the sort of lady gentlemen adored, and with few exceptions, her beauty blinded them to her myriad of faults. Yet Mr. Finch felt the opposite.

Puffing out his cheeks, the gentleman let out a breath, his gaze dropping away from her to drift around the area as he shifted his weight once more.

"Simon may not have noticed you before, but I had heard and seen plenty to know you were the antithesis of *that woman*. If Simon refused to marry for love—something I still think was foolhardy and ridiculous—at least he would have a wife he could respect. Someone with a good heart who could make him happy."

Mina stilled, staring at the fellow as he continued avoiding her gaze and fidgeting. Her tongue tied itself in knots, remaining completely useless in the face of such a declaration. She couldn't have been more surprised if Mr. Finch had declared his undying devotion to her. Thinking back to that evening, Mina couldn't reconcile the words she'd heard with the explanation Mr. Finch had given her, yet neither did they contradict it.

True, they'd been harsh, but Mina had used similar bluntness when faced with Simon's stubborn blindness. The man had a talent for obtuseness, and there were times when bald words were the only option. And even then, they didn't always work.

"I apologize, Mina. Had I known you would overhear me, I wouldn't have said..." Mr. Finch let out another puff. "I like to think I wouldn't have said such things, but I was in a particularly foul mood that night, and I cannot say with any conviction that I would've softened my words. Simon was being so insufferably pigheaded."

Placing her hands on her hips, Mina glanced up at the cloud-ridden sky, her thoughts cast back to those early days with Simon.

"My pride and vanity have been nursing this bruise for a long time, but I am grateful for your words that night," she murmured.

And now it was Mr. Finch's turn to gape at her.

"The truth is Simon had met me many times, and I hadn't made an impression. It was his guilty conscience that drove him to seek me out and apologize for my overhearing you. And it was that conversation that drew us together and planted the seeds of friendship."

Scrunching her nose, Mina winced and shook her head, dropping her gaze to the floor. "And whatever your faults, I have been unkind in my own right, and I apologize as well. Perhaps we might agree to forget the past and start anew?"

When she met his eyes again, Mr. Finch stood like a statue before her. His expression was muted, but his eyes shone with a desperate hope that made it impossible to hold onto any lingering resentment.

"It has been pointed out to me many times of late that I can be quite the dunderhead, and I am trying to do better," he said. "But I cannot guarantee I won't say something unintentionally, like laughing at your horse's name. Which I haven't apologized for yet. And I am sorry for it. I truly thought it was meant to be witty—"

Mina held up a hand before the fellow talked himself into another gaffe. "And I am far too sensitive at times. Like you, I am trying to be better at it. Perhaps we might both try harder."

Dipping into a low bow, Mr. Finch swept off his hat and said with a smile that was equally joyful and relieved, "Madam, if I were a Catholic, I would nominate you to be the patron saint of gentlemen who mean well but are too dense for their own good."

There was just the right hint of humor and earnestness so that Mina laughed out loud and motioned for him to join her as they strolled back to the house. Offering his arm to her, Mr. Finch guided her home with all the courtly air of a king.

"If nothing else, my good lady, I would adore you forever for freeing my dear friend from the clutches of that siren," he said with a slanted look. His eyes warmed as he added, "And I am truly grateful to see you are genuinely happy together."

She patted his arm with a smile before turning to his first statement. "I do not understand her appeal, Mr. Finch. She is wretched, yet men fall over themselves when she's around."

Mr. Finch chuckled. "I am at a loss to explain it."

And with that, Mr. Finch launched into a lively discussion of all things wrong with *that woman*, and Mina laughed silently to herself. They now had two subjects on which their opinions aligned: their love of music and their distaste for Susannah Banfield. That was a start.

Chapter 26

"Why are you not playing, Mr. Finch?" Aunt Imogene jabbed the ground with her cane, leveling an imperious glare at the fellow. "I have fed you, and now it is your duty to entertain me."

Felicity turned her wince to the wall. Lady Imogene Lovell was known for her forward manner, and the behavior was tolerated by most because of her rank and fortune. For those who truly knew her, they welcomed it because it was steeped in humor, as though the lady found great ridiculousness in her elevated status, both as the widow and mother of a baronet and as an elder of the village.

There were times when Felicity suspected that Aunt Imogene spouted audacious things simply to see if she could raise eyebrows. And normally, Felicity found great fun in watching sycophants feigning indifference when their inner thoughts were gasping and gaping, but the evening had already been so discomforting, which was the crowning event of a difficult week.

"Surely your refined tastes would find my musical offerings paltry, my lady," said Mr. Finch with a lazy grin.

"Nonsense," came the reply, punctuated by a snap of her cane. The poor maids would have to polish the floor tomorrow at this rate.

"As you command," he said, giving her a gallant bow.

"And you'd best prepare yourselves, ladies, for I will expect the same from you." Aunt Imogene gave both Felicity and Mrs. Kingsley a pointed look, and though the lady did blush, Mrs. Kingsley smiled at the older lady's antics.

Aunt Imogene leveled yet another gimlet eye at her niece, and Felicity sighed. It was the lady's prerogative to invite whomever she wished into her home, but there was no mistaking the motive behind the dinner invitation she'd extended to the Kingsleys and their all-important guest. The meddling biddy.

Buxby Hall was a grand old estate, and the building showed all the signs of grandeur one expected from a baronet's country residence. While there were formal rooms in which Aunt Imogene and Uncle Gilbert had entertained, those rooms that belonged solely to them eschewed the fine furnishings and decorations in favor of a more intimate and comfortable situation. The music room embraced the latter over the former.

Plush armchairs and sofas had been gathered around the pianoforte. Felicity wondered if Great-Uncle Gilbert had been fond of playing, for the instrument was of fine quality and showed signs of having been well-loved and well-maintained, though Aunt Imogene was no great musician.

Mr. Finch took his place on the piano bench, brushing his fingers across the keys. Felicity didn't know if or how Aunt Imogene had managed it, but her vantage point placed her directly in his line of sight when his gaze rose from the instrument.

"Something of substance, young man," said Aunt Imogene. "And play every movement. The composer intended it to be enjoyed as one whole, and it does his work no justice if you choose only a portion of it as so many are wont to do."

His eyes held a hint of laughter in them as he shared a silent moment of commiseration with Felicity over Aunt Imogene's antics, and for that brief moment, the pair of them shared a silent jest as they had so often done before.

The last few days had given Felicity adequate time to lick her wounds, and she was in no danger of weeping or swooning or any other such ridiculous behavior. Yet when Mr. Finch's brown eyes met hers, she could not deny how much she longed to heal the rift between them. She missed his friendship, advice, and support, but if he wished to cut ties, Felicity would not force the issue. She would soldier on as she'd done long before he'd appeared in her life.

Mr. Finch's eyes darkened for a moment, the light disappearing as he turned his attention to the keys. Shifting in his seat, he struck the opening chord, letting it hang in the air as more came haltingly after it, as though the composer wished to tantalize the listeners for several long moments before a run of notes drew the song along in earnest.

Felicity adored music as much as any and had middling skill at the piano, but she was not well versed in musicians and their compositions, so she could not identify the piece. It was a lovely blending of crisp trills and runs with moments of such passion that no one listening could remain unmoved by the music. But that had as much to do with the man playing it. Mr. Finch's love shone through each note.

He was such an interesting fellow with diverse interests and talents. In truth, Felicity felt awed by the breadth of his abilities, and every time they spoke, he gave more hints of the various skills he'd developed over the years.

But such thoughts were best left undisturbed. Mr. Finch no longer desired any closeness between them, and there was no good to be had by dwelling on her feelings on the matter. Felicity refused to be undone by it. Even if her heart ached over the loss.

It was her luck that the gentleman whose company she longed for was determined to avoid her while another seemed determined to hound her. Alastair Dunn had not approached her in person since the churchyard, but he made his presence known with little gifts and notes left for her. And if that wasn't enough, she found him watching her from afar as though pining for his lost love.

The whole thing was ridiculous. A megrim of the highest order. So, Felicity turned her thoughts away from gentlemen and focused on the music, allowing the melody to catch her up in its spell.

Following his orders, Mr. Finch played through every movement of the chosen sonatina, and only when finished did he stand and receive his applause, though he deserved more than what four people could give.

"Now, don't go scurrying away," said Aunt Imogene as the fellow turned to take his seat. Felicity's stomach sank at the lady's tone and the accompanying spark of mischief lighting her eye. "I think a duet is in order."

Mrs. Kingsley had the heart to give Felicity an apologetic smile, but the traitor chose to join in with Aunt Imogene's meddling. "Oh, yes. I would love to see you and Miss Barrows play together."

"Too right," said Aunt Imogene.

His wife poked him in the side, and Mr. Kingsley chimed in, "That's just what the evening needs."

"You are quick to press another into service, Simon," said Mr. Finch with a narrowed look. "Are we to be blessed by your musical talents?"

Mr. Kingsley laughed. "If I had any, I would readily offer them up whenever Lady Lovell demanded it."

"You are a good boy," said Aunt Imogene with a bright smile before turning an expectant gaze upon her guest and her niece.

Felicity remained in her seat as Mr. Finch strode over and held out his hand to her. She stared at it for a long second before her gaze rose to meet his and found the gentleman's eyes filled with a mix of humor and commiseration. She placed her hand in his, ignoring how much she liked the feel of it as he led her to the instrument.

Being as helpful as ever, Aunt Imogene produced the sheet music Felicity had been practicing of late. She'd begun learning the piece in the hopes of playing with one of her friends when she returned to Plymouth, but instead, she found herself seated on a piano bench that was far too small to share with Mr. Finch. His hip bumped hers as he took his place beside her, his leg brushing against hers, and Felicity attempted to give him more space, but there was nowhere else to go, as she was close to sliding off the bench.

"Don't fret," he whispered, slanting her a gentle smile.

"I apologize for my aunt's behavior," she murmured.

But Mr. Finch chuckled. "I happen to adore the old curmudgeon."

"I am not certain how I feel about her at present."

"All will be well." His voice was warm and soft, and Felicity knew he was only speaking of their performance, but some part of her wished he was speaking of greater things. She held back a chuckle at her ridiculous behavior and focused on the music.

Felicity hit her opening notes, but they struck out of step with Mr. Finch's, and her cheeks heated. They clunked along for a measure or two, and Felicity focused on the notes on the page as though that might hurry along the torture.

The piece was a silly little thing taken from one of Mozart's operatic duets and restyled for the piano. It was light and fun, and the exact opposite of what she felt with Mr. Finch so close. Her part was the less complicated of the two, but she struggled to find the notes in the proper order even though she managed it well enough on her own.

Yet their notes began to blend, and by the time they reached the end of the first page, Felicity fretted less and less about the situation and focused more on the performance. Mr. Finch easily sight-read through his part and even adapted here and there to cover her missing notes and mistakes, which took far more skill than he claimed to have. More than that, he radiated strength; it filled her, calming her nerves as she enjoyed the music as she hadn't been able to before.

Having picked through both parts, she'd had a general idea of what the piece sounded like, but hearing them together was gorgeous. Her primo part was mediocre on its own, but with the secondo filling out the harmonies, the song had more depth and beauty.

Felicity's eyes drifted to Mr. Finch's hands, his fingers running along the keys with far more ease than her own. With each measure, she felt his attention on her, and the bench grew smaller, drawing them closer than before. Her notes fumbled, and Felicity's attention shot back to the music, her eyes turning from her partner to study the page.

There was not a single flower adorning Miss Barrows' hair, yet Finch thought the lady smelled of roses and lavender, the scents blending in utter perfection like a garden in full bloom. It was only fitting, for Miss Barrows carried sunshine with her, bringing the world into perpetual summer.

Finch's life seemed as desolate as the winter night outside, for it was filled with nothing. Even when he'd had a profession, his days were dominated by monotony or waiting about; the law was little more than endless hours spent reading dry texts or watching his brothers at their work, and the army was punctuated with long bouts of nothing to do as they awaited orders. To say nothing of the years he'd spent in school learning facts and figures that had little use in his daily life.

Yet the last sennight had stretched interminably, feeling far more tedious than all those years. How had Miss Barrows become so important to him in such a short time? Most of his days had been touched by her, and her absence made the long hours of nothing seem even emptier.

This was for the best. Distance was necessary, and Finch just wished he had more at present. Fighting to hold his expression steady, he ignored the feel of her seated so close and the weight pressing on his chest.

His fingers marched through the piece, supplying the necessary notes with little thought, leaving him all too free to fixate on the lady at his side. His gaze drifted to her hands, which moved with less surety but a decent amount of skill, and though he tried to keep his thoughts in check, his eyes found their way up to her face.

Miss Barrows' pale skin held a hint of roses in her cheeks, and her gaze darted to him for the briefest moment before returning to the page. Finch longed to see her eyes. To see that spark of joy so constantly burning in their depths. Like a lighthouse calling sailors safely home, they drew him in, whispering hopes and possibilities he knew better than to entertain.

Brown eyes met his, and his breath stilled at the heart shining through them. Though Finch had tried to convince himself that these warm feelings were his alone, there was no denying the sight of them aglow in Miss Barrows' gaze.

Gooseflesh rose across his arms and neck as his pulse picked up to match the quick notes of the song. Worries and fears faded from his thoughts, leaving Finch overwhelmed by the realization that this lady cared for him. The man with nothing to recommend himself had somehow captured the fancy of this incredible creature.

Finch longed to rest his head against her shoulder and revel in her solace. To forget the world with all its demands and live in this moment with her. To make her his before she realized just how poor a deal that was for her.

Applause sounded, and Finch blinked, jerking his attention away from her as he rose to his unsteady feet. He offered her a hand of assistance, but Miss Barrows did not take it, stepping away from him as they took their bows. Without a second glance, she returned to her seat at the far end of the semi-circle.

"Mina, it is your turn," said Lady Lovell, and Finch moved out of her way, yet remained standing, staring at the seats.

To choose one's place ought not to be a difficult undertaking, but Finch faltered as he turned towards his original seat far from Miss Barrows' side. That was the safe place. The proper place. Distance was best, and one could not get more distance than his previous position.

Miss Barrows sat, smoothing her skirts, and turned her gaze to Mina at the pianoforte, though there was a stiffness to her posture that belied her casual pose, and Finch found himself seated beside her before he realized he'd moved. It was only for the evening, after all. A few final hours in her company.

"You play beautifully," she whispered so as not to disrupt Mina's performance.

"My thanks, but I am middling at best."

The lady stiffened, her gaze turning from Mina to stare at him with a furrowed brow. "Having sat through many home concerts, I can assure you that your talent is more than 'middling.'"

Finch held back a snort. Perhaps he was talented compared to the offerings of Plymouth or Bristow, but like the rest of him, his playing was neither masterful nor remarkable. He wasn't even the greatest musician among the Finch clan; Solomon and Phineas were more often called upon to entertain.

Shifting in his seat, Finch watched Mina, though his attention was not on her or the music. His eyes drifted to the side, studying Miss Barrows.

"I've missed your company." Finch's eyes widened and his stomach sank as the words slipped out.

Miss Barrows turned her head to meet his gaze, her eyes narrowing. "You made it clear that you do not wish for my company, and I have no interest in forcing myself upon unwilling companions."

"That is not true." Finch winced, fighting against the surge of frustration that forced his voice louder; the others darted looks in his direction, but they turned away with equal speed, feigning disinterest and ignorance of the pair's conversation.

"I came to you as a friend, in need of a listening ear and a bit of advice, and I was turned away, Mr. Finch. I believe that says it all."

Something in her tone and the pinch of her expression had Finch's heart sinking. "What has happened?"

Miss Barrows let out a mirthless chuckle, a wry smile on her lips. "That is not how friendship works, sir. You cannot ignore me one moment and expect me to tell all the next. I shall handle my problem on my own as I always do."

There was a hollow quality to her words, and though Finch didn't doubt her capacity to do just that, his heart ached at her having to shoulder troubles alone. Miss Barrows was one of two people on the planet who desired his opinion (let alone valued it), and he'd turned a blind eye to her.

Finch tapped a rhythm against his leg, his mind scrambling to know what to say to her. As much as he wished to ignore the accusation and pretend all was well, he couldn't leave things be. Perhaps if he hadn't seen what an honest conversation could do with Mina, he could've ignored the voice in the back of his thoughts begging him to tell her the whole truth, but as things had been so pleasant between him and Mina of late, Finch thought it best to forge ahead.

"It is not disinterest, Miss Barrows," he murmured. Sucking in a deep breath, Finch held it for a moment before letting it out in a rush, his words tumbling out with it. "The opposite, in fact."

Chapter 27

Swallowing, Finch forced his throat to loosen. It felt as though every eye were on him, though the others continued their impromptu concert, pointedly ignoring him and Miss Barrows. As he thought through what he ought to say, Finch's heartbeat sped, fluttering along like the trilling notes of a piano.

"I did not mean to..." Finch frowned at that poor start and the jumble of thoughts keeping him from seizing upon the right words. While Miss Barrows deserved to understand, declaring his heart would hardly improve the situation.

"A man in my position must guard his actions and behavior, so as not to give rise to expectations he cannot meet." Finch did not look at Miss Barrows, choosing to stare forward as though watching Mina's performance, though his thoughts were far from it.

"Such a man cannot hope to marry," he whispered, "and to foster feelings beyond friendship would only bring him and the lady pain."

Miss Barrows turned her gaze to him, studying his profile. Finch couldn't bear to meet her eyes, but he felt the breath catch in her lungs as she stilled.

"So, it is better for that gentleman to distance himself. Cut ties altogether, if necessary." Finch's throat tightened, but he could not keep the next words silent. "No matter how much he may wish otherwise, his fate is set, and it is better for them to part ways. It does no good to entertain feelings that cannot be acted upon."

Her voice barely carried over the music as she whispered, "And why not?"

Finch sniggered, shaking his head, his brows scrunching tight. "A gentleman without income cannot afford a wife when he can hardly afford to care for himself. The only thing he could offer his lady is poverty and suffering, and no man with an ounce of decency could do that. Even if the lady in question makes him happier than he thought possible and gives him reasons to smile when the world wishes him to weep."

A better man would not say such things, but Finch could not keep the feelings completely hidden. Speaking in hypotheticals had allowed him to be frank, and the added strain in his heart forced even more of his confession as this would likely be his final conversation with Miss Barrows.

The world blurred as Felicity stared at Mr. Finch. His lovely words filled her, weaving their way into her heart until they were a part of her very makeup: Mr. Finch loved her.

Perhaps he had not said those exact words, but there was no mistaking the meaning beneath them or the emotion filling his tone. His eyes remained trained on the others, yet she felt his control slipping, pulling free of his grasp as he spoke what was in his heart.

This wasn't the bland recitations so many had offered her. This was a gentleman fighting against what he thought was right and what he desired. Felicity felt like leaping to her feet with an exultant shout at the thought that Mr. Finch desired her. Not her money or position or all the other mercenary motives of the past, but because she made him happy.

"...the lady in question makes him happier than he thought possible and gives him reasons to smile when the world wishes him to weep..." Those scant words were worth more than the volumes of verse that spoke of love.

And it was as she reveled in this newfound joy that Felicity realized what Mr. Finch was truly saying. Yet again, her fortune was standing in the way of her finding matrimonial bliss, but this time it was her apparent lack of one.

Felicity's eyes slid closed, and she shook her head, leaning forward to rub her forehead as the weight of her lie pressed down on her. Good heavens, what had she done? Even as she tried to think her way through this mess of a situation, Aunt Imogene's voice taunted her, saying this was all of her own making, which was true but exceptionally unhelpful at present.

There was no way to maintain her dignity and keep Mr. Finch, and though her heart shuddered against admitting the truth, if it was between her pride and love, there was no contest. And though habit warned her to keep silent on the matter, Felicity couldn't—not with his tender and earnest declaration warming her heart.

"Mr. Finch, I feel like a fool," she whispered, straightening and turning in her seat to look at him. "As much as I wish I had not made such a mess of things, the truth is that I did, and the only way to remedy the situation is to speak the truth."

The gentleman watched her with a puzzled look, and Felicity sucked in a deep breath, letting it and a rush of words out in one gust. "I am not a companion to Aunt Imogene and do not need to earn my living. My uncle left me a sizeable inheritance."

Mr. Finch stilled, his expression slackening as he stared at her.

Taking another fortifying breath, Felicity continued, "I came to Bristow to escape the attentions of fortune hunters, and when I met you, I didn't expect us to become friends..." She lingered on that word, for it did not do justice to their relationship, yet it was the only word she could think of to describe it. "I wanted to avoid all that bother about money and inheritances,

so I lied about my situation. I am so terribly sorry, Mr. Finch—
"

"You are not a companion?" Neither his tone nor his expression gave any hint as to his feelings on the subject.

"I am not," she said. "I do hope you can forgive me—"

Finch was on his feet before he realized what was happening, and Miss Barrows followed, babbling things he couldn't follow as his disheveled wits attempted to make sense of this development. Mina stumbled over her notes, and though it was usually she who blushed, Finch felt a flush coloring his cheeks as he and Miss Barrows drew the attention of the others.

"Have I ever told you the history of this painting?" asked Lady Lovell, motioning towards a dramatic depiction of a man astride a horse. With Simon's assistance, she rose to her feet and ushered him and his wife to that side of the drawing room, which was as far from Finch and Miss Barrows as they could manage. With overly loud words, the older lady began a recitation of the history of the Lovell family while gesturing at the painting.

And Finch was left to stand there like the mute fool he was.

He'd spent far too many years with an intimate knowledge of the fickleness of fate to trust a sudden show of good fortune; Finch had long ago learned that the proverbial horse was more likely to trample than bestow gifts. And such a revelation certainly counted as providential.

"You are not a companion?" he echoed the question, and though the lady smiled and gave him all sorts of reassurances, Finch struggled to realign his previous worldview with the reality that lay before him.

Miss Barrows was an heiress.

Marrying for money held no appeal for Finch. Though he may have entertained mercenary fantasies as a very young man, they'd faded and vanished in quick succession. Of course, they were helped along by the fact that he had no enticements to secure an heiress, but the thought of approaching matrimony like a business venture sickened him.

And so, marriage had been out of reach. Or so he thought. But with her income, there was no reason they could not...

Finch stiffened, his thoughts pulling free of those fancies, and a weight landed on his shoulders, pressing down on him like a boulder. His legs gave out from under him, and he slumped down onto the seat.

"You lied to me," he mumbled.

Miss Barrows took the seat beside him, resting a hand on his forearm. Her expression was grim, a sorrowful shadow darkening her gaze.

"I did." Her eyes fell to the ground with a wince. "I've spent years being hounded by sycophants and false suitors. Though it is a poor excuse, I did not wish to be seen as a bank account..."

The lady babbled on about all the many justifications, but Finch's thoughts were not present. Casting his mind back through the weeks they'd spent together, Finch saw them in a new light. Though there had only been one blatant falsehood, it colored so many of their conversations in half-truths and misdirections.

A flush of heat swept over him, and Finch bit down on the inside of his cheek, hoping that pain might ease the ache that had taken hold in his chest. Tingles ran along his skin as he thought through his behavior. His cheeks burned, and he leaned forward to rub at his face, as though that might wipe away the past or hide him from the future.

"You sloughed off your privileged life for a few weeks, like some traveler wishing to experience how other cultures live. Did it amuse you to play pretend?" he asked.

Miss Barrows' hand tightened on his arm, but Finch's eyes remained fixed on the rug.

"It was not a playact, Mr. Finch," she whispered, though her voice faltered. "Well...yes, but not in the manner you mean and not the majority of it..." Miss Barrows continued to ramble excuses, her words halting and breaking while Finch wished the ground would swallow him whole.

Finch couldn't look at her. Couldn't look at anyone. Though he felt cold to the core, his face was flush with a heat that threatened to consume him, and he hardly felt fit to stand. His head dropped lower as he castigated himself. He had spent his life keeping his own counsel; why had he not done so in Miss Barrows' presence?

With panicked thoughts, Felicity struggled to find the right words. Surely there was something that would erase the hurt etched in Mr. Finch's face and the dejection rife in his posture. The gentleman rose to his feet once more, his gaze averted from her, and Felicity wished he would meet her eye. Perhaps then she might understand what was going on in his head.

"Please, Mr. Finch. I know I have hurt you, but can you not forgive me? Yes, I lied—a fact of which I am ashamed—but that does not erase the friendship we have built. Would you throw it away for the sake of a little white lie?"

Mr. Finch stiffened and turned his gaze to hers, but there was no comfort to be found in his eyes; like the frigid winter wind, his pain swept through her, chilling her heart.

"A little white lie?" he parroted in a tone as icy as his gaze. "I told you things I've never admitted aloud because I thought you understood my struggles. I trusted you with hidden parts of myself because I trusted that little white lie. You lectured me about finding joy in this life, acting as though you understood my situation. You made a fool of me, Miss Barrows, and now you dare to act as though that deception was an insignificant nothing. I assure you it is not."

Felicity wished she had some defense, but the twist of her stomach told her otherwise. Whether or not her deception had been justified at first, it did not negate her efforts to perpetuate the lie. On their own, each deceitful word had seemed unimportant, but together, they pressed down on her in a great mountain of guilt.

"I am sorry," she whispered as her vision blurred. "But everything else about me was true. My life may be different than yours, but I know what it feels like to be trapped by one's circumstances—"

Mr. Finch snorted, rounding on her with a fire blazing in his eyes. "I've spent my life hiding in plain sight, unable to speak a word of my troubles to anyone lest I disgrace the very family that deems me useless. I thought you understood. I thought..."

His voice faltered, and Mr. Finch turned away, pinching his nose. Taking in a shaky breath, he shook his head and strode to the door.

"Mr. Finch, please," called Felicity, but he was gone without a backward glance as the others pretended not to notice the sudden departure.

Pinching her nose, Felicity slumped down onto a nearby seat and closed her eyes. The full weight of her mistake settled onto her shoulders, pressing down until she felt ready to collapse beneath it. She cringed as Mr. Finch's condemnation played through her thoughts again and again, but she knew she deserved every ounce of the guilt.

Only a little white lie? Good heavens, what had she done?

Chapter 28

Seven years had passed since Father's edict had sentenced Finch to a life of solitude. He didn't like his situation, but there was no fighting the path he was on, so Finch had come to accept it. There was a peace in embracing the inevitable, however unhappy that future may be. Somewhat like the sleepy calm that takes hold of one before the cold saps the last vestiges of life away.

A chilling thought.

And the knife twisted in his heart at that unintended pun. It was the sort of ridiculous jest Miss Barrows enjoyed.

From his corner of the assembly room, Finch looked over the crowd, wishing he'd had the good sense to forgo the gathering. He'd managed to avoid everyone but Mina and Simon in the past sennight, yet remaining at Avebury Park alone had seemed a far worse fate tonight. Besides, Finch was well-versed in hiding his emotions.

The musicians were gathered on their dais, churning out merry tunes at one end of the room, and the dancers pranced before them, their joyful steps and claps punctuating the melodies. The fireplaces on either side of the long room blazed, helping to fight back the winter's frost, though the energetic press of people was doing a fair job on its own.

And Finch stood in a solitary corner, watching the whole thing, blending into the dark walls that were only a shade lighter than the pitch black of the world outside the window. Chandeliers shone above them, casting their light upon the crowd, yet they did little to stave off the night. A rather fitting comparison to the desperate attempt Finch made to cast aside the shadows clinging to his heart.

As much as he'd hoped to find some respite, it was impossible when the source of his torment was in the midst of the fray, dancing with gentleman after gentleman.

"Why did you insist on attending with us if you're going to stand in the corner, watching over the frivolity like a specter of death?" asked the gentleman who was supposed to be Finch's friend.

"Hush," said Mina with a frown befitting a governess.

Holding hands with some peacock, Miss Barrows chasséd down the line of dancers with a lightness of step that reflected her temperament. The lady's voice echoed in his thoughts, chiding him for being so severe and begging him to search out the joy hidden amidst his sorrow. But that was her talent, not his.

"Why don't you ask her to dance when you so clearly wish to?"

Mina followed that with a quick, "Simon!"

Her husband looked between his friend and wife with a put-upon sigh. "But surely Miss Barrows is not beyond forgiveness, and she is trying to make amends. Lady Lovell's cook must be baking day and night to keep up with all the peace offerings Miss Barrows has sent over."

Had Simon suggested forgiveness a sennight ago, Finch would've balked. The wounded pride that had driven him from Buxby Hall that night had certainly thought her betrayal a capital offense. But with time came perspective, and though Finch despised the dishonesty, he couldn't entirely fault Miss Barrows either.

Being well acquainted with the options granted a younger son, Finch knew many looked at marriage as a profession, and among their ranks were plenty who employed underhanded tactics to secure a prime position. Father had even suggested a few tricks with which to catch an heiress, though he'd surrendered that hope as readily as the others he'd harbored for his son.

Part of Finch's heart still shuddered because of all the truths he'd laid bare to her, but even that was easing with time. It was hard to hold onto his anger and shame when it had felt so wonderful to share those secrets. Whatever else may have happened and whatever else was to come, Finch felt Miss Barrows was trying to be his friend, and even if his confessions were gained through falsehood, the burden of silence had lifted for a time.

And in the privacy of his thoughts, Finch could admit that his desire to attend tonight had little to do with needing a distraction; there was little to be found when the source of his anguish danced before him. No, when the pain of betrayal and shame eased, a new clarity came with it: Finch had nothing to offer a lady like Miss Barrows. But he needed to see her.

For this last time, if nothing else.

"It is better if I keep my distance," mumbled Finch.

Simon scoffed. "With the dour looks you're both giving to the assembly, I find that difficult to believe."

Finch's brows drew together, and he cast a glance at Miss Barrows, who moved through the dance steps with a light heart, meeting each movement with a smile. Perhaps there was a tightness to her expression, but she chatted with her usual animation. No doubt the fellow had far more interesting things to say than anything Finch could manage.

"Miss Barrows is in fine spirits," Finch said with some reluctance. Not that he wished for her to suffer, but it was painful to admit that she was so unaffected by what had passed between them.

Mina's brows rose at that, and Simon scowled, turning to his wife and whispering *sotto voce*, "Was I this infuriatingly blind?"

"Hush," she repeated with a narrowed look at her husband, though she added, "but yes, you were, Simon. More so in some regards."

Then, turning to Finch, she said, "If you believe Miss Barrows is in fine spirits and pleased with her partners, you are not very observant."

With a true frown, Finch turned his gaze to the lady in question, but before he could give more than a cursory glance, Simon spoke.

"And so, rather than mending the rift between you two or hiding away in Avebury Park to lick your wounds, you choose to spend your evening torturing yourself by watching her from afar?"

Finch felt like growling. The subject of Miss Barrows had been avoided for a good many days, but apparently, the Kingsleys had only been lying in wait for the proper moment to spring the discussion on him. Perhaps they'd thought the assembly was the perfect moment for him to resolve all the issues of the past and dance off into everlasting happiness with Miss Barrows.

How little they knew.

"Does this have to do with your money troubles?" asked Simon while Mina sent another look of reproof at her husband.

Finch gaped. Though he tried to control the shock coursing through him, Simon's question was too sudden and unexpected to be met with anything but wide-eyed surprise.

"I am your closest friend, Finch," said Simon with a wry smile. "I know I am oblivious at times, but I'm not so dense as to overlook such a significant detail."

"I..." Finch's words drifted into nothingness as he stared at the fellow.

Simon chuckled and shook his head. "Do you truly believe I went to all the expense and effort of maintaining a box at the opera because I adore it so very much? Especially when I do not spend much time in London?"

Finch straightened while blinking and gaping like a landed carp.

"You seemed so intent on keeping your secret that I didn't want to press the issue," said Simon, lifting one shoulder in a shrug. "But that does not mean I am ignorant of it. And Miss Barrows—"

"Please, Simon," said Finch, holding up a hand. "I do not wish to speak of her."

"But she cares for you as you do her—"

Mina tugged on her husband's arm, pulling him towards the dance floor. "Stop pestering him, dearest, and dance with me."

"But he's being a fool—"

With a challenging raise of her brows, Mina silenced Simon and turned back to Finch, giving him a warm smile that held a tinge of sadness. "We will not pester you any further, but if you wish to speak, Simon and I would welcome your confidence."

Finch gave her a bow. "My thanks."

With a final considering look, Mina led Simon onto the dance floor.

Talking. What good would it do? What good had it ever done? His life was his life, and no amount of negotiating or conversing had changed the course of it. Words had done nothing to convince his father or to gain the respect of his superiors. A lifetime of experience had trained Finch to remain mute.

Except with her.

Tucking his hands behind him, Finch pinched his lips together, his gaze sliding to the ground. Even when it had appeared that their financial footing was equal, he didn't completely understand what had possessed him to lay his failures bare to Miss Barrows.

What sort of man was incapable of a profession? Not forgoing it because he didn't need the income, but forced into a "life of leisure" because he was unable to succeed. Laughing to himself, Finch wondered what sort of woman would give her heart to such a useless creature; it didn't speak well of Miss Barrows' faculties.

Finch's eyes sifted through the crowd, though it took little effort to see her amidst the crush of people. Miss Barrows' hair was like a torch, lighting the path to her. Even when she was otherwise blocked from sight, a peek of blazing red allowed him to track her as she danced with other men. But there was a stiffness to her smile that had him recalling Mina and Simon's words.

Watching her weave between the dancers, Finch studied her expression and movements.

Miss Barrows was a fine dancer with light and energetic steps. In truth, it was no less than what he expected, as she exuded lightness and energy at all times. Where others felt the exhaustion of so many sets already come and gone, Miss Barrows rallied, throwing herself into each dance with her typical vivacity.

Finch wondered at his first impression of her, astonished that the man he'd been had not seen the beauty etched in every facet of her. Perhaps her complexion had its flaws, but knowing the history behind her scars and the lady's feelings on the subject, Finch thought they suited her. Those little marks were a physical representation of the lady who bore them, and even if he could magic them away, he wouldn't want to part with them.

Finch stiffened, shaking free of those meandering thoughts that had pulled him away from his original one. But he supposed that was bound to happen when he was staring at her so intently.

Forcing his thoughts back to the subject at hand, Finch watched Miss Barrows, and a niggling sense of discomfort wormed its way into his heart. There were little signs of her discomfort if one wished to look. A tightness to her shoulders.

Boredom dimming her eyes. Her smile was at the ready, but it remained fixed in place, unchanging.

Miss Barrows was a lady of a thousand expressions, and her smile was no exception. It shifted and changed with every thought in her head, flitting between wry and warm, pleased and chagrined, and back again. Yet now, those ever-changing lips were stuck in one position, giving each of her partners the same kind but vacant expression.

And then she turned and her gaze connected with Finch.

In that brief moment, a flood of sentiments shifted her features, broadcasting more emotions than Miss Barrows had shown the entire evening. A flash of longing colored her gaze, wrapping around him like unbreakable chains yet with the gentle touch of silk and velvet. Then her expression pinched, her brows drawing together in supplication, like a sinner begging for absolution. Miss Barrows' expressions shifted and changed quickly from one to another, but it was the final flash of desperation, as though begging for rescue, that decided his course of action.

Chapter 29

Having paid no attention to the dancing as a whole, Finch had no idea how long this set had been going and how long it would last, but his fingers tapped in time with the notes, ticking down the measures until the song came to its conclusion, all while he refused to think about how inadvisable his action would be. It needed to be done, so there was no point belaboring it. Even as his cravat tightened around his neck.

The music signaled its fast-approaching end, and Finch moved from his place to fight through the assembly to the edge of the dance floor. Her current partner led Miss Barrows to one side, and Finch shifted his course to intersect theirs.

"I believe I have the next," said Finch with a bow, and Miss Barrows' eyes widened, a genuine smile tickling the corners of her lips.

"Yes, Mr. Finch," she murmured, taking his arm just as another gentleman came rushing forward.

"The lady promised me this one," he said in a rush of breath.

Though Finch detested dishonesty, the tightness with which Miss Barrows gripped his arm made the white lie slip out easily.

"I am afraid she promised it to me some time ago, sir. Miss Barrows must have been mistaken when she said she was free." A flash of mischief took hold of his tongue, and Finch added in a low voice (though not low enough for Miss Barrows to miss it), "Please do not think ill of the lady. Her wits are addled, the poor dear, and she often forgets such things."

Miss Barrows' foot shifted, the toe of her slipper settling over his foot and pressing down with just enough weight to serve as a warning.

Her promised dance partner glanced between Finch and Miss Barrows, his expression souring, and though Finch ought to have felt terrible about misleading the fellow, there was a covetous glimmer in his eyes that had Finch's heart chilling. Apparently, addled wits were an enticement for this gentleman, which on further reflection Finch ought to have anticipated; a lady of means with questionable faculties was a strong lure for fortune hunters.

Turning her away, Finch led Miss Barrows to their place in the figure. It would be another moment before this set started in earnest, but readying themselves was a good enough reason to put some distance between her and the gentlemen plaguing her tonight. As they faced each other, Miss Barrows held his gaze and let out a low breath; the tautness of her shoulders eased, and that polite smile stretched into a genuine one full of gratitude and warmth.

"I did not expect such a fine rescue, Mr. Finch." But her bright eyes dropped to the ground as she added, "I certainly do not merit such kindness."

"Nonsense." Recalling the words she'd spoken to him not long ago, he added, "I cannot stand to see you unhappy when I have the power to make you smile."

Miss Barrows' cheeks pinked, that ever-shifting smile of hers growing at those recognized words. But that joy was short-lived, and her complexion paled as she clenched her hands.

"You have ample reasons to be unhappy of late," she said, "and it pains me to know I play a large role in your suffering."

Finch nodded, considering the words she offered, and his gaze drifted to a few gentlemen scattered throughout the assembly, who looked upon Miss Barrows with greedy eyes. "If tonight is any indication of your struggles, I do not blame you for seizing a bit of anonymity here in Bristow. I am familiar with the machinations of fortune hunters, and if I were in your place, I imagine I might've done the same."

Miss Barrows stilled, her twisting fingers slackening as she stared at him. When she spoke, her words were little more than a whisper that barely carried over the noise around them. "Then you forgive me?"

But before he could reply, she closed her eyes with a wince and shook her head. "I ought to have spoken up sooner. I knew you were not like the others, but there was this silly little part of me that was terrified to damage the friendship we'd built, and then..."

Her shoulders and expression fell. "I suppose it doesn't matter why I waited so long to tell you the truth. Just know I am ashamed for having misled you and for causing you pain."

"I know, Miss Barrows." Speaking that truth aloud had a power of its own. The feeling had grown in strength during the days he'd spent pondering this situation, and giving voice to them wiped away any residual doubt. Finch trusted Miss Barrows' contrition, and it washed away the last of his anguish at having discovered the truth.

"I forgive you," he added, and Miss Barrows' eyes brightened at the words, glowing with joy and relief as only she could.

"Mr. Finch." His name was a whisper on her lips, but he heard it all the same. Her gaze glowed with her heart and soul, filling his own and binding him all the more tightly to her.

Finch jerked out of that daze as the musicians began to play, and he stepped back into place, uncertain of when he'd moved closer to her. The first bars of the introduction played in the background as he struggled to know what to say. The dance had the ladies stepping towards the gentlemen, and as Miss Barrows drew near, he stole the opportunity.

"Do not pin your hopes on me, Miss Barrows. Our situation is unchanged."

Mr. Finch's confession had Felicity pausing, mid-step, as she stared at him. This was not at all how she imagined this moment. Groveling had featured as the highlight of the conversation as forgiveness was not a guarantee, and Felicity had anticipated it taking much more effort on her part. Now, she'd gained absolution, yet there were no forthcoming declarations or pledging of troths.

"...Our situation is unchanged."

Someone jostled her, and Felicity's cheeks blazed red, her feet hurrying to catch up to the other dancers, only to stumble. Mr. Finch's strong hands were there to steady her, covering her misstep as best he could.

Coming to her resting place, Felicity watched the gentlemen as they completed their portion of the dance, and her mind spiraled into a quagmire of supposition, searching for the meaning behind his words.

Had she imagined his feelings? Heat swept over her, and Felicity closed her eyes, as though that might hide her from the others. But even as embarrassment overtook her, his words from that evening returned to her thoughts. Her heart was too engaged to trust its interpretation of his behavior, but more than the appearance of affections, Mr. Finch's words had all but admitted his admiration of her.

Puffing out her cheeks, Felicity groaned at her foolishness. Surely, at her age, she ought not to be overwrought by wild speculations into the logic and sentiments of men.

The dance brought them together for several steps, and Mr. Finch avoided looking at her as they moved together. Biding her time, Felicity waited for a pause.

"What do you mean, Mr. Finch? That evening, you made it clear that..." Felicity struggled with the words. Though the others paid them little heed, she did not like having witnesses to this conversation. Yet the moment the set was over, she knew the vultures waiting at the edges of the dance would steal her away again. This was no time to be a wilting miss.

"You gave me every indication that the impediment between us was our lack of funds. That is not the case. So, why do you insist the situation is unchanged?"

"I have no profession, Miss Barrows. That is unchanged."

Felicity's brows drew together. "What need have you of a profession when I have income enough for the both of us?"

Those words had Mr. Finch's expression hardening as his gaze slid to the floor. The hand at his side clenched as he murmured, "So, I go from being my family's ornament to being yours?"

Straightening, Felicity stared at him, but the dance pulled them away again, and she cursed the fool who'd choreographed the wretched thing. Could he not have given the couples a tad more time together before they went flailing about once more? As she moved about the dance floor, her eyes fixed on Mr. Finch, but he would not meet her gaze.

Did he truly think she viewed him as such? To her thinking, the role of spouse and parent was a far cry from being an "ornament." But was there more to his meaning? Various interpretations of his words sprang to mind, and Felicity itched to drag him from the dance floor so they could discuss this properly.

When the dance finally allowed it, Felicity pounced. "That is hardly a fair comparison, Mr. Finch. And I would think you would be pleased with this situation, for you would have work enough with our properties and investments. Even with a man of business and steward, there is so much work to be done, and I would welcome a partner."

"And an unequal match where the husband brings nothing to the marriage?" Mr. Finch did not look at her as he spoke the words, casting his gaze about the room as though searching for an escape. His teeth ground together, the muscles in his jaw tightening.

But Felicity's thoughts were fixed on his words, pulling them apart as she tried to grasp the underlying meaning. Was his pride pricked that others might believe him a fortune hunter? Unequal matches elicited some snickers and judgments, but surely that was no reason to forgo their joy.

"What does it matter, Mr. Finch? If we are happy together, surely your income is but a detail."

His gaze fell to the ground, his expression pinching as he examined the floorboards, but before he could reply, the dance drew them away once more, and Felicity struggled through the steps. Was this all a matter of masculine pride? That foolish quality pushed men to do idiotic things simply to prove themselves better than their counterparts. It had already left its mark on Mr. Finch's forehead; was it now to claim his future as well? And hers?

The pair moved through their set, getting only snippets of a conversation, but each reiterated the issue of the money. Felicity could not comprehend why it mattered so very much, but no amount of reassurances budged the fellow. A steady refrain of denials kept her at arm's length, and as their time together wound to a close, a weight settled in Felicity's stomach.

Mr. Finch was determined to cast her aside because of his lack of funds.

Taking her by the arm, the gentleman did his duty and led her from the floor without a word. The pair moved together, though a gaping void stood between them.

Felicity's breaths came quicker as she glanced at him (though he kept his face turned away from her) and realized that he saw her in the same light as the other gentlemen: Felicity Barrows was simply an heiress and nothing more, whose defining characteristic was numbers in a ledger. Where others used that as a reason to pursue her, Mr. Finch saw it as a reason to avoid her, but that did not negate the fact that men viewed her money first and foremost.

"So, Mr. Finch," she said as they came to a stop, "our situation is unchanged because yours has not."

He shifted in place, tucking his hands behind him while his eyes looked at anything but her. "I have nothing to offer you, Miss Barrows."

Her throat tightened, and Felicity tried to swallow, though it felt like someone had tied it in a knot. While there was an admirable amount of self-sacrifice steeped in his words, they simply reinforced the fact that he was no different than the others. Taking in a breath, Felicity tried to steel her heart against the prickles of pain, but it was like trying to stop the earth from spinning.

"I see," she murmured. "If you view one's value only in terms of money and income, perhaps we are not suited after all."

He flinched, though she could not fathom why those words mattered to him. This break between them was of his doing, and there was no point in belaboring the issue. Felicity would not beg him to love her.

"Miss Barrows," called Mr. Wilson as he arrived at Felicity's elbow. The fellow gave Mr. Finch a hard look before turning a smile to her. "As my set with you was commandeered by another, might I claim this one?"

A sigh lurked beneath her placid expression, begging to be let loose. Though Felicity wanted nothing more than to send him away rather than be subjected to his insipid conversation, there was nothing to be done.

"Of course, Mr. Wilson," she said, taking his proffered arm.

Though she wished she felt nothing when surrendering her place at Mr. Finch's side, Felicity's heart was as illogical as any. Even after his rejection, she still longed to be near him and bask in all the wonderful moments to be found with him.

A fleeting hope whispered that Mr. Wilson may prove more diverting with time, but he and several other gentlemen had pestered and preened around her for the entirety of the assembly, and he'd proven thus far to be as uninterested in anything she had to say as the rest of the fellows. That might be forgiven if Mr. Wilson was a source of entertaining conversation, but alas, he was far too enamored with his horse's bloodlines. Felicity forced a smile on her lips and nodded as Mr. Wilson began to drone on, listing off all his abilities and talents, as though petitioning an employer for a position.

At least Alastair had not approached yet. She caught glimpses of him lurking in the background, watching her with longing eyes that were likely meant to make her weak at the knees. But Felicity knew better than to think he would be content with simply gazing from afar.

Chapter 30

Content was not a word Simon associated with assemblies and dancing, yet there was no other descriptor to choose at this very moment. Standing to one side of the assembly rooms, Simon surveyed the crowd, his gaze lingering on his wife. Mina's dark eyes sparkled in the candlelight, her hands gesturing as she spoke to Lady Lovell with a smile stretched across her face in a manner that would raise the eyebrows of the posh ladies of London.

Yes, Simon Kingsley was quite content.

Casting his thoughts to the changes fate had wrought in his world, he was startled to realize that it was almost a year ago that a ball had brought Mina into his life. That Simon of the past had foolishly thought marriage would free him from the demands of bachelorhood, such as dancing at balls and assemblies. Instead, it had taught him to cherish these moments.

Even as he contemplated that, his feet itched to lead Mina around the dance floor again and see her spirits soar as she skipped through the steps. His wife was a fine dancer and even though Simon didn't care for the activity itself, he adored dancing with her.

Wouldn't Finch laugh if he were privy to Simon's soppy sentiments.

But thoughts of his friend drove away that peace and drew Simon's gaze from his love to the gentleman in question. Finch and Miss Barrows were among the throng, looking as pleased with their situation as a prisoner facing transport to New South Wales. Crossing his arms, Simon watched the pair, his fingers rapping against his arm with a frantic beat.

Finch was making a muck of things. Simon had hoped a dance might heal the breach between them, but when his friend deposited Miss Barrows into the care of another, both gentleman and lady appeared to welcome the separation.

Fools, the both of them.

Phantoms of the past cast a shadow over his thoughts as Simon remembered that dark time not too long ago when he'd believed all was lost. He'd spent nearly a sennight on horseback, hunting for Mina to beg her forgiveness, and though his body had ached from that abuse, his heart had fared worse. Those days of travel offered nothing to occupy his thoughts but his sins of the past and the bleakness of a future devoid of his wife.

Without caveat or equivocation, Simon could say those days were the darkest of his life. Mina had given him a glimpse of a joy he'd never thought to find, only to have it ripped away, leaving his world all the bleaker for its absence. Though Simon had attempted to do so, there were not words enough to describe his gratitude at having found forgiveness at the end of that journey.

For both Finch's and Miss Barrows' sakes, Simon hoped the fellow would follow Mina's example.

Turning on his heels, the gentleman in question strode from Miss Barrows, his expression shuttered, though Simon knew his friend well enough to see that Finch was in turmoil beneath the placid facade. The fellow's gaze swept the room, and when it landed on Simon, he moved through the crowd with more expedience than care and arrived at his friend's side in a trice.

"You must ask Miss Barrows to dance," said Finch.

Simon straightened, his gaze darting between his friend and the lady. "Have you two mended things?"

Finch waved that away. "That is of no importance."

"I would say it is. Miss Barrows made a poor choice, but I cannot believe her unworthy of forgiveness."

Puffing out his cheeks, Finch shook his head, his eyes darting away from his friend. "Forgiveness is not the issue, Simon. Nor does it have any bearing on the favor I am begging of you. Miss Barrows is being pestered by unwanted attention, and I have done as much as I can without raising eyebrows. Would you step in for me? Or would you rather stand around like a lump?"

Simon scoffed and gave him a wry smile. "That is one way to ask a favor, though not terribly effective—"

Finch scowled. "There is no time for jests. The set is about to start, and she will be trapped."

"If she already has a partner—"

"Make some excuse. Any excuse," he said with a vague wave. "Mr. Wilson doesn't seem bright."

Simon gave a low groan. The Wilson sons weren't sensible, nor did they have the social acumen to cover that deficiency. Not bad lads per se, though Simon would not want them courting his daughter. *His daughter.* That thought brought a lopsided grin to his face as he wondered how soon it would be until Avebury Park rang with children's laughter.

"Simon!" Finch barked, bringing the fellow back to the present.

"I would like to help you, Finch, but I don't know if that would be wise. I do not dance with anyone but my wife." Simon's gaze drifted from Finch to rest on Mina. Even without his friend's petition, Simon wanted to help Miss Barrows; she seemed a fine lady who did not deserve the unwanted attention of fortune seekers. However, an uneasy shiver held him captive. Surely it was only a dance and could not be construed as anything more. Yet could he be certain?

"Please, Simon," said Finch, and even without the additional supplication, Simon was decided. If the roles were reversed, he would hope for Finch's assistance. As long as he gave no indication of a particular preference towards Miss Barrows, all should be well with Mina.

"Of course, Finch," he said with a nod. "Whatever I can do to help the two of you."

But his friend stiffened, his gaze dropping to his feet. "Ignore whatever imaginings you've concocted. Nothing has changed between us. Miss Barrows deserves better."

Before Simon could question that further, Finch stepped to the side, nudging Simon forward. "Get a move on it."

The musicians struck the introductory notes, and Simon scurried forward and came to stand before the lady.

"Do forgive my tardiness, Miss Barrows," he said with a bow.

"Pardon me, Mr. Kingsley, but we are about to begin a set," said Mr. Wilson, but Simon smiled at the young man.

"I apologize for the confusion, but Miss Barrows promised this one to me." A wicked thought slipped into his mind, and Simon couldn't help but add in a pointed whisper to Mr. Wilson, "The poor dear has trouble remembering such things ever since the accident."

If Finch was going to put him in this unenviable position of playing rescuer to someone else's damsel, it was only fair that Simon be allowed some enjoyment. And Miss Barrows provided that amply when she narrowed her eyes at him.

Mr. Wilson's brows rose, and he glanced between Simon and Miss Barrows. Unfortunately, Simon had miscalculated his foe, for the young man didn't move from his spot.

For good measure, Simon added, "I understand Miss Hensen is asking after you."

The young man's expression lightened, and luckily, the opening notes struck as he was debating his options. Simon slid into his place, leading Miss Barrows through the steps as Mr. Wilson was shunted to the side. Having already danced a few sets with Mina, he didn't wish for another rousing turn about the floor and was grateful he'd lucked into a dance with a moderate pace.

"I see you and Mr. Finch are of a like mind when it comes to teasing me. I don't know whether to thank you or scold you for that," said Miss Barrows. "While your intervention saved me from his exasperating company, you've only encouraged him to pursue me more. Being a lackwit is considered an enticement for an heiress, after all. Far easier to snare into marriage."

Simon winced. "I did not think of that. Though Mr. Wilson isn't a bad sort."

Miss Barrows and the ladies opposite moved forward, passing Simon and the other gentlemen as they switched sides and back again.

As she came close, Miss Barrows muttered, "He isn't a good sort, either, Mr. Kingsley. Whether or not he is a conniving and selfish creature, I do not wish to be pursued solely because of my inheritance."

The lead couple in the dance moved down the center of the line and back, and as he and Miss Barrows wove around that pair to take their place at the head of the line, she added with pink cheeks, "I didn't mean to sound ungrateful. I do thank you for your rescue, Mr. Kingsley. I fear I am out of sorts tonight."

Simon's heart thudded against his ribs, reminding him all too acutely of a time when he'd been in the lady's position.

"It is understandable, Miss Barrows. Regaining that which was lost is a painful endeavor."

Miss Barrows turned a sad smile to him, her eyes devoid of the brightness usually found there. "There is nothing to regain, Mr. Kingsley."

"Give him some time, and he will forgive you—"

"Forgiveness is not the issue," she said with a hint of mockery that made it sound as though she were parroting the words. As they sounded identical to those Finch had spoken a few minutes ago, Simon guessed their source.

But Miss Barrows continued before Simon replied, "Our situation remains unchanged because a certain gentleman has shown he is no different than any of the other wretched men who hound my every step and equate one's value with one's bank account. Such a man won't settle for something as plebeian as love."

The lady's tone sharpened, and Simon was quite grateful the gentleman in question was not standing before her, for Finch would've been flayed. As it was, Simon was relieved when the dance separated them again, giving him a blessed moment to sort through his thoughts.

With time to reflect, Simon saw more clearly the truth behind Finch's words and behavior, and his steps became heavy as he thought of the struggles the poor man faced. Perhaps he ought to have been more forceful with Finch, pushing him to speak. Then they might not have arrived at this point. The best he could do was to give Miss Barrows insight.

"You have every right to be angry," he said as they came to rest, facing each other. "But the reasons behind his actions are not what you think."

"Do his reasons matter?" The lady's jaw was tight and set against his friend, but there was a spark of curiosity in her gaze that allowed the knot in Simon's stomach to loosen.

"Certainly they do, but as that was your wounded pride speaking, I will ignore it and say that Finch has every reason to believe he is not good enough for you."

A hard glint gleamed in her eye, and Miss Barrows opened her mouth, but Simon held up a staying hand to hold off any protest she might mount.

"It is not your doing, so do not take his actions personally." The dance drove them apart, and Simon was forced to pause, waiting for the next opportunity to add, "It is not the money that upsets him."

Miss Barrows' forehead wrinkled as her brows drew together, but she did not interrupt him. The steel in her gaze softened a touch, and Simon prayed she would listen and understand. With a few more steps, they moved down the line of dancers, taking their part as needed before coming to a rest again.

"His family are not cruel people. They do not belittle or abuse him in any overt fashion, but they do not value or respect him." Simon's brow furrowed, his expression twisting at the memory of those few interactions he'd had with the Finch clan and all the little things his friend had told him over the years. None of it painted a happy picture. "A person cannot be surrounded by such low opinions and remain unscathed."

The lady's gaze drifted from Simon, as though she were sifting through her memories, and he hoped she saw the little signs that showed a broken but genuine soul.

"It was Finch who begged me to chase off Mr. Wilson." Simon's words drew Miss Barrows' attention once more before her eyes flew to the edge of the ballroom, and he hoped she was searching for the poor fool; Finch deserved some credit for his gesture. "And while doing so, he made it clear he thinks himself unworthy of you. I believe his precise words were 'Miss Barrows deserves better.'"

The lady shook her head, speaking in an off-handed tone. "He said something similar to me a few minutes ago, but I don't understand why he feels it is so important for me to find a man with money. I have enough of it as it is."

Simon shook his head. "He wasn't speaking of income, Miss Barrows. He was speaking of himself. His family has him convinced he has no value."

Her expression pinched and her voice rose. "That is ludicrous!"

Dancers on either side jerked their gazes towards Miss Barrows, but the lady waved a hand in their direction, as though dismissing the lot of them. Their attention waned, but Simon felt their regard as they feigned disinterest.

Tugging at his cravat, Simon tried to loosen it as he prayed the others would pay them no more heed. The last thing he needed was to stir up rumors about a heated discussion between him and a lady who was not his wife. The gossipmongers were still feasting on the mess he'd made with *that woman*, and there was no need to throw them fresh meat. His gaze turned to Mina, but she was still in discussion with Lady Lovell.

Miss Barrows was caught up in her thoughts, and Simon was pleased to let the silence linger between them as the dance moved along. The steps were simple enough that they required little thought, and he was grateful for the respite. He cleared his throat and resisted the urge to remove his cravat (though the wretched thing seemed determined to strangle him).

Simon prayed Finch would forgive him for having spilled those secrets, but he couldn't remain silent when the fellow was determined to be a fool.

"My thanks, Mr. Kingsley."

"For rescuing you from an unsuitable dance partner or for the insight into my dunderhead of a friend?" Simon asked with a smile, which she answered with one of her own.

"I don't know if I can give thanks for the first, as you called my wits into question while doing so," she replied with a narrowed gaze, though her eyes sparkled with laughter.

"Perhaps if we expand on your poor qualities enough, the fortune hunters might leave you be. We could invent a whole list of revolting habits bound to scare them away."

Miss Barrows sighed. "I fear it only entices them. The less desirable I seem, the more they believe they have a chance at gaining my favor."

"I knew a fellow who loved to drone on about himself without a dash of inflection. Few could stand his company for more than five minutes."

Miss Barrows gave him an arched brow. "So, I am to bore my suitors away?"

Simon's own brows matched hers. "Perhaps. Or you could prove yourself unsuitable for society."

Her smile grew. "I could take up smoking and fisticuffs or riding astride and cursing like a sailor."

Simon laughed at that image and shook his head. "Perhaps not. Unless you wish to become a pariah."

"Best not then," she said with a chuckle, her steps growing lighter. "I suppose patience is the only answer. No doubt I will find some peace eventually."

The last strains of the song came to a close, ending their set, and Simon gave her a low bow. "I do hope your peace comes far sooner than that, Miss Barrows. Yours and Finch's."

Miss Barrows curtsied and squeezed his hand. "I live in hope."

Before he could escort her from the dance floor, Mr. Drake appeared at Simon's elbow.

"Would you mind introducing me to your charming dance partner, Mr. Kingsley?" he asked with a pointed look to Simon's left. Miss Barrows did not see it, but Simon followed the gaze to see Finch standing there with an expectant look, nodding at Simon to do as Mr. Drake asked.

Simon provided the necessary greetings, and Mr. Drake immediately seized the opportunity to claim the next set with Miss Barrows. A younger gentleman had been moving in their direction, but he veered away when Miss Barrows took Mr. Drake's arm. The gentleman gave Miss Barrows a kindly smile, and Simon left the pair to their conversation about Mr. Drake's wife and children and Miss Barrows' visit to Bristow.

Chapter 31

"That was nicely done, Finch," said Mina, as the two of them stood to the side, watching Miss Barrows and Mr. Drake take their place in the figure.

"I have no idea what you mean," he said, though they both knew that was a fib.

Let him pretend if he wished. Matters of the heart resolved in their due course, and Mina felt no need to hurry them along. Unless the pair proved incapable of mending things, in which case she felt no compunction over prodding them in the proper direction. But it did her good to see Finch making the effort. Hope was not lost as long as they both cared, and a gentleman did not go to such lengths without his heart being engaged.

Simon left his former partner in Mr. Drake's care and turned his attention to Mina. His gaze held hers as he wove through the assembly room, and her cheeks pinked. She could not help it. Her husband could discompose her as no one else could, and Mina grinned like a fool as he joined her.

"Miss Barrows is a fine lady and an enjoyable companion," he said with a decisive nod, as though expecting some opposition to that statement.

Holding her breath, Mina prayed her husband would leave it be. The adorable man meant well, but pestering Finch or Miss Barrows was not the solution. Simon gave his friend a pointed look, but Finch refused to meet his eye, choosing to watch the dancers. Or rather, one particular dancer.

"Simon." She detested chiding him, but he was so determined to swoop in and resolve everything immediately, and these situations were far too precarious for heavy-handed approaches.

Her husband straightened, meeting her gaze with a wide-eyed look. "Not that I hold Miss Barrows in special regard."

Mina's brows scrunched together as she stared at Simon while Finch leveled a narrowed look at his friend.

"She is pleasant enough but not of particular interest to me," added Simon as his hand crept up to fiddle with his cravat.

At that, both Mina and Finch's heads cocked to the side, staring at Simon as the fellow hemmed and mumbled on about Miss Barrows, jumping between praising her and noting how unremarkable she was. The whole halting, awkward speech chilled Mina, filling her with a dread she refused to name. All his bizarre behavior of late surged into her memory, giving strength to the shiver running down her spine.

Then Simon stopped and straightened. Giving her a bright but brittle smile, he changed tack and said, "Mina, you look radiant tonight."

Glancing down at herself, Mina wondered at the inordinate amount of awe in his tone. Not that she thought herself a fright, but neither had she put much effort into her toilette this evening. Her pale blue gown was a simple cut, and Mina adored the dark blue embroidery edging the bottom half of the skirt, sleeves, and neckline, though it was mostly unremarkable.

Simon's tone was unsettling, with a determined tinge as though willing his words to be believed. And Mina's breath caught at the implication.

Taking her hand in his, Simon gave her knuckles a buss and said, "Surely you are in want of some refreshment."

And he hurried away in search of the drink she hadn't requested.

"Is something amiss between the two of you?" asked Finch, who apparently had no issue with wandering into sensitive subjects as long as they were not his own.

Mina shook her head with a wry smile. "I fear men are an unsolvable riddle."

"I believe you are speaking of women," he retorted with a hint of humor, though his gaze remained dull.

"Both are hopeless. It is a wonder anyone finds happiness in marriage," Mina said in a dry tone.

Finch slanted her a look. "But you and Simon have. I've never seen my friend as happy as he is with you."

Mina's expression fell. "Not of late, it would seem."

The gentleman shook his head. "That is a hard pronouncement, and wholly inaccurate. Simon has been out of sorts to a degree, but as a whole, he is happier today than he was a year ago."

Reaching out a hand to squeeze his forearm, Mina gave him a wan smile. "Thank you for that."

But a niggling worry rested in her thoughts, squirming its way through that reassurance. Was Simon truly better off? The answer to that question was an unequivocal affirmative if Mina posed it about herself, but could the same be said of Simon?

Standing there amidst the revelry and merriment, Mina pondered that profound question. Once she'd posed it, her chest tightened, giving rise to fears that said it wasn't true, but as she thought about the man she'd met last year, the pressure eased. The edge of fear softened, and a wave of peace washed over her. Whatever else had happened in their lives, Mina trusted that this marriage had been a blessing to them both.

"If you are concerned about things, you should speak to Simon," said Finch in a low voice.

Mina glanced at the gentleman she'd thoroughly disliked a short time ago. It seemed odd that he was now advising her on such personal matters. More than that, she couldn't help but agree with his sound advice, even if she wished to lock away her worries and ignore their existence.

"And if it should lead to unpleasant conversations?" she asked.

Finch shrugged. "I have come to appreciate the importance of honesty. For good or ill, it is better than deception. But why should you fret? Simon adores you. Whatever is amiss, I'm certain you two will right things again."

"I am glad someone is confident of that." Mina's eyes widened at that admission, her cheeks flaming as she stumbled to cover her confession, but before she could get too far, Finch stopped her.

"Why do you feel so uncertain?" he asked as he watched the dancers.

Mina's brows furrowed. "Have you ever felt unworthy of another's affection, Finch?"

Jerking his gaze to her, Finch stiffened and stared at her, which brought another flush of color to her cheeks. Sucking in a breath, Mina waved an airy hand as she tried to gather her muddle of thoughts into something coherent. Then, dropping her hands to her side, she twisted her skirts, worrying the fabric.

"It may appear silly to you, Finch. Men are built never to doubt or waiver from their convictions and have an endless supply of confidence. But I do not."

"That is absurd," he said with a shake of his head. "What reason do you have to view yourself in such a poor light?"

Mina gave a short burst of laughter that was rife with disbelief. "I hate to recall the mistakes of the past, but you had some rather unflattering words to say about me not too long ago, and they are not the first time I have heard such criticisms."

Finch's jaw clenched, his gaze falling away from her.

"I do not mean to shame you," she said with an apologetic smile. "It was merely an illustration. Throughout my life, people have told me I was worthless because I did not fit their ideal.

And one cannot hear such cruel judgments for so long and not take them to heart."

Slowly, Finch's eyes rose to meet hers for a brief moment, but in that instant, Mina saw a flash of pain. Not the shame of his past deeds, but a whisper of some hidden scar etched into his heart, and an echo of the agonies she'd suffered throughout the years. Though it was only a brief glimpse into Finch's heart, Mina recognized it in an instant.

She had been wrong. Some gentlemen doubted themselves. And if her instincts were correct, she'd wager it was no minor issue for Finch. As that revelation struck, her words shifted and changed, speaking as much to him as she was to herself.

"It is difficult to cast aside a lifetime of fear. When one has been treated poorly for so long, it can be impossible to trust kindness. Even when another is professing his undying love, it is a struggle to believe it. How can anyone love me when so many others despise me?"

Mina paused, closing her eyes against the truths wriggling beneath the surface. Then she added, "How can he love me when I barely love myself?"

Groping about for the proper reassurances, Mina struggled to know what to say; her thoughts raced with various possibilities, trying to predict Finch's reaction to each.

"But then I remind myself that their opinions hold no sway over my worth," she said, a ghost of a smile curling the edges of her lips. "Just because I lack in one aspect, even if it is something everyone prizes, that does not mean I am wholly insignificant or repugnant. Everyone has intrinsic value. It may not be obvious to others, or it may be buried or forgotten, but it is there if one is willing to look."

Mina's hands relaxed. Her poor skirts were wrinkled beyond repair. Taking a deep breath, she held onto those words, realizing that she'd needed to give them a voice as much as Finch needed to hear them. The tension in her chest eased, and her heart warmed as she contemplated those truths she too often forgot.

"It's not easy to remember, but I try," she added.

Finch remained mute, but there was an intensity to his expression and posture that spoke of one clinging to every word; his brow was pulled low, and his eyes burned a hole in the floorboards.

"I do apologize for taking so long, dearest," said Simon, handing Mina a cup of punch. "I was waylaid by Mr. Caldwell. He has an interesting proposition for your school that might keep a certain troublesome lady at bay."

Glancing between Finch and Mina, Simon's brow furrowed. "Is something amiss?"

Finch hid his pain behind a lazy smile. "We were bemoaning your absence."

Tucking Mina's free hand through his arm, Simon chuckled. "Pining after me, were you?"

"It was as though our very reason for being had disappeared, leaving us empty shells," he replied.

"Too right," said Simon with a nod before giving his wife a rascally grin. "I read somewhere that wives sit about all day waiting for their husbands to return, lost without their guidance and attention."

Mina slanted him a narrowed look, and Simon had the decency to grimace, though it was too impish to be believed. The gentlemen continued to chat, leaving Mina's mind to wander through the previous conversation.

Unfortunately, she knew too little of the man to be certain her words were the ones he needed to hear; her wretched pride had kept her at a distance, leaving her hindered at present. Mina could only hope and pray she had done some good.

And then her thoughts drifted to Finch's advice. As much as she wished to ignore it, Mina knew she could not. Waiting for things to sort themselves out was doing no good, and she and Simon were falling back into that familiar pattern of the past. Silence and fear were now in control of her marriage, and the time was long past for her to have a frank discussion with her husband.

Chapter 32

Slipping through a side door, Felicity scurried away from the heat and noise of the assembly room and out into the cold; this winter had been so terribly frigid, but her skin was so flushed that the nip was exactly what she needed. Touching a hand to her forehead, she dabbed at the droplets forming there and took in a deep breath of the frosty night air.

With more leeches and less happy resolution, this evening was a far cry from the one she'd hoped to have. Though the past few sets had provided more interesting partners, it was difficult to enjoy the reprieve with her heart aching so.

Perhaps it was time to return to Plymouth. Her month-long visit with Aunt Imogene had stretched into six weeks, and no doubt she was needed at home. Yet her silly, aching heart sank at the thought of leaving Bristow.

Felicity didn't know what to make of Mr. Finch. Worse, she didn't know if she wanted to puzzle him out. Was he the stubborn fool he seemed to be? Or the flawed man Mr. Kingsley described? With all the attention turned her way, she'd hardly had a moment to think about either of those conversations. And as footsteps echoed behind her, Felicity suspected she wouldn't get an opportunity now, either.

"You are as graceful as I remember." There'd been a time when Alastair's voice had entranced her, but now it felt like oil dripping down her skin.

"And you are far more irritating than I remember," murmured Felicity with an inward sigh. Raising her voice for him to hear, she said, "I would like to be alone, Mr. Dunn."

Coming up behind her, he leaned forward and gave a soft chuckle. "Mr. Dunn, is it?"

Felicity stepped away.

"Do you wish to tease me further? You've tortured me for nearly a fortnight, but I have endured it, for I deserve your censure." Mr. Dunn's voice rose, his tone filling with the agony of lost souls. Had she ever truly believed this melodramatic balderdash to be in earnest? Felicity shuddered over her past ignorance.

"In truth, you deserve my gratitude," said Felicity, though there were other, more painful and humiliating things the scoundrel deserved as well. "You taught me not to give my heart foolishly or trust in hollow words. If not for you, I might've made a terrible match with some other mercenary man."

"You think me a liar?" Mr. Dunn's tone was filled with unshed tears, and Felicity rubbed at her temple, hoping to ease the pressure there. When his palms brushed her arms, she leapt away, spinning and putting out a hand to ward him off.

"I know you are a liar," she said with narrowed eyes. "Did you think I wouldn't realize your letters were falsified?"

Mr. Dunn's brows shot up, his eyes darting away from her; that spark of surprise was enough to tell Felicity how little he thought of her intelligence. Her revelation discomposed him for only a heartbeat before he met her gaze once more with a pained smile.

"I admit it." His shoulders dropped with a heavy sigh. "They were the letters I always wanted to send you, but I couldn't afford the paper or ink then. But neither could I arrive on your doorstep after all this time without an offering. *When* I wrote them may be untrue, but surely those missives demonstrate how much I still adore you."

Clearly, his opinion of her wits was even lower than she'd realized.

"For goodness' sake, Mr. Dunn. You are embarrassing yourself and irritating me. For both our sakes, leave it be."

"But you are my whole existence. I've dreamt of this moment for years. Do not say that you are lost to me." Taking her by the forearms, he held her there, that once handsome visage aimed at her as though that and his false ardor would sway her. And they might've, once.

If it weren't for the pains pricking her temple and the general exhaustion pulling at her as though gravity itself had strengthened its hold on her, Felicity might've been impressed with the fellow's acting ability. In some ways, it eased the embarrassment that tainted her memories of him, for Alastair Dunn was quite convincing as the forlorn lover. It was like he'd stepped forth from the pages of a novel, determined to carry the heroine off into that perfect fantasy of eternal wedded bliss.

Felicity twisted her arm, breaking his hold on her. "Why do you love me, Mr. Dunn?"

Stepping forward, he swept her into his arms, leaning in until she felt his moist breath on her cheeks. "I think my letters say the words well enough."

Pushing against him, Felicity wrenched herself free again and put another few paces between them. "They conveyed your intentions quite clearly, but I wish to hear it from you."

Dipping to his knees, he took her hand in his, placing a kiss on her knuckles. "You are the most radiant woman I have ever laid eyes on, my darling. I have traveled across this country, and none could compare with your beauty and grace. It is as though Aphrodite herself fashioned you..."

Felicity yanked her hand away and wiped his token of affection on her skirts. Had his lips always been so soggy?

Mr. Dunn continued to drone on about the same things those fools always said. He was far more gifted with his flattery and managed to avoid breaking into bouts of poetry, but Felicity was finished with the moderate politeness she'd been bestowing.

"Enough, Mr. Dunn. I count myself lucky that my uncle stopped our ill-advised elopement all those years ago, and your renewed attentions have done nothing to change my mind. I will never marry you, so please maintain your last shred of dignity and leave me be. Your petitions have moved from irritating to insulting, and I am done allowing you to waste my time," she said, turning away with a dismissive wave.

"Felicity, please!"

Hearing that informal address was enough to set her teeth on edge, and Felicity fought against the urge to berate him. Not that she cared about bruising his feelings, but to engage him in conversation once more would only prolong his presence in her life.

With pounding steps, she marched back to the assembly room door and was met by a figure in the darkness. Stepping into the moonlight, Mr. Finch glanced at her and then at Mr. Dunn, his eyes narrowing. But when his gaze returned to Felicity, the hardness fled, leaving them filled with concern.

"You are interrupting a private conversation, sir," said Mr. Dunn.

Felicity sucked in a breath, closing her eyes and letting it out through her teeth. When she opened her eyes, Mr. Finch was staring at her, his brow pulled low.

"I am here to claim my set with Miss Barrows." Mr. Finch's voice was quiet, but it carried through the night air. "And it is monstrously rude for you to keep her out here in the cold without a proper cloak, sir."

"You've had your set," replied Mr. Dunn as he straightened his jacket.

"My first, but not my second."

Mr. Dunn stilled at that, and the gentlemen's gazes locked. Felicity let out another exasperated sigh. Turning away from the pair of them, she made a straight line through the doorway and into the crowd as her thoughts cursed all menfolk. But Mr. Finch was at her elbow an instant later, and he guided her onto the dance floor.

"Will you not give me the courtesy of asking before you force me into another set?"

Mr. Finch's brows rose. "Do you object to it?"

"To the dancing or to your rescue when none was needed?" Some part of her heart prickled at the tartness of her tone and the hard words, but that organ was so twisted and shaken that Felicity could hardly move through the steps, though the dance had a languid pace with simple movements. Her feet were heavy, plodding things, doing their best to stay on the beat despite the terrible weight that settled on her.

Felicity was so very tired of feeling like a coin purse and not a person. But though Mr. Finch was a source of much of the present heartache, he did not deserve such censure.

"I apologize, Mr. Finch," she murmured as they passed down the line, weaving between the others. "You were trying to be of assistance, and I have repaid it poorly. But you needn't worry about Mr. Dunn. He is a pest, but I am used to unwanted suitors haranguing me. They are irritating but harmless, and he will leave when he realizes I will not budge. He may be more persistent than most, but my will is stronger than his."

Mr. Finch's blonde brows twisted together, his gaze holding hers with such concern that Felicity felt like crying. But there was no point in spilling tears: her life was her life, and she would make the best of it somehow.

"You needn't suffer alone, Miss Barrows."

"Not entirely alone, true. But alone enough." A smile tinged with sadness drew up the corners of her lips, but she met his eyes with an empty gaze. "My family is gone, and I live in a great big house with only servants to break the silence. I have friends aplenty, but they have lives of their own to live with husbands and children who are their priority. More often than naught, I am left to soldier on alone."

Cringing, Felicity rubbed at her temple and sucked in a breath. "I apologize. I am not usually so maudlin. I adore my life, and I am very blessed, but there are times like these when I struggle to remember that."

Felicity cast a look around as a blush stole across her cheeks. It was bad enough to be overtaken by such melancholy thoughts, but to do so in front of an audience was excruciating. The others paid her little heed, but her heart would not calm itself. Not when faced with the gentleman whom she'd hoped would fill that hole in her life.

"Miss Barrows, you are as capable and content as any person I've met before, but everyone has their moments of weakness. There is no need to feel embarrassed by yours."

His voice hardly carried over the music, but the words settled into her heart, drawing her gaze to meet his. Mr. Finch's eyes warmed as he held her there, the pair moving through their dance while the other distractions faded away. There was nothing she wanted more than to remain in this moment with him. To keep the world and its troubles at bay and seal the two of them in this peaceful bubble.

Mr. Finch cleared his throat, turning his gaze away from her and breaking the connection they'd shared. "You are an elegant dancer."

Felicity's heart dropped to her toes, and her cheeks puffed out as she let out a heavy breath. It would not do to forget that neither the world nor circumstances were keeping them from claiming this happiness as their own. No good could come from harboring feelings for someone who did not want a future with her.

"It helps when one has a talented partner." Though Felicity did not think Mr. Finch held any particular love of dance, he was one of the finest she'd ever stood up with. Like with so many other things, it seemed effortless for him.

"You are too kind, Miss Barrows."

Straightening, Felicity slanted him a glance as they passed each other, switching sides while weaving through the others in the line. It was not so much what he'd said as how he'd said it. The casual words had a weight to them, as though they were more than a polite deflection.

Felicity sorted through the past few weeks, including all that Mr. Kingsley had told her (what little that was), and tried to make sense of it all. The ideas planted by Mr. Kingsley took root at that moment, spreading through her memories and twisting them into something new.

"Why do you do that?" she asked. At a questioning raise of his brows, Felicity amended, "You always cast aside compliments as though they are empty and meaningless."

Mr. Finch gave her a wry smile. "You are kind, Miss Barrows, but I am well aware of my lack of talents. No amount of false flattery will change the truth."

Pausing in her step, Felicity nearly collided with the lady behind her, but she scrambled to arrive in her proper place.

"I was not stretching the truth, Mr. Finch." When she spoke, Felicity examined his features for the sentiments lurking beneath his calm facade. There were little movements. The set of his jaw. Tightness to his shoulders. Doubt coloring his gaze.

The gentleman did not believe her.

Taking his arm, she spoke out louder than she ought, casting her voice to the busybodies listening in. "I'm fatigued, Mr. Finch."

Without waiting for his reply, she tugged him away from the dance floor.

Chapter 33

The assembly room was full, which made it difficult to find privacy, so Felicity settled on private enough. Leading him to a section of wall near the musicians, she planted herself in front of the gentleman and studied his face. Mr. Finch met her gaze with lifeless eyes, and Felicity's heart shivered at the sight of his resigned acceptance. As though his low opinion were a fact she would not dispute.

A man without hope.

"With that one notable exception, I have always been honest with you, Mr. Finch. No false compliments or niceties." The notes of the song filled the air around them, masking much of their conversation from the others. "As you are so often forthright, I will ask you bluntly: what has you believing otherwise?"

"I am well aware I have little to recommend myself."

Felicity scrunched her nose. "That is patently false."

Mr. Finch met that with an arched brow. "I have a lifetime of experience to contradict that. One doesn't earn the moniker 'jack of all trades' by being remarkable."

Her head jerked back, her brows shooting upwards. "What do you mean?"

Mr. Finch shrugged. "A jack of all trades is someone who does not excel at any particular skill—"

"I know what it means," she said with a swipe of her hand. "But what moniker? I have never heard Mr. Kingsley call you that."

Tucking his hands behind him, Mr. Finch shrugged again. "My father dubbed me the family jack of all trades some years ago, and the Finch clan took to calling me Jack. But it's fitting, as I have many interests but few skills of any value. What good are they when I cannot use them to earn my bread?"

Standing there in silence, Felicity struggled to know what to say in response. Her thoughts stuttered and strained to grasp the reality standing before her. It was so difficult to believe a man of his years held such a low opinion of himself, but memories of their conversations combined with the insight Mr. Kingsley shared, testifying it was true. Felicity's heart shuddered and ached like an old tree buffeted by the wind as she considered him.

Yet quick on its heels came warmth. It lit her heart and spread through her, bringing tears to her eyes as she thought about how blessed she was to have had her family. She could not imagine what it would've done to her fragile ego if those who were meant to love and support unconditionally chose to lob insults and disparage her worth. Felicity's own history was littered with those who mocked her scars and denigrated her looks, but it was her family (though few they may be) that buoyed her spirits. Tears had fallen, and they were the ones who dried them. What confidence she had was due in large part to their support.

Speaking of tears, Felicity's eyes began to water at the thought of Mr. Finch's aching soul. He spoke matter-of-factly as he enumerated his flaws, giving support to his family's opinion of him. Felicity wanted to throw her arms around him, as though to shield him from his twisted self-image and his family's invisible barbs.

"What sort of a man cannot make a go of the many opportunities afforded him?" he said in a casual tone, as though it was of little consequence. Then, with a huffing chuckle, Mr. Finch shook his head with a wry smile. "I ought to have a sign hanging around my neck that reads, 'Does not suit.' I have heard that phrase often enough in my life."

Felicity winced, her lips burning as she recalled how carelessly she had said that very thing this evening. How she longed to turn back the clock and approach that earlier conversation with the knowledge she'd gathered this evening.

"Mr. Finch." Felicity's voice faltered, and she swallowed, though her throat was dry as a desert. Clearing it, she tried again. But the comforting words she wanted to speak fled from her thoughts as a flare of anger burned in her heart. "Your family is wrong. They are inexcusably, horridly, and altogether infuriatingly wrong."

The gentleman's brows rose. "And my schoolmasters? My employers? My peers? Are they as well?"

"Yes." She barked the word, her teeth clinking together as her jaw snapped shut. Felicity took a breath through her nose, filling her lungs as she willed herself to calm, but the thought of all those fools judging her Mr. Finch in such a heartless manner made her long to storm about. "They are wrong."

Mr. Finch gave her a half-smile that held more than a touch of pity, as though her faculties were lacking instead of his. "It is kind of you to think so—"

Felicity drew up a rigid finger, her expression hardening. "No, sir. Do not dare try to convince me of something I know to be false. You are not an 'ornament.' You are not useless. You are not worthy of derision."

His brows rose, but his gaze still shone with disbelief.

"I am awed by you, Mr. Finch. The more time I spend with you, the more capable you seem. If anything, it is those talents and abilities that first caught my eye." Felicity let out a breath, the fire in her burning out as she thought through all the many moments they'd shared, leaving her with a deliciously light sensation as she stared into the eyes of the man she loved. "Your skills may not fit into your family's or employers' mold, but that does not lessen them."

Mr. Finch's eyes dropped to the floor, and Felicity stepped closer, drawing his gaze to hers once more.

"I arrived in Bristow exhausted and seeking peace of mind and clarity, and you are the one who gave that to me." Reaching forward, she placed a hand on his forearm, willing him to believe her. "Your friendship and counsel have blessed me. You are intelligent and thoughtful, and the sort of man my uncle hoped I would find."

Drawing a hand upward, Mr. Finch rested it atop hers, gazing at that touch. Felicity prayed with all her heart that he would see the truth and understand. Her breath stilled as she watched him.

"You are very kind, Miss Barrows," he murmured, and her chest shrank, squeezing her heart, for his tone was not one of acceptance. As he met her eyes, his features were set as though carved from marble, giving strength to the words he spoke. "But I am certain your uncle would've wished you a better husband than myself."

Forcing air into her lungs, Felicity held her chin still, not allowing it to wobble or release a flurry of words that cursed the stubbornness of men. But even as the light in her world dimmed, leaving her heart heavy and cold, she saw a spark of doubt in his eyes that was directed inwards. Small though it may be, Felicity sensed it there. Whatever his lips may say, some part of Mr. Finch was wondering whether her words might be true.

Perhaps she was a fool for clinging to it, but Felicity grabbed onto this hope with both hands, holding it close to her heart. She would not beg a man to love her when he was determined not to, but it was himself that he did not love. And that was something worthy of patience.

"If you are resolved, Mr. Finch, then I will honor that. But might we remain friends?" Another lie of sorts, but one with far better intentions than the last. She did wish to remain friends with him forevermore, but there were grander plans for them in the future. Time and love could do a world of good, and she trusted in that.

Mr. Finch smiled, though it lacked its usual warmth, and he nodded. "I would like that, Miss Barrows."

His hand lingered atop hers for several long moments before he dropped his and tucked them behind his back with a nod. "I still owe you an apology for not seeing you when you came to visit Avebury Park last. Would you please forgive me and tell me what is weighing on you?"

Felicity forced her lungs to maintain a steady breath as she smiled and nodded.

...

After an evening of dancing and socializing, there was nothing better than tucking oneself away in a bedchamber. With the door closed tight to intruders and the crackling fire filling the space with its light and warmth, Mina's bedchamber was a sanctuary that belonged only to her and Simon. But stepping into her haven tonight brought none of that comfort.

True, it was better to address the issues clinging to their marriage than to let them fester, but Mina was not confrontational. Cowardly was a better descriptor.

Having rushed through her evening ministrations, Mina perched on the edge of the bed, her hands twisting the edges of her robe as she waited for her husband to emerge from the dressing room. She'd spent the evening fretting and fussing about the words to say, how to broach the subject, and every possible outcome or argument that might arise from it, but she did not feel adequately prepared to embrace honesty.

Even now, that frightened, fearful part of her begged Mina to remain silent. With cruel efficiency, it brought to mind those wretched days after the last time they'd had a frank discussion about the issues haunting their marriage, whispering to her that history would repeat itself tonight. Though she knew she needed to trust in herself and Simon, it was far easier to do in the abstract.

With shaky breaths, Mina's lungs heaved as she tried to calm the frantic beat of her heart. Her fingers twisted and worried the fabric of her robe until she was certain it would need mending tomorrow.

Time might sort it out in the end. Did she need to be direct? Such foolhardy action might lead to disaster. But Mina shoved that cowardice aside. They'd spent their marriage stuck in this horrid cycle of Simon hiding his darker emotions while Mina pretended not to see them.

This needed to be done.

That one thought kept her seated on the edge of the bed, but no matter how prudent and necessary the conversation may be, her nerves would not calm. By the time the valet took his leave and Simon entered the bedchamber proper, Mina was twisted into knots.

"You are not in bed," he said, coming over to place a kiss on her forehead before wandering to his side of the bed. He rambled on about Finch and Miss Barrows as he pulled back the bedcovers, but Mina did not move.

"Something is amiss, Simon." Mina winced at that, grateful he couldn't see her expression. The movement at her back halted, and she felt her husband's gaze burning into her back.

"I thought we had aired our concerns and moved forward, but something continues to trouble you," she continued, closing her eyes when she heard him coming to her side of the bed; it was so much easier to speak when not looking into his gaze.

Though her nerves had not calmed, Mina forged ahead. Now that she had begun the thing, the words slipped out, her tone straining and rising with each admission.

"I have tried to divine the source, but the only thing that makes any sense is that your feelings have changed, and you feel guilty about it. You compensate by lavishing me with presents and compliments as though trying to convince yourself that you still care for me. But you must tell me the truth. Have you grown tired of me?"

Chapter 34

Simon stilled, staring at Mina as he struggled to know what to say to such a question. His thoughts stuttered, struggling to tell him what to do. It felt like an eternity passed as he gaped like the fool he was.

"I swear I have no feelings for Miss Barrows," he said, the words pouring out of him as he babbled on about his exceptionally unexceptional sentiments for his friend's love. "She is a fine lady for Finch, but I have no designs on her. That dance meant nothing. I promise you. It was merely a favor for Finch."

Mina's eyes flew open, and her brows twisted together. "What are you talking about, Simon?"

"It was an innocent conversation. She is engaging, but she is nothing compared to you."

Head slanting to one side, his wife stared at him as though he was speaking gibberish. "Are you trying to convince me or yourself?"

Simon's hand reflexively went to his cravat, but there was nothing there, so why did his neck feel so wretchedly tight? His throat closed, and he fought to clear it. "I promise it was innocent, Mina. There is no need for you to leave."

Straightening, Mina stared at her husband, wondering what in the blazes he meant by that. "Why would I leave?"

With wild eyes, Simon gestured towards the door, his words clipped and staccato as though he struggled to get them out. "You did it before, and it is only a matter of time before it happens again."

Turning, Simon paced before her, his hand rubbing at his forehead as though it might erase the fretful thoughts clogging his mind. "I never meant to hurt you, but I did. I sensed you were struggling at the time, but I never thought things were so wrong that you would leave me without a word."

In all her planning for this moment, Mina hadn't expected such a confession, and her wits were too frazzled to formulate a gentle response. Instead, she blurted out, "You have no reason to fret as long as you desist from flirting with other women."

Simon spun to face her, and his voice rose to a panicked pitch, his eyes wide. "I didn't know I was flirting with Mrs. Banfield! Perhaps I was more friendly than necessary, but I was trying to be a good host. I couldn't see how others interpreted my behavior."

He resumed pacing, his feet moving at a frantic pace, as though all that he'd kept bottled up for so many months was spilling out all at once. "Am I laughing too hard at a lady's joke? Paying her too much attention? Is my behavior going to drive you away once more? My nights are plagued with dreams of you leaving again, and I am left alone, unable to find you and beg your forgiveness. Without word or explanation..."

With a heaving sigh, Simon pinched his nose and that raging energy seeped out of him. It was as though her husband deflated before her eyes. Inching towards the bed, he turned to sit but slid to the ground beside her.

Mina closed her eyes, holding back the pain radiating through her chest. Simon's head leaned back to rest on the edge of the mattress, yet she could not look at him. Her thoughts replayed the past few weeks, seeing each gift and word anew, and her cheeks flamed. Sliding off the mattress, Mina nestled into

Simon's side, his arm coming around her and clinging to her as though she might disappear that very moment.

"I am sorry, Simon," she whispered. "I did not realize how much damage I did that day."

Her husband shook his head with a tense jerk. "You hold none of the blame, Mina. The fault lies squarely on my shoulders."

Mina gave him a tiny smile. "I am not laying claim to all of it, but I am equally responsible for the current state of our marriage."

Closing her eyes, she sucked in a breath, steeling herself. "I am a coward, Simon. I was so afraid to speak to you, so instead, I allowed my fears and hurt to fester and spread. And on that awful day, I vanished rather than face you. If you hadn't chased me down, I would never have given you any explanation for my leaving. That was wrong of me."

"Mina—"

"And I continue to hide my feelings rather than simply speaking to you about my fears and worries." Swallowing past the lump in her throat, she added, "If your behavior was wrong, then so was mine. We have both made this mess."

Tears gathered in his eyes as she spoke, and Simon did not fight them. Each one was a testament to the agony he felt at hearing his beloved Mina's confession. She hid away from him still, keeping her eyes closed as she unburdened her heart, and Simon could guess at the reasons behind those fears. She had all but admitted it already with that heart-wrenching question, *"Have you grown tired of me?"*

Despite his greatest efforts, Mina still doubted him.

Simon brushed a finger across her jaw, drawing her eyes open once more. Her warm brown eyes were rimmed with unshed tears, but it was the bone-deep fear mirrored there that had his heart twisting.

"Why do you think my love is fleeting?" he asked, giving voice to his most pressing question. Surely he had shown her in so many ways that his heart belonged only to her, yet still, she harbored those fears.

Mina flinched and tried to pull free of him, but Simon held firm, repeating his question.

"I watched as you pined for another," she whispered, and Simon ignored the wrenching pain in his chest; as much as his guilt demanded his attention, his feelings were not the more pressing matter.

Mina raised a hand to rest against his as his thumb caressed her cheek. "And then a miracle happened, and your heart changed, erasing her from existence and embracing me. I don't doubt your love is real, but what if one morning you wake to find it changed again?"

Holding her gaze, Simon wished there was some token or sign he could give her to prove his constancy. It was impossible for him to love anyone else, for no other woman compared with her. Mina's eyes shone with the goodness of her soul, and kindness blazed in her heart, giving warmth to his cold life.

"I spent years searching for love, Mina," he whispered. "I was convinced it existed but didn't find it until I met you."

"But she—"

Simon shook his head. "That woman never had my heart. What I feel for you is nothing like that pale imitation of affection I harbored for so long. You say my heart turned suddenly, but it didn't. I loved you love before I said it, though I did not understand what I felt."

His throat tightened, and he blinked to keep himself from being overcome by the memories of those dark days.

"I don't know what assurances I can give, but I do love you, Mina. More than anyone or anything in my life," he whispered. "It is no fleeting thing. I love you because of who you are, and a world without you is dark and cold."

Mina's gaze darted away, her lips twitching as tears spilled down her cheeks. "But I am nothing special."

"You are to me."

Closing the distance, Mina pressed her lips to his, and the pressure in his chest eased as he reveled in her affection. Simon could never hope to articulate the feelings in his heart, but they expanded and wrapped around him, filling him with utter joy.

This was his wife. His Mina. His one and only love. A man could ask for no greater gift than to spend a lifetime with her.

Mina wondered if Simon understood the power of his touch. The simplest graze and Mina could hardly think straight. Her fingers ran along his jaw, and Simon pulled her closer, as though begging for more of her. But even as her heart pushed her to keep kissing him, she needed to give voice to other feelings longing to be known.

"I am sorry for doubting you, Simon." Wincing, Mina shook her head. "There are times when I cannot believe you love me, even though you give me so many reasons to trust it. Can you forgive my weakness?"

Simon released her face, bringing his arms around her to hold her close as they leaned against the bed. The cold of the wood seeped through her nightclothes, but she was in no hurry to leave that position.

Pressing a kiss to her head, he murmured, "We are a pair. Both so petrified of losing the other that we behave irrationally, which only feeds into the other's fear."

Mina rested her hand on his chest, playing with the edge of his nightshirt collar. "What are we going to do with us?"

"Perhaps we can go back to the beginning and start afresh..." Simon's voice trailed off, his hold on her tightening. "But I suppose I did not fare so well when we first spoke, either. Why did you agree to marry me in the first place?"

Lifting her head, Mina met his puzzled gaze, his eyes asking for an answer he could not work out himself. She gave him a teasing smile and said, "I was a touch desperate."

A jest at such a time was a gamble, but luckily, Simon chuckled, turning a wry smile inward.

Mina clutched his robe's lapel, pulling his attention to her, and she answered honestly, "It wasn't the best of starts, but I do find it humorous now."

Her husband grunted and did not seem amused at all. "My obtuseness knows no bounds."

"No more of that, sir. I think it time for a negotiation, so to speak. We both had expectations coming into this marriage, and none of them have unfolded as we hoped, but it was because we were not honest with one another. Not truly."

Straightening, Mina turned to face him directly and took his hand in hers. "Simon, if you promise to be free with your thoughts and feelings, then I promise I will do the same. I will no longer hide what is bothering me."

"I am utterly rotten at guessing your thoughts," he replied with a sad smile.

"And you shouldn't have to," said Mina. "I kept expecting you to intuit my feelings, rather than telling you, and that was wrong of me. No more secrets between us."

Simon reached around to pull her into his arms. His eyes were glistening and bright, capturing Mina and warming her through. "I promise." He placed a kiss on her cheek. "And I promise that you are the only woman I have ever truly loved." He followed that with another press of his lips at the corner of her mouth. His voice softened, growing huskier as he continued. "And you are the only woman I will ever love. My beautiful wife."

Mina blinked away her tears at that declaration. The words were nice to hear, but it was the utter conviction in his voice that wrapped around her heart and soul. At that, he met her lips, kissing her with such abandon that Mina's mind cleared of all thoughts, reveling in the feel of him and his love. It filled her, and she was certain she could say the same of him: Simon was the only man she would ever love.

When Mina settled back against Simon, the pair of them stared at the wall opposite, deep in thought as they enjoyed the peaceful moment together. His arms were wrapped around her, and Mina thought there was no better place in the world to be.

"Thank you for speaking up, Mina," he said, his fingers tracing a pattern along her back. "I shouldn't have followed Finch's advice."

Lifting her head, Mina sent him a questioning look, and Simon shrugged and added, "A few weeks ago, I asked him what I should do, and he said it was better to let things be as everything would settle in due course. He didn't think any good would come from dredging up such unpleasant subjects."

Mina stiffened, her eyes widening. "He said that?"

Chapter 35

Impoverished gentlemen could not afford to travel, but a stint in the army and visits to his family allowed Finch some opportunity to see places outside of London. True, his time on foreign soils had been of short duration, and he'd yet to see any British city that was not home to a Finch or Kingsley, but Finch had seen enough to say The Four in Hand was identical to any number of coaching inns that dotted their country.

He wagered the exterior had been altered to match the more modern exteriors of the adjacent buildings, with plaster painted over the old Tudor framing. The interior still showcased the thick wooden beams, and likely the owner hadn't bothered modernizing the interior due to costs and the fact that covering the timbers would lower the considerably short roof to untenable levels. But Finch liked the charm of those architectural details.

Bristow was of little significance to travelers, other than a quick stop to change over the horses, which meant most of the patrons frequenting the pub were locals. Finch sat beside a tiny square of glass that served as a window, but his eyes were trained on the door. His drink sat untouched, for he had only bought the thing to appease the barmaid.

His thoughts drifted as he waited, and Finch wondered if he ought to purchase some sweets before he returned to Avebury Park. Perhaps some licorice or lemon drops might sweeten Mina's disposition. Certainly, a peace offering mightn't go amiss.

Finch chuckled to himself and took a sip of his drink as he watched the doorway; his view from the window was far too obstructed to be of use.

Apparently, he could not maintain equanimity with Mina if everything was well with her husband. For the past three days, Mr. and Mrs. Simon Kingsley had been in alt, but Finch's hard-earned goodwill had vanished. Of course, it was justly deserved; his horrid, long-forgotten advice to Simon had only served to extend the couple's torment.

However, Finch was pleased to note that most of Mina's ill-will was reserved to merciless teasing and the occasional narrowed look, both of which held no true animosity. And a peace offering might smooth the last of Mina's ruffled feathers.

But as Finch thought through what form his penance might take, his quarry stepped through the door.

"Mr. Dunn," said Finch, nodding at the fellow and then motioning to the seat opposite him. "Might I buy you a drink?"

With narrowed eyes, Alastair Dunn dropped onto the chair across from Finch with the look of a man facing his rival, but with a cool assessment that echoed his true feelings for Miss Barrows. Another surge of forgiveness swept through Finch as he contemplated that poor lady; no wonder Miss Barrows had to hide her true self when surrounded by such manipulative regard.

"So, we've arrived at the point of negotiation," Dunn said with a dimpled smile that had likely won him many hearts. "How much will it take for you to leave her be? Or are you wanting to offer a similar bribe to me?"

Finch did not deign to answer. Lifting his drink, he took a long, silent sip as he examined the fellow.

"I've invested years in Miss Barrows, and I do not intend to cry retreat so easily," said Dunn, taking the cup the barmaid offered him.

Dunn had the decency not to leer at the young woman, though there was no mistaking the appreciative gleam in his eye as he glanced at her. Perhaps his behavior ought to upset Finch. He certainly did not care to hear Miss Barrows spoken of in such callous terms, but knowing what was coming next allowed him to ignore the indignation and anger flaring in his heart.

"So, make your offer," said Dunn before taking a swig of his drink with an arched brow. "From what I've seen, you've made good strides with Miss Barrows, but I was her first love. She may be angry with me at present, but I will work my way back into her good graces."

Chuckling to himself, Dunn met Finch's gaze with a challenging glint before adding, "I've had plenty of practice luring her into my embrace, and I have no doubt she will be eager to return to it."

Tapping his fingers against the table, Finch focused on his plan. As much as he longed to wrap his hands around Dunn's throat, there was a better retribution coming that did not require Finch to become a brute. Of course, his heart still wanted to deliver swift justice to Dunn's nose, but a brawl between two men connected to Miss Bristow was bound to raise gossip. It was better this way.

So, Finch let him speak, giving Dunn a moment to crow over his victory: it would make his defeat all the sweeter for it.

"I gather you are a fellow gentleman of great desires and limited means," said Dunn. "So, you understand this is nothing personal, but I do have a prior claim on her. What will it take for you to clear the field? I will make certain you get it once Miss Barrows and I are wed."

Giving a tight smile, Finch finally spoke. "The lady wishes you gone. As you refuse to honor that, I am here to force the issue."

The fellow let out a bellowing laugh, and Finch held onto his tight smile, meeting Dunn's smug look with narrowed eyes.

"You have some gall, Mr. Finch," said Dunn with a shake of his head. "Threats? You hardly look like the sort to grapple in the inn yard."

"I assure you my time in the army taught me more than enough. And I will admit that I am quite tempted to follow George Barrows' example and simply hire a few strong lads to assist me with a more direct means of persuasion. A few weeks in your sickbed might give you time to reassess this foolhardy course of action."

A frisson of pleasure ran down Finch's spine as Dunn's complexion paled. The fellow made a good show of remaining unaltered, but there was no ignoring the flash of panic in his eyes. No doubt, he was thinking about George Barrows' efforts on his niece's behalf, and Finch gave Dunn a moment to recall each agonizing detail.

Fiddling with the cup before him, Finch gave Dunn a genuine smile, for there was nothing feigned about the joy he felt about his brilliance.

"But as much as I admire that fellow's *thoroughness,*" said Finch, lingering on that word and all the pain it entailed, "I decided on a different approach."

Finch shifted forward, leaning his elbow on the table as he held Dunn's gaze. "You see, I possess knowledge and experience George Barrows did not. I am like you in that I am a younger son who is struggling to make his way in a costly world with little income. Though I never borrow a farthing, I know many of our kind do, and I am familiar with the moneylenders they frequent."

Straightening, Finch gave Dunn a false look of confusion. "Imagine my surprise when I wrote to some of my colleagues in

London and discovered just how many debts you've amassed during your hunt for a well-dowered wife."

With a shake of his head, he leaned forward and whispered conspiratorially, "Mr. Bartlet seemed especially keen to speak with you. I must say it's quite bold of you to seduce the daughter of your moneylender."

Dunn stilled, his eyes widening. "So you mean to tell them where I am if I do not leave Miss Barrows alone?"

Finch's smile widened, his laugh echoing Dunn's earlier one. "I did not come here to threaten you. I came to warn you. By my calculations, the earliest they could've arrived was this morning, and as you are still intact, you have an important decision to make: cut all ties with Miss Barrows and run or suffer at their hands. And you can be certain I told them of your fondness for Plymouth, so do not think to follow her home."

Dunn sat in stunned silence for only a moment before he leapt from his seat and ran to his room, calling to the innkeeper for a horse.

With a wide smile, Finch leaned back in his chair, crossing his arms. A shadow of disappointment flitted across his contentment at the realization that his plan had worked without any need for fists. For Miss Barrows' sake, it was better this way, and the abject panic in Dunn's eyes filled Finch with warm satisfaction, but he had to admit that George Barrows' more violent approach to punishing cads had its appeal. Miss Barrows deserved retribution.

His friend.

That was such an interesting word. Friend. A truth and a lie all wrapped in one, for Miss Barrows was one of his truest and dearest friends, though his feelings expanded far past such a small word. It made him long for and loathe London. As much as Miss Barrows seemed to believe they could maintain a friendship even after they parted ways, Finch didn't think it likely. And he couldn't help but wish for the distance, for being with her was a beautiful agony that brought him both joy and pain.

A shiver ran down his spine, and Finch leaned away from the window. But it was not a draft or nip in the air that had his heart sinking. Refusing to allow future sorrows to color this moment, he shoved away those dark feelings and raised his glass in a silent toast to Miss Barrows.

Though his efforts were few, Finch hoped they granted her some of that peace she sought. There was little else he could do for her.

Chapter 36

Some snowy days were filled with gusts of wind that kicked up flurries and sent them skittering along, twisting through the air in ribbons of white. But then there were days without the barest breath of breeze, when all was silent and the light reflecting off the snow cast the world in pastel hues, as though a painter had washed the world in purples and rosy blues.

Spring ought to have arrived long before now, but the ice and snow refused to give way, and Felicity didn't care about the bite to the air, for such beauty begged to be seen.

But even in foul weather, she couldn't prefer the warmth of the parlor—not when Mr. Finch accompanied her on their favorite route. The paths around Bristow had become old friends, and Felicity knew them as readily as any, which was no great surprise when one considered how many hours she had spent exploring them of late.

It was one thing to pass the time with Mr. Finch indoors, but there were always others about, whether the Kingsleys or Aunt Imogene. Even when they allowed the pair privacy, it was never private enough. Out here in the open air, they could meander about on their own, and even if it wasn't entirely acceptable, neither was it scandalous for a lady of Felicity's years.

It was discomforting to know that others assumed nothing untoward would happen because of her age, for they could not imagine any gentleman wanting to court a spinster. And it made no sense that such was acceptable when out of doors but not in them, for couples could get themselves into trouble anywhere. But as these bizarre societal norms allowed her a level of freedom not afforded during her younger years, Felicity wouldn't complain.

The gentleman at her side was quiet, watching the passing landscape as they meandered along the countryside, and Felicity didn't know how he remained so calm and stoic. Friendship was a good thing, and she counted him as one of her closest confidants, but Felicity was ready to burst whenever she looked at him.

All had been well when she first proposed this platonic lunacy. Though not renowned for the virtue of patience, neither was she devoid of it altogether. Mr. Finch merely needed time, and she felt certain their future was less a matter of "if" and more about "when." But after a fortnight of this torture, Felicity felt ready to burst. Far too often, she found herself seized by an impulse to throw herself into his arms and kiss him soundly, which was altogether inappropriate for "friends."

Mr. Finch slanted a glance in her direction, that corner of his mouth quirking upwards in a lazy grin, and Felicity's breath froze. As she held his gaze, her heart pressed against her ribs, and every particle of her shouted at him, begging him to break through his walls and embrace her, as though her sheer force of will might compel him to act.

But Mr. Finch's feelings for Felicity were not the issue, and she struggled to know what to say or do to help him out of the darkness of self-doubt.

"I don't know if I can ever thank you enough for your assistance with my man of business and steward," said Felicity.

Mr. Finch's brows rose. "You have said so many times already. I assure you it was nothing."

Felicity held back a growl at that all too familiar refrain. "And I assure you it was not. I am waiting to make a final decision until I meet the candidates in person, but I feel confident I have found the pair that will do me and my properties justice."

"I only gave you a few names, Miss Barrows. That is hardly worthy of praise."

Heaven save her from stubborn lackwits. Mr. Finch was determined to cast all his accomplishments in a poor light, and each time Felicity longed to shake him and his wretched family.

Patience. She'd had to remind herself of that many times over the past fortnight, and the only thing that granted her the strength to do so was knowing Mr. Finch was well worth the wait. Even if he could not see it.

Puffing out her cheeks, Felicity let out a heavy breath.

"Is something amiss?" he asked, slanting her another glance.

Plenty, but nothing she would tell him at present. So, Felicity shook her head.

But Mr. Finch watched her with a worried brow. "Are you certain? You would tell me if something or someone was bothering you?"

Felicity waved a hand, dismissing that. "Of course, but truly, things have been pleasant of late."

Except for Mr. Finch agitating her, things had been perfect. The bachelors of Bristow seemed to have accepted her dismissal, and even Alastair Dunn had been surprisingly quiet. Straightening, Felicity cast her thoughts back through the past fortnight and realized it was more than that. Since his reappearance, Mr. Dunn had not gone more than a day or two without some token or sign of his "affection," but it had been well over a sennight since he'd bothered her.

Narrowing her eyes, Felicity studied Mr. Finch's profile. "Things have been wonderful, in fact. Mr. Dunn seems to have accepted my rejection."

"Good." The word was short and spoken like an off-handed reply that mattered little to the speaker. Yet the corners of Mr. Finch's eyes crinkled, and a hint of a smile tickled his lips.

Felicity pulled him to a stop and faced him. "You had something to do with that, didn't you?"

Tucking his hands behind him, Mr. Finch shrugged. "I may have given him an incentive to leave you be."

And the other fellows in Bristow, no doubt.

Felicity blinked at him, her brows drawing close together. "I was handling matters."

Mr. Finch rocked on his heels and nodded, his gaze dropping away from her. "But you didn't need to do it alone. I saw something I could do for you, so I did it. That is all."

"That is all?" she parroted, her words clipped as her heartbeat picked up its pace. Felicity stared at the fellow, though he did not meet her gaze. Straining her nostrils, she took a deep breath and shifted her shoulders, easing the tension that had gathered there, and dear, sweet logic came to her thoughts, reminding her that he needed time. Mr. Finch could not change overnight.

Patience. Time. Bit by bit, she would help him see the truth of who he was.

But those calming thoughts were drowned beneath his words echoing in her mind, and the last strand of her forbearance frayed. The world blurred, and Felicity turned on her heel and marched away from him; she needed to leave before she said something foolish.

Mr. Finch called after her, but Felicity pointed her toes towards Buxby Hall and moved as quickly as the snow and ice would allow.

"What is the matter?" he asked, hurrying around to stand in her path.

"Pigheaded fools!" she replied while trying to step around him, but Mr. Finch took hold of her arm and faced her once again.

"What—"

But Felicity didn't let him finish that question. "I swore I would not force matters. I vowed to allow you the time you needed to discover the truth. But so help me, Mr. Finch, I cannot remain silent when you refuse to see the world as it is."

His brows rose. "And what do I need to see?"

"That my world is better with you in it."

Mr. Finch dropped his hand from her arm and straightened, watching her with wary eyes. There was something in his posture and expression that made him look like a child uncertain as to whether he was about to receive a reward or punishment, and Felicity's heart broke anew for him. But it did not quench the frustration flaming inside her.

"You believe you are unworthy of being my husband, but what gives you the right to make that decision for me?" she asked, jabbing a finger at him. "I could accept your rejection if you did not care for me, but I refuse to accept your twisted view of your worth. I view you as more than good enough. So isn't that enough?"

Mr. Finch's gaze dropped to the ground, and he murmured her name in a tone that spoke of more arguments to be made.

"No," she said, cutting off his ridiculous objections. "Do you not see how perfectly you fit into my life? From a practical standpoint, you are excellent with money and investments with a broad education that would serve us well in managing my uncle's estate. But the truth is, I don't *require* a husband. I can live a happy life as a spinster and manage it all on my own if need be. But I *desire* companionship and love. I want someone who will help me not because they think me incapable, but because they can and want to—something you have done time and time again."

Miss Barrows' heart burned in her gaze, lighting her like a winter's bonfire. That passion filled every syllable as she talked, enumerating all the many things she saw in him, and the world around Finch shrank away. Hearing those words was like being told up was down and right was wrong; it was so incongruent with his view of the world that his foggy brain struggled to accept it.

In all honesty, Finch thought Miss Barrows' wits must be lacking for her to view him in such a light.

Yet something warmed in his heart. Tiny echoes of it had come and gone during the past weeks. Something so faint and distant that Finch struggled to understand it. But hearing Miss Barrows' defense of him fanned those faint sparks into a genuine hope.

"Why do you care for me?" she asked with a tone and expression that spoke of a lady so stubborn that she was bound to follow him around until she received a satisfactory answer.

"I haven't said that I 'care' for you," he mumbled.

Any other person might be offended by such a statement, but Miss Barrows merely straightened and narrowed her eyes at him, and as much as he wished to deny the truth, it was impossible with it standing before him.

"Why do you care for me?" she repeated.

"You are kind," he murmured, dropping his gaze from her once more. "But that's not right exactly..." Finch sought for the right descriptors, but he fumbled about like a man struggling to light a candle in the pitch black of night. "You are more than kind. Your heart is big and full. The sort that seeks to make others happy because it cannot stand to see them sad."

He wanted to sneak a glance at her and see if she would be pacified with that, but Finch knew it would be a useless endeavor. So, sucking in a deep breath, he sifted through his thoughts.

"You make me laugh even when I am sullen."

With another deep breath, he continued. "You have ample reason to be melancholy yet you view the world with joy and gratitude. And it's not that you ignore the bad or pretend it does not exist; you simply choose to see the good in it."

Finch sighed and shook his head with a huff. "And I adore those silly jests of yours, even though they would be tedious if anyone else recited them."

Taking in a final fortifying breath, Finch opened his eyes, forcing himself to be brave as he said, "You make the world brighter simply by being in it. You are sunshine personified."

The fire burned out of her, and Felicity stood there, blinking like a fool as her gaze blurred. Her chin wobbled, and she tried to chase the tears away with a deep breath, but there was nothing to be done as one trickled down her cheek.

How did one respond to such a compliment? No amount of carefully crafted verses could compare to such a simple and earnest declaration spoken in the tone of a man facing an endless winter without her.

"You speak as though you have nothing to offer me, Mr. Finch, but I assure you those words mean everything," she whispered.

His head dropped, and Felicity drew closer, forcing his eyes to meet hers. Her hand rested on his arm, and she filled her gaze with all the certainty she felt in her heart.

"You do not view my worth in terms of worldly possessions, Mr. Finch. Do you truly believe it impossible that I feel the same about you?"

The spark in his eyes said he had not considered that, and Felicity felt a strong urge to thump him on the head for it.

"I care for you because you are blunt but not cruel," she said with a hint of a smile. "You laugh at my ridiculousness—even when you think me a fool. You give me strength and comfort, and in the two months since we first met, you have become my closest friend and dearest confidant, whose opinion matters so very much to me."

Felicity huffed, throwing her arms wide. "You are perhaps the most capable and talented person I know. Every time we speak, you share some new interest or skill, adding to your massive list of accomplishments."

Taking his hand in hers, Felicity drew as close as she dared (she could not trust herself any farther while her irritated heart was begging her to kiss him), and the world faded from her view as she held his gaze in hers, willing him to trust her words.

"I understand you may not be ready to embrace our feelings all at once," she whispered, "but can we not welcome the possibility and see where it leads? If we discover we do not suit, then I can accept that, but it seems foolish not to—"

Mr. Finch's arms came around her, pulling her tight in a sudden movement that had her squeaking. And then his lips came to hers, and Felicity was lost in his touch. Whatever sentiments she'd felt in the past for other men, they were pale constructs of what a foolish young girl thought how love was supposed to feel. This was not heady attraction or the thrill of being adored. It was as though her world had been washed in grey and that veil lifted to show her a whole new spectrum of light and color.

Logic and rational thought had no place during a kiss, which was a good thing, for Finch was tired of holding firm to what he ought to do. Now was the time to embrace that which he longed to do. Perhaps a better man might hold himself aloof and free Miss Barrows to find someone else, but Finch was too selfish a creature to let her go now. A man would have to be much stronger than he to turn away from such tender petitions.

And now, he was fully ensnared by her. Her touch wove a spell around his heart, binding it tighter to hers, and Finch couldn't say he was unhappy about it. Still, he didn't understand why Miss Barrows loved him so, but he would be a fool to turn that bright, joyful heart of hers away.

A sliver of decency worked its way through the fog, and Finch slowed the kiss, knowing that though he did not wish to end it, this was only the first of many to come. Holding her flush to him, Finch gazed into her eyes, which were as dazed as his own.

"Does that mean you are willing to see reason?" she said in a breathy tone.

"It means I am tired of fighting you. I still believe you could do far better than me," he murmured with a self-deprecating smile, and she pressed her fingers to his lips, holding back his protests.

"I believe enough for the both of us," she whispered. "That will do for now."

That sliver of hope buried deeper into his heart and whispered that maybe—just maybe—Miss Barrows might be right. And with her so close, Finch lost himself in her embrace and the bright future she painted.

A life together. He and his Sunshine.

Epilogue

Sussex
Five Months Later

It had been many years since Finch passed an autumn at Dewbourne, yet the view from his father's study was exactly as he remembered it. The leaves were shifting from greens to yellows and reds, looking as vibrant and colorful as a sunset, and Finch smelled the subtle scent that signaled the coming of winter.

Standing at the window, Finch gazed at the scenery and was struck by an odd sensation: peace. Not that the sentiment itself was unusual, but feeling tranquil while standing in a room that held far too many unpleasant memories was surprising. And welcome.

Father came to his side and placed a hand on Finch's shoulder. "I am proud of you, son."

Finch might've smiled at that, except he knew the source of that pride.

"You will be master of your own estate and investments," he said with a half-smile and shake of his head. That grin grew and he squeezed his son's shoulder before returning to his seat. "I couldn't be prouder of you."

Yet even with that rather irritating assessment, Finch's good mood did not diminish, for his heart was aglow with the promise of his impending nuptials.

Of course, Finch wished he'd earned his father's approval on his own merit (he supposed a part of him always would), but he felt no need to defend his worth to his father. Finch poured out his heart in gratitude that his path had intersected with Felicity's, for he knew full well that the whole of his present joy and peace was due to his Sunshine.

"It is a shame that Miss Barrows' pedigree doesn't boast more—"

"Father," said Finch with a warning tone, and the gentleman held up his hands.

"I do not mean to impugn her honor or any such nonsense. Miss Barrows is a fine lady, and she will do you and this family credit." Father paused, his eyes narrowing as he considered things. "And she is the cousin of a baronet..."

For all the strength he'd gained over the past few months, Finch still felt a strong swell of resignation take hold of him as Father spoke. He crossed his arms and embraced it; there was little to be done about Father's snobbery.

"But that is neither here nor there," the gentleman said, giving his son a wide smile. "I am simply pleased with what you've done with yourself, my dear Jack."

Finch's jaw set, his fingers digging into his arms, but he remained silent as Father droned on about his pleasure over his son's "accomplishments." But even as he thought to speak out, his heart grew heavy, that initial anger seeping out of him until he felt empty inside.

"...my dear Jack..."

For all that he'd learned and grown, Finch was still the family's jack of all trades. He may have now gained their respect, but only because he'd snagged himself a wealthy bride-to-be. There was no point in fighting his place in the family. There never was.

His thoughts spiraled into that darkness, his throat constricting until it felt as though he would never be able to swallow again.

But a pinprick of light glimmered in his heart as Felicity's voice echoed in his thoughts, chasing away the shadows and filling him with that measure of peace once more. Her words reminded him of all the things he'd come to understand over the past five months, recalling all the many things he'd grown to love about himself. And that helped him seize hold of his hard-won sense of self-worth, even in the face of old habits.

"That isn't my name, Father," said Finch, getting to his feet.

Father chuckled and waved the protest off. "I mean no offense, my boy. I know your wife-to-be despises our pet name for you, but it is only a jest."

Straightening his jacket, Finch held his father's eyes. "Call me Lewis, Finch, my boy, son, or any variation of those, but my name is not Jack."

Father straightened, his brows drawing tight together, but before he could say anything more, Finch turned and walked out of the study. Though regret settled in a quiet corner of his heart, he felt light—like one of those hot-air balloons, rising into the heavens.

Going from room to room, Finch searched the house, wondering where everyone had gotten themselves to. Just as he was about to leave the library, he caught sight of a familiar green skirt sticking out from the bottom of the curtains. Moving to it, he pulled back the heavy fabric to see Felicity hiding there, her finger flying to her lips as she pulled him close and shut the curtains behind him.

"Did you see the girls?" she whispered, but Finch didn't bother answering that question, wrapping his arms around her and pressing his lips to hers. Her brows rose, but she leaned into him, accepting his embrace with her usual enthusiasm.

Sunshine personified, indeed. Felicity Barrows was a blazing light, and Finch didn't know if he could ever give enough thanks for her appearance in his life. With every tender touch, he wished he could properly express the joy she'd brought into his world. Finch released her lips, resting his forehead against hers and breathing in her scent.

"I suppose that means the conversation with your father went well?" she asked with a grin.

Finch straightened but did not release his hold on her. Locking his hands at the small of her back, he gave her a wide smile, though he shook his head. "It went as expected."

"And that makes you happy?" she asked with a quirk of her brow.

Leaning in to kiss her cheek, he whispered, "*You* make me happy."

Felicity's hands rose to his chest, and Finch counted the hours until the wedding. They ought to have eloped.

"But," he continued, "I am happy to report that I defended myself."

He hadn't thought it possible, but Felicity's grin widened even further, filling her whole being with radiance. "You did?"

With succinct words, he relayed the conversation, his heart growing lighter as he recalled his part in it, and his joy mirrored in Felicity's expression. Before he could even finish, she closed the distance, capturing his lips with eagerness.

Finch wouldn't say it aloud. Not now. He knew Felicity would not accept it. But the truth of the matter was that his father had been correct. The best thing Finch had ever done was to win the heart of this dear lady. What finer accomplishment could he claim than securing this incredible lady as his wife? And that joy would only grow as their family expanded.

Husband and father. Surely no man could ask for greater or more important roles.

Tears gathered in Felicity's eyes, not tinged with sorrow but born of a heart fit to burst. The past months had wrought such changes in Lewis, and she only wished there was some better or grander manner in which to express her pride and joy in witnessing it. Though Lewis claimed it was she who lit his world, Felicity knew he had blessed her life in equal measure.

"Lewis Finch," she murmured. "The jack of all trades, and master of my heart."

A broad grin stretched across his face as he shook his head. "That is a terrible pun, Felicity."

"Yes, but it made you smile." Leaning forward, she rested her head on his shoulder.

Lewis's chest rumbled with a chuckle, his arms holding her tight.

Her Lewis. Her love. Her husband-to-be. Wrapped in his embrace, she was awed to know that this was just the beginning of their life together, and there was so much more to come. Years stretched before them, and Felicity knew they'd be filled with the sort of joy and warmth that grew exponentially, turning two cold, lonely lives into one eternal summer.

About the Author

Born and raised in Anchorage, M.A. Nichols is a lifelong Alaskan with a love of the outdoors. As a child she despised reading but through the love and persistence of her mother was taught the error of her ways and has had a deep, abiding relationship with it ever since.

She graduated with a bachelor's degree in landscape management from Brigham Young University and a master's in landscape architecture from Utah State University, neither of which has anything to do with why she became a writer, but is a fun little tidbit none-the-less. And no, she doesn't have any idea what type of plant you should put in that shady spot out by your deck. She's not that kind of landscape architect. Stop asking.

For more information about M.A. Nichols and her books visit her webpage at www.ma-nichols.com or check out her Goodreads page (www.goodreads.com/manichols). For up to date information and news, visit her Facebook page (www.facebook.com/manicholsauthor).

Exclusive Offer

Join the M.A. Nichols VIP Reader Club at

www.ma-nichols.com

to receive up-to-date information, freebies, and VIP content!

Before You Go

Thank you for reading *The Jack of All Trades*!
If you enjoyed it, please write a review on Amazon and Goodreads and help us spread the word.